Peep

It's a miserable Friday afternoon in autumn and me and Christian are snuggled into a cosy booth nursing brimming pints of rejuvenating hair of the dog.

And off I go. 'You know I like spying on people . . .' I start in a sing-song-y voice.

'Yes.'

'Especially people having sex, men having sex, gay men. Like, that's my super-kink . . .'

'Or men masturbating,' Christian adds, with a cheeky grin.

'Well, yeah. Anyway you know that. Well, there's something else I like to do that's sort of similar but different.'

'Ooh,' says Christian in a tone of semi-faux excitement. 'A new chapter in the book of my sexy girlfriend's deviant tendencies.'

Sometimes, I think the thing that Christian finds most attractive about me is the fact that I'm 'naughty' – like, textbook naughty. It's not so much what I desire, as the fact that I act on those desires; the fact that I am ipso facto a Naughty Girl.

Peep Show
Mathilde Madden

BLACK LACE

Black Lace books contain sexual fantasies.
In real life always practise safe sex.

First published in 2005 by
Black Lace
Thames Wharf Studios
Rainville Road
London W6 9HA

Reprinted 2006

Copyright © Mathilde Madden, 2004

The right of Mathilde Madden to be identified as the Author of
the Work has been asserted in accordance with the Copyright,
Designs and Patents Act 1988.

Design by Smith & Gilmour, London
Printed and bound by Mackays of Chatham PLC

ISBN 0 352 33924 1
ISBN 978 0 352 33924 9

1

Only the tiniest dappling of light from the street lamps ghosts through the tree canopy here – just enough to see what's what. Orangey speckles dance on the grass, looking like some fancy lighting effect. It reminds me of a production of *A Midsummer Night's Dream* I once saw. And that is so very appropriate, as there is something quite dreamlike in the air tonight.

It's so quiet. The foliage all around seems to deaden the noise of Friday-night chatter spilling out of the pubs and the bars, and the distant traffic could almost be the roar of the ocean waves breaking dark blue on the shore.

And I'm in heaven, even though I'm crouched in a clump of bushes. I'm in heaven and I'm looking at the face of God. And God, he's fit. He pulls a blue and white stripey T-shirt over his head and gazes down, his egg-box abs and sculpted pecs standing out in all their sodium-edged glory.

I inhale sharply, taking it all in, and silently congratulate myself on picking so well. I get a warm glow in the pit of my stomach when I choose the right ones. Slowly and quietly I ease my hand into my knickers as I look at him. I'm already a tiny bit wet, just from the anticipation of what's to come.

He starts with a long kiss, then slips away to plant haphazardly lust-driven pecks on his partner, nibbling and coaxing until he elicits moans and an almost desperate scrabbling for more. But he's good, and he teases it out. He makes it last a long, long time. And when he's done I wait for him to leave with his companion, before I slip out of my damp hiding place and sneak away.

Christian sticks out his neat little serge-clad arse and swings it back and forth to the loud rock music that's making the whole flat throb. He's bending over my dressing table, applying hair wax more expertly than I ever could, creating just slightly spiky dark-brown waves that any casual observer would swear had simply flopped into place by themselves, and I'm lying on the bed watching him sleepily, one hand slipped down the front of my knickers.

He catches my eye in the mirror and watches me for a moment, frozen mid-coif, before reaching over and flicking the volume down on the stereo. 'What are you looking at?'

I give a little laugh. He so knows; he so loves to be told.

'You,' I mouth, smiling coyly before raising my arms and stretching. I'm tired from work. Work, and my busy weekend lurking in a soggy bush, which is still catching up with me.

'Oh really?' he says with a saucy wink into the mirror. God, he's such a flirt.

'Yes, really. I like ...' I ponder for a second or two. 'I like you in that suit. I like men in suits.'

'Well,' he says thoughtfully, picking up a tube of lip balm and smoothing a minuscule dab over his mouth, distorting his voice as he goes on, 'if you like, you can have me in this suit when I get home. I've got no underwear on, you know.' A beat while he ponders something. 'Easy access.'

I make an appreciative noise. Although, truth be told, he hardly ever wears underwear – but that doesn't mean I can't appreciate it.

Setting down the opalescent tube of gel he moves his head from side to side, surveying himself from all angles, pouting and gurning with satisfaction. And he has every reason to be pleased. He looks hot, smart and deviant. Finally he stands up and turns to face me. 'Good?'

I raise my eyebrows. 'Yum. Sexy, yet professional.'

He smirks. I'm glad. 'Well, it just so happens that that is just the look I was going for. So, I take it you're not coming?'

'What gave me away?' I ask.

'Oh, the being in bed. The not being dressed.'

I smile and stretch, wallowing in my comfort zone. 'Well, you did describe the event as "dull networking with brainless PR types at The Pear Tree",' I point out. The truth is I'm already planning my evening alone as I speak, and a boyfriend in a Pear Tree just doesn't figure.

'OK, babe.' And he takes a detour to drop a kiss on the top of my head before he leaves the room.

A moment later the door of our flat slams and I stretch out on the bed, revelling in the delicious silence. Christian is so very, very noisy. When he's at home he seems to fly, singing and shouting and banging, from room to room, switching on radios and televisions as he goes, an all-conquering crash-bang-wallop hurricane of sound. So being alone in this beautiful peace is just precious. Free champagne and nibbles are all very well, but so not me. And certainly not in the mood I'm in right now.

But before I begin working my way down the mental list of indulgences I have rushing around my head like eager puppies, I close my eyes and take a little nap, because there is simply no rush. No rush at all.

It's properly dark when I wake up. It's still September, but the nights are already starting to tumble in before the evening has got itself going. Leaving the lights off, I wander into the kitchen and make myself some peanut butter on toast. Delaying the pleasure is one thing, but there's no point in wasting time cooking a proper supper. In any case I'm not that hungry. A full stomach is the last thing I want right now.

I eat the toast sitting at the folding table by the kitchen window. It's a very nicely positioned window, this one. It looks out over the central area of Maple Court, the block of flats where we live. And I can see window after window on the other three walls surrounding the so-called 'courtyard' (a small square of tarmac, flower beds and the parked cars of privileged space-owning residents).

This is the best time of year for watching people – early autumn – because people aren't used to the early dark yet. Hardly anyone has drawn their curtains. More than half the windows glow with pretty artificial light, creating a super-size mosaic pattern of yellow and black squares. But this pattern doesn't interest me at all. I like to look closer. See the details. And I can see so many details I almost don't know where to look first.

My eyes slide over cosy domestic scenes: a couple eating, a lone figure watching Channel 4 news, another couple eating, a couple rowing. Unsurprisingly, I choose the argument as worthy of further inspection. She's shouting, and he's sitting on the sofa, trying not to make eye contact. They're both really, really good looking. I wonder what he's done. She's holding something in her hand. I squint to make it out but can't.

Standing up, I snag the binoculars that live on top of the fridge. She's holding a mobile phone.

Ah ha! I think to myself – naughty text messages. Either she checked the saved messages on his phone, or he sent her one he meant for someone else. Bound to be.

OK, I'd better confess here, I'm not Sherlock Holmes or

anything, far from it. This is more than random guess-work. I'm pretty sure I'm right, though, because I've known for ages that the chap on the sofa is having an affair. I've seen the woman from a couple of floors above sitting in his living room drinking wine with him. I've seen him in her flat too. I've not actually seen them do anything – probably because neither of them is actually dumb enough to have full adulterous sex with the lights on and the curtains open. Unfortunately. But I've known what's been going on for ages. It was getting obvious. Well, obvious to any close neighbour with a pair of high-powered binoculars and an enquiring mind.

With a well-practised flick of the binoculars I light on the reason for all the misery two floors above. She's wearing a bathrobe and putting on make-up. Looks like she's getting ready to go out. Perhaps she has a Monday-night date. Perhaps Mr Two-time downstairs was just a fun diversion. Perhaps his main plus point was his location.

I have the option right now of retiring to the bedroom with my glasses, where I can get a much better and very comfortable view of any further goings on. But already the relationship meltdown melodrama has started to bore me. They seemed to have reached some kind of stalemate with her crying and him frozen to the spot. I cast around with my binoculars for something else to watch, but nothing grabs me. And besides, I remind myself, I've got plans. My toast is done, one slice eaten, the other cold and unappetising. I brush crumbs from my mouth and stand up. On a mission.

I make my way into the spare bedroom, to the bottom of the wardrobe there, and find my dirty little secret. My buried treasure. I don't know why I keep it hidden, but I do. It's not like Christian would actually mind if he knew about it. He never minds; he lets me be what I am. That's number one on the long list of reasons why Christian and I work. But I like my secrets. I like my privacy. I don't like people to know what I'm watching.

From a black bin bag under a pile of old clothes, meant for Oxfam but long forgotten, I pull two precious unboxed videotapes. I only have two. But I only need two. I hug them close, shut the wardrobe and tiptoe away, excitement already banging through my chest.

Cocooned in my living room, I slide the first cassette into the machine and flop onto the floor, before the heads of the player even engage. A familiar, slightly degraded image fills the screen: a crane shot of an army barracks and seconds later, in a dated typeface, the words *Private Punishment*.

It's difficult for me to explain how much I love this film. It is beyond words. And I can't really describe it in a way that would do it justice. This being a porn film the plot is, of course, ridiculous unbelievable drivel. But porn has never been reliant on a good plot. I'm not sitting here worrying about character motivation. Porn is about moments, and this film has moment after moment.

Like the one where our hero, an angel-faced new recruit, gets tied down tightly over a vaulting horse and given very special drill by the Sergeant Major on his first morning. Or the one where the poor fucker is made to kneel and suck the cocks of all the other boys in the platoon, as they march in tight uniformed formation around him, waiting their turn. Or the one where he tries to protest about the treatment he is getting and is put on humiliating naked toilet duty as a punishment. Cue lingering shots of him scrubbing the urinals with his toothbrush and later, when that is confiscated, his tongue. (And he does this all while other cute soldiers wander in when they please and use it, not bothering to avoid pissing all over the young soldier as he scrubs.) And the very best moment of all, the climax in every sense, when he is staked out in the exercise yard, naked and blindfolded, to be used over and over again, by all and sundry, until he swears his loyalty to the platoon and, by this time, loves it, of course. The end.

Yum. *Private Punishment*. And when I finally press eject, after three little flurries of rewinding and rewatching, I stay where I am, spread-eagled on the carpet for a while, and just come down a little. I don't want to peak too soon; after all this is just a warm-up really. The main attraction is still a long way off; *Private Punishment* was just to get me in the right mood.

I get up, walk into the kitchen and put the kettle on. Nine times out of ten, when I have a night in by myself, I make the tea after the first tape. It's not a ritual or anything as super sad as that. It's not set in stone, like it's 'my-porn-watching-system', because that would be cringeworthy, but it is what I usually do. So, moments later and brew in one hand, choccie bar in the other, I head back for the living room and the second part of my double bill.

I slide the second tape into the machine slowly and lovingly. It's probably my most prized possession: *Hidden Camera Studs*. Now, I love this one. I know I said I loved *Private Punishment*, and though I do, I love *Hidden Camera Studs* with a burning passion that eclipses my love for *Private Punishment* in a heartbeat.

Now, I am well aware that the title is super naff, but somehow that just adds to its dirty charm, especially when the content is such sex-dynamite. It starts off tame and playful; all horseplay in changing rooms and hot wet mouths crushing together in dirty alleys, supposedly all filmed unawares. (Of course, I'm sceptical, I'm not an idiot, but I can suspend disbelief for ninety minutes – especially these particular ninety minutes.)

And then, it slowly gets filthier and kinkier. There's a great part which is (supposedly) an SM rent boy with his client. The film quality is awful, but it doesn't matter a bit because the client really works the skinny little whore boy over so deliciously, so perfectly, that it almost feels like they're both right in the room with me. He ties the squirming cutie's hands behind his back, before spanking him and then slowly fucking him, until he is screaming, actually screaming out loud, for a hand on his cock.

The final scene, though, is my absolute favourite. If it really is secretly filmed they must have used some ubercool piece of kit to get the pictures, and I know something about spy cameras. It's a twenty-minute set-piece, a trip round a nightclub, but a very specialist nightclub, as becomes clear as the show goes on.

The camera (and the picture quality is very good on this part of the tape) starts outside a large and imposing building, at night. Slowly it pans up to reveal the word 'Schwartz' in gothic wrought-iron lettering, fixed to the frontage and lit by dainty little white spots. That established, the camera moves inside, through a tiny foyer and out onto a sweaty, packed dance floor. The lens steams up momentarily, the crush of half-naked men dancing jerkily in the strobe-lighting blur, disappearing into the mist. Then something too fast to make out wipes the picture clean and everything is pin sharp again. The whispered promise that was whisked away by condensation is back; it's everything it could possibly be. It's bacchanalia.

On the expansive dance floor bodies move against bodies, hip to hip, groin to groin and lip to lip. No one is exactly naked, but they don't need to be. Tight leather and tighter underwear make the dancers seem more exposed than if they were wearing nothing. No one is actually engaged in actual sexual activity either, but, again, they don't need to be. It's visible in the air, obvious in the driving, throbbing beat of the anonymous German industrial house. I swear I can smell it. Sex. Coming off the walls, the floor, the ceiling, hanging there in great clouds in the air, everywhere.

But the camera doesn't stay long on the overheated, overcharged dance floor. Pushing through the crowds of hot sticky bodies, it heads for a red-curtained doorway at the back of the vast space. It takes a few seconds of blurry flesh and tantalisingly fleeting images to get there and then the curtains sweep aside and the pace changes completely.

On the other side of the curtain everything is rather cool, sedate even. We're in a cobbled courtyard, with fantastically clever lighting that looks just like daylight. There's even a water feature, a stone fountain, looking as if a fountain being in a nightclub is perfectly normal. Groups of men, still in outlandish costume, are sitting around at wrought-iron tables, chatting and drinking cocktails. Apart from the clothing it looks rather like a refined garden party. I love this sudden change of pace, like a little interlude; it just makes the watcher totally on edge. It gives the impression that anything could happen.

And then, it does.

The camera settles on a couple sitting at one of the tables. Just like the earlier rent boy and his client, they are a pairing of a young skinny boy, probably in his early twenties, and an older, more well-built man. The younger of the two is topless above a pair of tight jeans and has rather dated floppy hair, circa 1991 I'd say. His companion is all in leather, jacket and trousers, and bare chest. He is, I guess, somewhere in his early forties, but he looks pretty good on it. The atmosphere seems pretty lightweight, like they are making small talk I think, although they cannot be heard. After maybe a minute of this the older man stands up, takes the younger by the hand and leads him away.

Shakily, the camera follows as the couple head through a swing door and into a darkened corridor. The soundtrack on the tape is not usually anything special, pulsing music or muffled conversation. Clearly no one is properly miked up, so there's nothing much to hear. But here, in this shadowy corridor, all that changes. Clearly audible are sharp smacking sounds, whips cracking, leather on flesh. All the signs were there all along, from the opening shot, but now it is confirmed. It's that kind of nightclub. Yum.

Our couple are barely visible in the low red lighting, just confusing shadows, and there seems to be some kind of reception table, half out of shot. The older man is bending down, probably talking to someone. When he stands up, he has something in his hand. A key.

He grabs his companion, who is leaning against the wall, roughly this time, not by the hand but by the scruff, and manhandles him down the corridor, unlocking a door quickly and throwing his property inside.

This is, I admit, where the whole 'covert filming' thing starts to get tenuous. The camera jerks a little as it follows them, but follows them it does, right into the room. Now, I'm not dumb, I know full well that this camera couldn't follow them the way it does unless it was attached to a person, so I know that person must be known to the twosome on screen. After all he's right in the private room they have just hired. So I know it can't be a completely secret coverty thing. But I do wonder if they know they were being filmed. They might not have been, just happy to have some lucky guy in to watch them play. I like to think this was the case, because that way I'm still spying on them unawares. So even if the camera operator himself is invited, I'm not.

The little room is smart, neat and functional. Smooth white walls, smooth black floor, very perfunctory furniture and an ominous black wooden chest in the centre of the floor. There are several heavy-duty metal rings fixed to the walls in a variety of geometric configurations. Big guy wastes no time in getting his slave's wrists locked into mounted manacles.

Then, once his prisoner is strung up and rendered pretty helpless, I watch the master take his time, pacing the small space, opening the chest and removing his selection of toys, occasionally letting his eyes run hungrily over the naked back of his helpless victim.

He starts to lay out his chosen implements on a low bench. The camera dances teasingly over them, hinting and promising first, before delivering, in long lingering close-up. The first object is a pair of bright nipple clamps, little jagged teeth tessellating together, sweet and neat. Next to them lies a smooth pear-shaped metal weight with a hook protruding from its narrow neck. Then a long thin cane and, next to that, the final item.

This last thing is the most fascinating. Not just because it's cool and sexy in its own right, which it undoubtedly is, but also because this is the only time the viewer gets a really good look at its awesome beauty as, once it's in use, it's well hidden. It's a black rubber penis attached to a wide leather strap. It's not very long, only an inch or two, but that's for a good reason.

The master takes it and walks over to his partner, yanking him roughly by the hair to angle his head just so. He then wraps the leather strap firmly around the slave's head, pulling the buckle tight and thus forcing the penis deep into his slave's mouth, gagging him securely. The camera lingers on the poor slave's face for a moment. All that can be seen are his wild brown eyes and the strip of leather completely obliterating the rest of his features. Obliterating him.

Next come the clamps, and the master teases and teases as he rubs them around the writhing slave's chest, before snapping them home to a scream and a wrench. And it's then that the purpose of the mysterious hooked weight becomes clear. It is a fiendish addition to the chain that runs from one harshly clamped nipple to the other. The master hooks the weight onto the chain and lets it drop, swift and merciless, and the chain pulls the nipple clamps agonisingly taught under the sudden tension.

And then, with the vicious clamps applied, the camera pulls back. The slave is still wearing his jeans and the crotch of them is clearly visible in the frame, straining against an erection and already soaked with pre-come.

Gently, the master turns the slave to face the wall, before securing his ankles to rings set into the floor, spreading him taut and immobile. He comes up close behind his helpless prey and holds him from behind, the master pressing his chest against the slave's bare back and encircling him easily with his meaty arms. And they both pause, for almost a minute, the gagged and bound slave almost hidden from view in the tight bear hug.

Finally, and barely breaking the contact, the master reaches down and around, and the slave's trousers suddenly hit the floor. Snap. Gear change. The master turns and takes up the cane and the blows begin.

The slave's beautiful high arse is only on screen in its mouth-watering unblemished state for seconds before the cane leaves its first bright red wheal straight across the middle. And, as the blows continue and the poor helpless slave attempts to struggle in his bondage, the camera occasionally manages to angle itself to give a slight sideways view of the victim, reminding the viewer of his clamped and weighted nipples and strictly gagged mouth. And pretty as the gag is, it's a shame at this particular moment that it is muffling the obviously delicious sounds the slave is making as he struggles.

The master appears to be a mind reader, though, because it isn't long before he pauses, for just long enough to remove the gag, and the slave's shouts of painful pleasure and pleasurable pain echo through the tiny room.

Eventually the master sets the cane aside and approaches the slave, reaching out to caress his face. When the slave turns his head and looks back at his master, there are tears in his eyes and his shaking lips form one word: 'Please.' There's a moment's pause, where the poor slave looks expectant, before his master fetches him a ringing slap around the face, hard enough to turn him right back to the wall, and sets about him even harder. And after a few strokes the camera moves around to show that the slave is crying in earnest.

However, this second wave is mercifully short and when the beating is done the master releases the slave with a series of wrist flicks, unfastening his bondage casually, as if it were no more substantial than thistledown.

And even before the limp slave drops to his hands and knees on the floor the master inches his foot forwards towards his exhausted and broken slave's face. No words are spoken. The order is obvious and he complies, beautifully. The camera gets in really, really close. So close that as the slave's tongue comes out, all the little red chafes at each corner of his mouth, made by the tight penis gag, are clearly visible. His swollen lips get to work and the camera angle is, in fact, so perfect that I can

13

actually see boot black staining his tongue, as he licks slowly and lovingly over and over.

An easy pull-back reveals the master standing above, watching his diligence and pain-striped back, while firmly stroking his own hard cock. As his slave boy works, he bites his lip, and I do the same.

Just before he comes the master reaches right down with his free hand and grabs the slave roughly by the hair. With a sudden sharp movement, he pulls him from his diligent boot worship and yanks his head back, exposing his face and throat just in time to catch the sudden jet of semen that arcs from the master's cock, and splashes over the slave's flushed cheeks and panting mouth. And then, in a moment that takes my breath away time after time, the master leans in closer and licks every last drop away from his slave's face, as tender and loving as everything else was harsh and brutal. It's the perfect ending.

And it is the ending. Suddenly they both disappear and the screen is full of static.

I don't know where the club Schwartz is, or even if it's real. In fact I know very little about either of the tapes. *Private Punishment* is boxless, but it does have credits and a proper label. I looked it up on the net to find it is quite well known. But *Hidden Camera Studs* was just a lonely little tape, no box, no label outside the handwritten title on its spine. I've always supposed this is because it is a pirate copy, but sometimes I like to think it is because this tape really is someone's private collection of illicit filming.

I have tried Googling for a nightclub called Schwartz and, trouble is, there's about two hundred. It seems to be a popular name.

Of course, if I knew where the tapes had come from it

might help, but I don't. I wouldn't know where to buy this kind of video, or even if they are legal. The truth is I found the tapes. They were here when we moved in, in just the spot where I keep them now: in a bin bag at the bottom of the fitted wardrobe in the spare room. I have no idea if they were forgotten or abandoned. They may even pre-date the people we bought the flat from. All I know is they are mine now, and they could have been chosen for me. Perhaps I have some kind of pornography fairy godmother.

Hidden Camera Studs, even its delicious final sequence, isn't the main attraction of tonight, though. The two videos, however luscious, are still just a warm-up for the real fixture of the evening.

As I stand up and switch off the telly, stretching happily and enjoying the warm buzz left by the three orgasms I have had so far this evening, I let my eyes wander across the room, to the laptop.

We have quite a fancy sparkly computer. With me working from home quite often and Christian's latest freelance exploits, it's justified, just about, which is good for me because, as someone who likes sneaking around in the shadows, the online world is easily my biggest playground.

So if one night a crouch in some damp bushes just doesn't appeal, it doesn't mean I need to miss out. These days there's no need to leave the flat if I'm not in the mood to – every flavour of voyeuristic thrill is just a clickety-click away.

And the online equivalent of that convenient bush-shaped hidey-hole is a mask, a creative bit of profile, a fake ID that can take me right up Schwartz-cam close to the action. OK, it might involve a bit more giving than is usual for me, but it's so totally worth it, because when it comes to the best seats for my favourite kind of action, frankly, this is it.

I watch people from behind a fake profile, pretending I am a slutty little boot boy like the one I love to watch get worked over in my Schwartz video, and I go online and see who wants to play with me. Currently I'm 24 and looking for an older man to take me in hand. Does that sound cheesy? Well, maybe it does but, believe me, that type of thing works like a charm. I'm something of an expert here.

But now, and here's the real confession, my alter ego is called Christian, named after my own boyfriend. And actually, because if this is true confessions time I might as well be really honest, in my mind (and this is cyber sex remember, it's all in the mind) he actually is my boyfriend. I'm pimping my boyfriend out to other men – in a virtual sense at least. What can I say? I'm just a very unselfish girl.

My, or rather Christian's, current beau is called Dark Knight, again super cheesy, but if I'm in the right mood – the mood that an evening watching my videos can create with ease – then that name sounds very sexy to me. Dark Knight.

Dark. Knight. Yum.

What's more he's new. New-ish. I've only spoken to him three or four times before, so it's all fresh and sparkly still. We are still at the teasing stage, all tantalising conversations about what I or rather what Christian likes and dislikes. And after all the groundwork we've done over the last week or two, I reckon tonight could be the night. Cybersexy.

It's tennish now. He's always online about this time. In fact, I haven't been logged on a minute when a flashing window pops up. It's him.

<Good evening, Puppy. Fancy seeing you.>

<Hi> I reply. And it's sad, I know, but just this little exchange is enough to get me wet as anything. At least it would be, if I weren't still wet from earlier. This is what I've been waiting for all evening. This is the reason why I had no intention of going out to Christian's stupid schmoozefest.

<Good day?>

<Not bad. Slow day in the shop, pretty dull.>

<What's the name of the shop where you work again?>

<Again?>

That's one of Dark Knight's little quirks. He always pushes for personal stuff. Course, I can't tell him any personal stuff. If he finds out who I really am (i.e. 100 per cent woman, XX chromosome and everything) he won't want to play any more. But it's cool. It never seems suspicious that I won't give anything away because tons of people online like to play it safe when it comes to personal stuff. So it's become sort of a game. He's always trying to trick me into giving away some detail or other about my personal life, and I'm always hauling him up on it and ticking him off.

So, he thinks I work in a shop, because that's what I told him, and it's not exactly a lie. It's half true. But of course he's thinking maybe it's somewhere in the Trafford Centre, and that's where he couldn't be more wrong. It's a fair enough assumption on his part though. We met on a gay Manchester site, so he knows I'm local and that's the biggest shopping centre around. Oh, that's another thing: I do like these games to be with local guys. Not quite sure why and I know a lot of people would just think, what the hell? Why not talk dirty to someone in San Francisco or Singapore? But I think what it is, is I like the fact that I can talk dirty all night to a bloke and then pass him in the street the next day, and neither of us would have any idea. That's such a sexy idea. I could even be talking to someone I see every day. Dark Knight could be my dentist. He could be someone who lives in my building, someone I could see from my kitchen window.

<Oh, you didn't tell me the name of the shop? I'm sure you did.>

<I'm sure I didn't.>

<Well, you should. I could pop in and see you. Your boring days wouldn't be half so boring then, pup.>

<I'll bet.> I lick my bottom lip. This sounds promising. I think my knight in shining armour could be going somewhere.

<You have a stockroom in your shop don't you, pup? I bet you do. A nice stockroom where your Master can take you if he happens to drop by.>

<Yes.> It's true. I might not work in a shop in the way he thinks, but we do have a stockroom.

<Yes, what?>

<Yes, sir. Sorry, sir.> And God it turns me on to type that. He does that, see, he switches from small talk into full-on dominant mode and catches me out. That way I'm already on the back foot, fumbling and apologising, and he hasn't even started.

<So, pup, tell me about this stockroom of yours. What's it like?>

<Messy. No one clears it up. There's piles of stuff everywhere. Boxes of junk and old stock. The auditors go mental.> I hit return before I remember, so I have to add on the next line: <Sir.>

<Hmm, big piles of boxes, that sounds good. So when I drop by your shop I can shove you into the stockroom and bend you over a pile of boxes.>

<Well, no, sir, you couldn't do that. Not while I was working. I wouldn't let you.>

<Oh, is that so, pup? Are you saying I would have to force you?>

<I'm afraid you would, sir.> Have I made it clear how hot this guy is? My God, he's just wonderful. He's so good.

<Force you? Really? In front of your customers? I'd have to grab you from behind your counter and slap you and call you a little slut before marching you into the stockroom, with the whole shop knowing exactly what I was going to do to you?>

And my hand is in my knickers then because, although I might be the most devoted voyeur around, my cyberself, for some reason, is a hopeless exhibitionist.

Somehow I manage to type. <Yes, sir.>

<Really, pup. Well, I can't say that's a big surprise. So in this messy stockroom of yours is there something I could use to tie you up?>

<Yeah, there's leads and stuff. Like electrical leads.>

<Oh, very good. They're good for flogging too. Did you know that, pup? Well, you will soon. And they sting like hell.>

<Oh, sir, you wouldn't do that to me, would you?> I know, aren't I terrible? But you got to give a little. Right?

<Maybe I would, that all depends.>

<Depends on what, sir?>

<I want to know what you look like first, pup.>

I pause, because this isn't the response I was expecting here. And then I let the words sink in. Oh shit. <How do you mean?>

<Email me a picture, silly.>

<Oh.>

<Come on, pup, I don't like to play sight unseen and besides your description sounds great. I'd love to see a pic of my cute five seven brunette aged 24.>

<I'm sorry, sir. I don't have a scanner.> Worth a shot,

but I'm very worried suddenly. Worried I'll miss out on my jollies. Worried, frankly, that the game is up.

<I want to know what my pup looks like. You must have a digital pic somewhere. Everyone does.>

Dammit. <Sorry, sir, I don't have any.>

<OK then, pup. Well I gtg. Later.> And before I can even wish him goodnight he's logged off.

When Christian gets home I am in bed, nestled well down in the duvet against the encroaching autumn. He slides in beside me, snuggling close, still in his suit – all soft cloth and cigarette smoke – just like he promised, a world ago.

'I wish you'd come, it would have been a laugh,' he murmurs, rubbing up against my back.

'Yeah, sorry, I fancied a quiet one, you know.'

'It's OK. It was nothing special, just the average.' His snuggles become a little more urgent, and I can tell he's trying to persuade me to turn over.

'Yeah, I thought so.'

'So what did you get up to?'

'Nothing much.' I'm tired and I don't bother to stop it showing in my voice.

'Oh, Genny, don't be sleepy, please. You know how I get after networking. I'm all tense. I need a bit of a wind down.' Still snuggled in bed, he shrugs off his suit jacket and tosses it onto the floor, then starts on his shirt.

I roll over to look at him as he peels the shirt away. Christian's nude shoulders are suddenly clearly visible in the street light coming through the half-drawn curtains. He's etched in orange, all soft muscle and peachy skin below the dark holes of his night eyes. I can't help thinking about the best moments of my evening's video watching and the hints dropped by Dark Knight, and those little thoughts start to get me hot.

'Yum, yum,' I sigh into his ear, moving closer in the dark.

'Oh, babe, that's more like it.'

'I was thinking about you while you were away.' And it's not a lie really, just because it was actually online Christian I was focussed on. And both of them, both versions of my boy, are so beautiful. Which is handy right now as I snuggle into his arms and he crushes his hard cock against my thigh, because there'd be no way I would be going for this, after the evening I've had, if he wasn't so irresistibly fit.

2

EYE-SPY, the shop the Dark Knight is so keen to discover the identity of, sells, well, for want of a better word, stuff.

Gadgets. Boy's toys. Electronica. A whole slew of over-engineered, overpriced bits of tat, mixed in with one or two items that are truly ingenious. Sadly, most of it is innovation of the tawdriest kind, unusual without being special or even useful: very small televisions and pens that have MP3 players in the cap. But the range of palm-top computers is pretty good, exceptional even. And one or two items I covet like nothing else on this earth: the listening devices and the mini-camera mostly. What I could do with one or two of those placed in strategic locations. No more hiding in damp bushes ever again then. In Tomorrow's World, I'd never need to leave the flat.

Now, the reason why poor old Dark Knight is never going to find the shop where I, or rather where Christian, works in the Trafford Centre, or any other centre he's likely to look, is because the shop doesn't really exist. Well, not in the whole bricks, mortar, have-a-nice-day sense. EYE-SPY is an online store.

It's funny, when I got this job I thought working for an internet company would be every kind of heaven. Not only did the place sell merchandise that fitted in rather well with my hobby, but I would also be able to glide around on their high-speed internet connection on slow days, chatting, emailing and maybe, just maybe, downloading porn. Course, I figured totally wrong. This is a technically savvy operation. They know how to clamp down on employees surfing on the clock. They have an all-but-impenetrable firewall and super-secure net-use spyware. Bastards. Just about all I can look at with impunity is the company's own website.

What's more, the merchandise here that doesn't get me wet bores me rigid. And this morning's first on the to-do list was a case in point: proofreading some copy about a range of ridiculously macho watches (and trying to avoid catching the eye of any of my colleagues while I'm at it, because I'm just not in the mood).

I'm deeply submerged in this less than thrilling task when Frank, my boss, calls me into his office.

He's sitting on the edge of his desk. Probably because he's been told to do that in a training course. Frank likes going on training courses. I think he thinks that that's what managers do.

'Imogen, I haven't got your timesheets for, uh . . .' He flicks through a sheaf of paper attached to the clipboard he's holding for no apparent reason. 'Well, the last three months it seems.'

I roll my eyes. Timesheets. Bloody hell. There is little in my dull paper-shuffling job I care less for than filling in my timesheet. Waste-of-fucking-timesheets I call them. But, obviously, I don't say that. 'Oh sorry, Frank, I must have forgotten.'

'Yeah, well just do them today. I need them for the bookkeeper.' Self-consciously, Frank crosses his arms low, over the place where his belly makes his shirt gape revealing a hairy patch of skin. Perching on the edge of the desk really isn't working for him as a look.

So it's a relief a moment later when he slips off his desk and stands up. And when he does this I can see his computer monitor. And I can't help but notice a series of small windows open, showing grainy moving images. Oh God, not web cams. In fact, the shocking thing is how little this shocks me. Because this isn't the first time for Frank. At least twice before he's planted these little wireless web cams in the office. But the location of this one is something of a step up.

'Oh my God, Frank. The ladies' loo!'

Frank gives me an embarrassed grin. 'Ah yes, just a test, you know, humid conditions.'

'Oh my God,' I repeat as I watch. The door of the stall in which one of the cameras is placed opens as a woman comes in, moving jerkily in a series of stills. From the odd angle only the top of her head is really visible. I stare. 'Those black roots look familiar. Is that?'

'Elaine,' says Frank, creepily. He is so gross, I feel like I need to wash just standing here. And I so don't want to watch, because even to me spying on a colleague like this is wrong, even if it is Elaine. But I do watch. I watch in breathless silence until Elaine stands up, pulls up her knickers and leaves.

'Well, it seems to work fine,' Frank says with a nod. His balls! He's a fully paid-up dirty old man. In fact, even before today's events I'd checked in the loos for recording devices more than once. Never found anything, which doesn't mean that there'd never been anything there, of course. Bloody Frank, he gives people like us a bad name.

Course I'd spy right back on Frank if it wasn't for the fact that he was the last person in the world I wanted to see more of. Ew.

He turns to me. 'Nice little rig, don't you think? Has its own transmitter thingy so it doesn't need to be plugged into a laptop. You can set it up to send its signal back wherever. Five-mile range apparently. I need to test that of course.'

'Hmm, yeah,' I say. (And I'm ashamed to confess that

even though I know Frank is the grossest I'm being monosyllabic partly because 'Gimme!' just sounds so inappropriate at this moment. So I try desperately to sound nonchalant when really a significant part of my mind is racing with the many, many uses I could put such a camera to.)

'They sent me some publicity about a new model. Same company have this camera coming out which is just like this one except instead of being the size of a golf ball it's the size of a five pence piece.'

'Really.' Oh-my-God!

'Yup. You could wear it on your lapel.'

Later I'm back at my desk, still reading the same copy, having wasted most of the morning being creative with my timesheets. I keep finding myself glancing over at Elaine on the next desk. She looks up and smiles as she catches my eye.

'Do anything fun last night?' she says. Almost certainly not caring, but very few people can just lock eyes at adjoining desks and not make boring small talk, and Elaine is anything but exceptional.

'Nah, I stayed in, quiet night, on my own.'

'No Christian?' I strongly suspect Elaine, like the rest of the world, fancies Christian. As I said, not exceptional. She asks after him far too much.

'Some PR bigwigs' do at The Pear Tree. Sucking up to the big knobs. I didn't fancy it.' I grin. 'I can see him begging at home.' Yes, I am so bored I am teasing Elaine. But she warrants teasing, in my opinion. If she had the capability, she'd whip Christian out from under my nose in a heartbeat. I'd lay an awful lot of money on her not having those capabilities, but just the fact she would if she could is enough to raise my hackles. What about sisterhood, Elaine?

Of course, it's oh-so-sisterly to be complicit in some dirty old man's spying on the ladies' loos. Pot. Kettle.

Thankfully I knock off at lunchtime, before my brain dies. A while ago I wangled Tuesday afternoons working from home. And this was for a very, very good reason. That reason is called Mr Fox.

(Well, that's not his real name, obviously. That's just what I call him because of the book *Fantastic Mr Fox*, because, well, yum.)

Mr Fox lives in flat seventeen, Maple Court. I know this because one lazy afternoon I sketched a little map of all the windows I could see across the courtyard and worked out which flat was which.

Mr Fox is a lifeguard. I know this because one Saturday morning about six months ago I found myself on the same tram as him and, because I was at a bit of a loose end, I followed him to work.

Mr Fox has every Tuesday afternoon off from the saving of floundering kiddies at the swimming pool. I know this because I watch him through binoculars. A lot.

He has a beautiful body. Small neat muscles from swimming, long legs and very little body hair. And he usually spends his afternoon off flicking through his extensive collection of pornographic magazines in the nude. He likes a really eclectic mix of things, does Mr Fox: gay kink mostly (my kind of guy) and then some rubber and leather stuff and sometimes a bit of added weirdness for spice. Around the time *Gladiator* came out, for example, he had some magazine full of images of Roman Centurions sucking each other off.

And I watch him. I watch him stroke himself and part his flushed lips to show me his wet red tongue. I watch him writhe against the bedclothes and arch his back. I watch him come in his hand and scream out loud. I watch.

So this Tuesday afternoon, like every Tuesday afternoon, I'm lying on my bed in my work jumper and knickers, with my best pair of binoculars and a flapjack (well, I don't always have the flapjack) and I'm watching Mr Fox.

Mr Fox is naked, splayed on his stomach on his unmade bed. I can see the sweet little curves of his tight arse peeping out from under a crumpled sheet and his long legs are flexed, ankles crossed. He's reading one of his favourite magazines and already quite flushed. And I can tell straightaway that he's got a hard cock, just from the way he's moving slightly, rocking his pelvis into the linen nest he's made. I know him so well.

Snuggling into my deep pile of pillows, I gaze lazily at him. I know he likes to draw things out – which is fine, I like that too – and I know he's going to wait as long as he can before he even touches himself.

He starts by doing this lovely little thing with his arse though, so I don't get bored. He keeps tensing and relaxing the cute cheeks, making them look so luscious I could bite them. He's looking at a kink magazine and I can't help wondering if he's imagining getting a spanking. Those well-shaped cheeks would look so good pink and sore. And when I think that, I can't help thinking about Dark Knight, because Dark Knight is inextricably linked with all things spanking shaped in my warped little mind. And then the combination of Mr Fox's frustrated squirming and my random thoughts about Dark Knight and me/Christian in the stockroom of EYE-SPY means that I suddenly realise that if I'm not careful I'm going to come before Mr Fox does.

And that's just not polite.

But then my fantastic Mr Fox saves the day by upping his game. He rolls onto his back, allowing his huge and very pretty erection to spring out from its cramped position crushed under his stomach. I almost squeal in delight at the sight. It's not just his cock that I'm looking at though, it's the whole package: his cute little nipples, the little line of hair that leads from his navel to his groin, the sharp way his hip bones jut out at either side and, best of all, his face, like a purring cat in a sun trap as he stokes himself.

And I mark him as I always do, matching him move for move as far as my shaky and suddenly one-handed binoculars will let me.

I don't have to manage like this for long, though, because it's my lucky, lucky day.

I suppose I was so wrapped up in what I was doing I didn't hear the door latch click when he came in. So I don't know he's even in the flat until I feel a hand on mine, the one that's working between my legs, gently lifting it away and placing it where it should be, back on my binoculars, steadying them for a better view. And then I feel a soft tongue take its place between my legs and I just melt.

This is about the perfect set-up for me, this is as good as it gets: spying on a gorgeous naked man pleasuring himself while someone who knows what they're doing gives me oral.

Because I love oral with a ridiculous passion, to the extent that sometimes I find it hard to be enthusiastic about any other sexual activity. No one will ever convince me, frankly, that any other sexual position in the world is going to touch oral for sheer screaming pleasure. Well, it isn't, is it?

And Christian, bless his heart, likes to give oral, and

he's so good at it too. He knows not to rush it or push me too hard. He starts so gently, tongue like a feather, practically ignores my clitoris and just keeps it right there, gas mark one, until I'm half insane, frantic for just a touch more pressure.

Across the courtyard Mr Fox arches his back, just as he always does, his right hand a blur and his face a picture. I can almost hear him gasp as he speeds up for the home straight. I gasp too, bucking into Christian's mouth and he responds by finally increasing the pressure and giving me what I need, with a stroke of his tongue right on the button. Right on my straining clit. Mr Fox's eyes squeeze even tighter shut as he comes explosively, thrusting over and over into the empty air. I scream and close my legs tightly around Christian's ears, locking him in place as if I am scared he might suddenly leave me hanging, as I come and come and come into his mouth.

When I open my eyes Christian is grinning at me from between my legs. I smile back. 'Thanks.'

'How's Mr Fox?'

'Much as usual. How're you?'

'Well, I'm fine. A little too fine, actually.' And he nods at his crotch, indicating that he wants my debt repaid in full. Tch.

I make a face, but roll over and kneel up while Christian flops onto his back and wriggles into the mussed duvet. 'Do you ever wonder,' he says as I take hold of the button at the top of his flies. 'If there are other girls like you out there, watching. They could be watching me right now.'

I unzip him and slip my hand inside. His cock is glassy smooth and hot. He smells all pheremoney and as my fingers close around him he gasps and stops talking. 'Well,' I say, moving my hand lightly and slowly, 'what if there are, you certainly wouldn't mind.' I hear his breath catch a little at this. God, he is such a naughty little exhibitionist.

'Mmm.'

I grip him a little more firmly. 'I bet there are lots of them. A whole audience out there. Watching you. Waiting for you to come.' I dip my head and feel his soft hard heat fill my mouth. He is so delicious. He tastes like salt and smoke. And I suck.

He bucks his hips as I start to move. 'Oh. Oh yes.' But I put my hand on his belly and slow right down, letting my mouth go so loose I barely graze him, while he keens softly in the back of his throat. I tease him up and down for as long as I can bear, holding him at the brink and pulling him back, over and over until I feel his hands on the back of my head, hauling me gently up to look at him. And when I do I know just what he's going to say.

He pauses, panting, and then says, 'Imogen, will you?' and then stops talking and purses his lips, almost shy. It's funny how some things never lose their power, their wrongness, their desire to stay unsaid. He swallows, and he knows he has to say it. He knows I like to hear the words.

One beat, and then another, and then: 'Imogen, will you fuck me, please?' He shivers as he speaks, almost as if he is aroused by the very words.

I don't even need to answer out loud.

I pull my jumper off, pausing and struggling as my bra top comes with it, and then I lean forward to snag the box under the bed. As I do one of my nipples grazes Christian's lower lip. He flicks his tongue across it so suddenly I almost lose my balance and collapse on top of him. I feel my exhausted clit start to purr gently as he keeps sucking and suddenly I'm scrambling, desperate for my little box of tricks.

Now, I have to confess the strap-on is mainly Christian's thing, but that's not to say I don't enjoy it. I like the idea of my boy getting nailed in the arse, and I certainly like being there to see him squirm and pant and beg and lift his hips to meet each thrust. But, really, I have to confess I'd rather be across the room in a comfortable armchair with an unobstructed view of Christian lifting up his arse for a hard fucking. But this is close and close enough.

With well-practised deftness, I pull the leather straps around my waist and thighs, snapping the buckles tight against my sweat-slicked skin. Christian's eyes go glassy and distant when suddenly I'm looming over him all flushed cheeks and a very substantial dildo jutting from my crotch. I smile softly.

'Tell me,' he whispers.

'Turn over, bitch,' I say, getting hot and wet as I suddenly imagine that I am Dark Knight and Christian is my latest plaything.

Christian performs a little for me, biting his lip in apprehension before he flips and I lean in close over him and rub the head of my cock up and down against his naked arse.

'Do you want it?' I hiss lightly in his ear.

I can feel him melting under me. 'Yes, yes, please.'

I stroke his arse. At first I use a fingertip, and then I lower my head and use my tongue. Pressing so close to him, so very real and loving. A perfect deep kiss, right where he is most vulnerable and most masculine. I lick him and kiss him until he is way beyond the point of being ready. And then I reposition. I slicked the cock with lube when I strapped it on and it glides wetly against him, both teasing and threatening.

Christian writhes. I can feel him trying to angle himself so I rub right against his tight little hole, but I make

31

it tricky and pull away every time he thinks I am about to slide inside. Waiting for it. Waiting for . . .

Right there. I find my angle, just the right position that makes the blunt end of the dildo butt up against my pubic bone and massage my now wide-awake clit, and finally I slide inside.

Christian moans like an animal and pushes back against me, making sparks rush from my groin to every part of my body. I rock inside him, pressing close to run my tongue over his smooth baby pink back. He tastes lovely here, not pheromone crazy like his cock, or musky dusky like his arse, but just him – clean and smooth and salty fresh.

With a groan Christian starts to shift. I struggle to stay inside him as he hitches his knees up, making a gap underneath his body. He snakes a hand inside and begins to stroke himself, matching my rhythm as I find purchase again and begin to fuck him, hard and sure. The sounds he's making and his frantic masturbation, panting and wanting, spur me on to give it to him harder. I pound into him, frantic and merciless. My clit is screaming for attention and I twist slightly, giving me a shade more friction where it counts. It's enough and just as I start to come I hear Christian begin to cry out his orgasm.

A few minutes later we lie together and I've come down enough to start noticing things, like the fact the bedroom now looks and smells like the end of the world. But it doesn't matter, because my boyfriend is so fucking sexy and he's smiling at me like I'm some kind of sex goddess myself.

'Where did you learn to fuck so well?' he asks for the millionth time.

'Gay porn.'

* * *

I don't get to lie around in the afterglow and eat biscuits for long because Christian leaps from the bed less than fifteen minutes later. Apparently he has to pick something up, something to do with the company he keeps telling me he is setting up. Christian and his business plans: I'm sure world domination is only a huge great slab of hard work and an even huger slab of flukey luck away.

I, on the other hand, have no such burning ambitions. So after some further brief bedroom acrobatics, otherwise known as changing the sheets, I snuggle down for a nap.

When I wake up, I'm confused for a moment, not sure what time of day it is. And what's more I can hear loud, slightly tipsy voices. I pull on my fleeciest pyjamas and go to investigate. I don't need to go far.

Christian and his wannabe business partner Dan are both stretched out on the living-room carpet, a huge pool of glossy little photos spread all over the floor between them and half onto the sofa, like weird confetti. The two of them, all oversized shoes and oversized mouths, are laughing as they point out a particularly gormless expression or candid shot.

As I cross the threshold, yawning blearily, Christian turns his head to look at me, a suggestive smirk on his face. He knows how much I love looking at photographs.

Returning his look with a knowing expression of my own, I bend down and snatch the picture Dan is holding and ask the obvious. 'What's all this?' I'm holding a photo of Christian, shirtless and intense looking, a bit out of focus, but very promising.

'For our company. We wanted some pictures for the website, so I got this guy William to take them. Good, aren't they?'

'Hmm, who's William?' I grab a handful of pics. These

are for a business website? About half of them seem to be of Christian semi-naked.

'Some faggy photographer with a crush on Chris.' Dan laughs, rolling onto his back.

'Oh, will you shut up about that.' Christian faux slaps Dan's chest, then looks up at me. 'He's just this photographer I met on a job once. He used to do me freebies now and again for my portfolio. So I asked him to do the web pics. And then we did a few fun ones too, for old time's sake.'

'So that's what it was. Old time's sake. Looked more like old fuck buddies to me,' says Dan. Dan is boring. He is so boring he ought to hook up with Elaine. He is one of those blokes that never seems to bloody shut up. I couldn't care less about this photographer and whether or not he fancies my boyfriend. Frankly, everyone fancies my boyfriend. I've learned to deal.

Christian bunches his legs underneath his body and sits up, looking at Dan with his head cocked. 'What the hell is wrong with you, Dan? Just because he's gay and he's nice and he's done me a favour once or twice, it doesn't mean he wants to fuck me.'

'So you admit he's gay then?'

'I know he's fucking gay. I've been out for dinner with him and his boyfriend.'

'Well, you never told me he was gay,' Dan replies sulkily from his position on the carpet.

'Yeah, and I never told you he was half French either. You wanted website pics, we got website pics. Professional quality. Dirt cheap. Now why don't you stop being such a homophobic cunt about it?'

Dan gives a pout that could be straight from page one of the textbook of petulant pouts, it's kind of sexy, and he says, 'I wish you wouldn't use that word, Christian, it's so offensive. And you know bloody well why.'

Reluctantly, I put the photos I'm looking at down on the table and turn my attention to the squabbling boys. 'Why?' I ask, nosy as ever.

Christian crouches over the heap of photos and starts to scrabble through them. 'Dan is pissed off because William, who I admit is a little fruity but nothing to write home about for an ex-fashion photographer for God's sake, wanted to take a couple of shots of the pair of us.'

'Two shots. Fucking porn shots.' Dan sits up and joins Christian in the rifling. Dan finds one of the offending pictures first and holds it out for me. 'See.'

I take the glossy pic in my hands, holding it by the edges, and say, 'Oh, oh I see.' And I do see. I really do.

Without taking my eyes off the first picture, I reach out for a second, which Christian is offering.

'Yeah you do, don't you. You see everything,' Dan half snarls.

I stare at the pictures for what seems like a long time. In the first one, Christian and Dan are topless and laughing, and Dan is giving Christian a piggy back. The photo is nothing worse than you see boy bands doing now and again when they want to snag the gay market. It's playful rather than porny, but it is definitely from the drawer marked 'homoerotic'. It has something of a mood about it. To put it bluntly, it seems to be clearly suggesting that Dan and Christian are a couple. And it's yummy.

The second is more dubious and far hotter. The two of them are basically in bed together. Dan is leaning back smoking a cigarette while Christian rests his head on Dan's bare chest. It's about as post-coital as a photo can get, and I'm wet just looking at it.

And yeah, I can see Dan's point, but surely Dan realised how this photo would look when he posed? He's not stupid, well, let's qualify, he's not that stupid. But, I suppose, if I were a homophobic repressed little posh boy, I wouldn't like this pic much, either, and I certainly wouldn't be happy about . . .

'It's going on the website,' Christian announces and then smirks at the noise of sheer indignation with which Dan greets this announcement. 'Sorry, Dan, but it is. It's the best shot.'

'Even if it was even slightly appropriate, which it isn't, it is not the best shot, and can I remind you I'm the webmaster?'

And so it goes on. With Christian baiting Dan and, in my opinion, flirting with him ridiculously (which is no biggy, as Christian flirts with everyone. Christian would flirt with the cat, if we had one). Meanwhile poor Dan just gets more and more confused and enraged. And I'm off in my own little world as I sit down at our big blonde wood dining table and spread a few of the best shots out in front of me in a pretty little arc.

So I'm not really listening, I'm looking at the pictures and grabbing handfuls from the floor and flicking through them again and picking yet more favourites. All because as I look at them – not the ones of Christian and Dan, but a selection of the semi-naked ones of Christian alone – I have such a terrible idea.

An idea so terrible and so tempting that I have to push it to the back of my mind straightaway, but once thought I can't un-think it, and no matter how hard I push it away, it's still there. It's an idea about how the Dark Knight wants a picture and how suddenly I have oodles of very suitable, seductive piccies of Christian (no doubt Christian has the lot of them on CD somewhere too), but even I have limits. There's a definite edge and, like Frank's lavatorial web cams, this is right on the precipice.

(And it would definitely help my do-the-right-thing resolution right now if I hadn't just been looking at photos of my delicious boyfriend all post-coital and snuggled with the not un-eye-pleasing Dan.)

Later, at bedtime, when I'm tucked under the duvet, flicking through a celeb gossip magazine, Christian finally emerges from the bathroom, licking his freshly scrubbed teeth. He's wearing a very lovely pair of little white underpants. I set my magazine aside and watch him as he fusses about, picking up dirty laundry from the floor.

Since the rather scary thought I had about the photograph situation earlier, I have decided my only option, as far as the Dark Knight situation is concerned, is to get out. To run away with my tail between my legs before I do something so stupid; before I even think it again. I am going to delete Christian's profile for once and for all. It's sad, but it has to be done.

I smile at Christian as he finally finishes his business straightening up the bedroom and slides between the sheets, snuggling his chilly body close to my warm one. And there's one thing I really have to know before I can settle down to sleep.

'Christian,' I say, twisting round in his arms so we are face to face, 'these photos of you and Dan . . .?'

He breaks into a huge grin as he interrupts. 'I knew you'd like them. That's why I brought them here instead of the office.'

'Yes but . . .'

An even huger grin. He loves it when he can read my mind.

'I was having a drink with William a few weeks ago. Maybe I did bitch a bit about Dan and how he annoys me by saying things he doesn't like are "gay" or "don't be such a fag". I guess William must've felt like yanking him about.'

'So it was all William's idea? The, er, the homosexy stuff?' I raise my eyebrows and purse my lips in an expression that I want to be chastising but is almost certainly just comical.

'Yeah,' Christian replies and gives me a little kiss on the lips before rolling over and turning off the light.

3

It's such a nice day that we are sat outside, breakfasting al fresco. The weather is excellent, squinty bright, which has given me an excuse to wear my beloved dark glasses.

Our metal chair legs scrape and squall on the uneven pavement as Christian smears some day-glo eggy mess around his plate with a toast crust, and I peek through my shades across the road to one of my favourite parks. The deserted grass is quiet now, although awash with happy memories. (Even a city as decadent as mine manages to restrain itself at 9 a.m. on a Wednesday morning.) At night, though, it would be a different story. Though not exactly a cruising ground, the park is dark enough and well positioned enough to be a favourite for my kind of romantic entanglements: couples who had just linked lips and couldn't bear to wait a whole taxi ride before lush consummation and uber-decadent twosomes, threesomes and moresomes who just didn't care about anything as bourgeois as privacy.

But, as I said, right now, it's just a park. So, in need of additional distractions, I pick up a teaspoon to flick around my coffee foam, and it's then that I realise that Christian is talking and I'm not listening.

'Huh? Sorry, baby.'

My baby smirks. 'I said "have you ever heard of Cruze?"'

I frown.

'It's a big gay nightclub. In the village.'

I put down my spoon. 'And it's called Cruze? Talk about exactly what it says on the tin.'

Christian laughs. 'Well, I met this bloke at that networking do on Monday and we got talking and when I told him I was starting my own PR company, he says he might be able to put some work my way.'

'Great,' I say, but what I'm thinking is rather less supportive. What I'm thinking is: Oh God, not this again.

It's starting to plague me, this entrepreneurial dream thing of Christian's. He's so hyped up in the media world. I'm convinced it's just a pipedream too – the no-clock, no-boss ideal. And, what's more, I thought I'd had my weekly quota of Christian and Dan's business ventures yesterday with those photos.

And who is this so-called bloke anyway? The one offering the work. He sounds rather dubious to me: he's thinking of employing my nearest and dearest on the basis of what, exactly? I cock my head. 'So how does big gay nightclub Cruze come into this?'

'Well, that's the thing he needs the PR for. He's starting up a club night at Cruze called Fandango.'

Bingo. So that's why mystery guy wants my boy on his team: it's his cock thinking, isn't it? Oh, Christian, Christian, why do you have to break all their little hearts?

And on another note, what a bloody stupid name for a club night. 'Fandango? What the fuck?'

'Yeah, I know. But think of the cash. No agency, just moi. Well, moi et Dan.'

'You moonlighting little devil.'

'Yeah, but can you help me out? I mean, when I say just "moi et Dan", I could do with a little bit of hand holding. Make me look together.'

I'm wary. My precious free time. 'Maybe.'

Christian wipes the last of his yolk up with a toast

crust just as the waitress appears and swipes the plate away, along with my half-empty mug. 'Will you at least be there on the launch night?'

'Sure. When is it?'

'First Thursday of October, that's . . .' He purses his lips a minute, doing a mental calculation. 'God, that's one week tomorrow.'

Sadly, work beckons, real work that is, so we cut this short and head for the tram stop. We're half-way down a narrow street next to one of the canals when Christian points out Cruze, but I don't even look because I am already staring at another building opposite. A building covered in scaffolding and with a tatty grey and black banner hanging above the door.

And the banner says: 'Coming Soon – Schwartz.'

The rest of the week whistles by, and the Thursday of Fandango's launch night rolls around without further incident. I don't go online, not through any great exercising of will power on my part, but simply because Christian is around every evening and I don't ever go online when he is home, because, well, it's obvious why.

We have some really excellent sex most nights. I like to do it in our bedroom with the lights out and the curtains open, watching all the neighbours through their tiny windows, like a bank of televisions; like Frank's little web-cam windows. Watching their yellow-outlined backlit shadows, knowing they're right there, almost touchable, while Christian twists and flicks his tongue against me and I thank my lucky stars for a boyfriend who knows his way around a cunt.

But I don't so much as touch the computer. Which means the whole week slides by without me doing the thing I swore I'd do first chance I get: and that's delete Christian's profile. He might not be doing much with me otherwise occupied, but to all intents and purposes, online-Christian lives!

On Fandango launch night, Christian's big moment, I arrive early at Cruze to do my hand-holding duty. Not as early as Christian and Dan, of course, both of whom are milling around chattering into their mobiles and looking frazzled, albeit in a rather immaculately well-groomed sort of a way. They've both been there all afternoon doing whatever PR types do that takes at least half a day and about forty fags a piece. The nightclub is still not open to the public though and feels strangely cold and cavernous as I make my way across the grimy dance floor towards the bar. Christian bounds over excitedly when he sees me.

He kisses me then laughs. 'Are you ready, baby? This is going to be awesome.'

And it is.

My boyfriend is really not at all bad at his job. At any rate, he knows how to fill a nightclub with exactly the right faces while cute boys in tiny gold-lamé shorts waltz around them filling their champagne glasses. Everyone who matters in North West's gayest in-crowd seems to be here, from local DJs to pin-up girls (and boys) and journalists from every gay paper, free sheet and porno mag I can name (and quite a few I can't).

And right in the middle of it, my boyfriend, on sparkling form as he bats his eyelids and fingers the stem of his wine glass like a well-trained concubine. Everything is laid out on a plate, and from the look of the salivating crowd around him, hanging on his every word, appetites are well and truly whetted.

But after half an hour of watching this blatant scrotum tickling of Manchester's pink-tinged movers and shakers, I'm actually somewhat bored by the spectacle.

And my hand-holding skills are really not required. I spot Dan lurking uncomfortably in a corner and make for him (which says a lot about my level of boredom), but by the time I pick my way across the packed dance floor he's gone. There's an exit right by where he was standing, so I slip through it, thinking maybe he's gone that way.

In the corridor there's still no sign of Dan, but I am quite glad of the fresher air. The testosterone level in the club proper was getting stifling; even here I can still feel it prickling my skin.

In front of me is a flight of stairs. And to my left is an emergency exit. I slump with relief against the hum of the vibrating wall as the DJ strikes up yet another pulsating club classic, and I weigh the options: up or out. Then with a snap of decisiveness, I press the release bar on the big metal security door and tumble out into the night.

It's freezing outside and my coat is . . . I'm not even sure where. Somewhere in the Cruze staff room I think. I shiver.

The change in temperature aside, however, outside is very like in. I'm standing on one of the tiny cobbled streets that make up Manchester's gay village, and a dozen or more different house and pop beats jangle in the crisp air, mixing with the gossamer wisps of cigarette smoke and a cacophony of voices. Although none of this really registers with me for very long because, right in front of me, rising up like the only port in a hormonal storm, is Schwartz.

And there's a light on.

After jamming the automatically locking door with a half brick, I make my way across the street, trying to sneak, but in reality having all the grace of a carthorse as my kitten heels twist on the cobbles.

There are three steps up to the entrance of Schwartz and I slide up them and wait in the shadows, where I can see inside through the open doorway.

The lobby has a very odd feel to its décor. It looks like a European hotel circa 1985, all fake wood veneer, orangey-yellow recessed spots and bright brass fittings. Two blokes are inside, blokes that are really nothing short of Tom of Finland cartoons made flesh. They are leaning on a small reception desk, examining the contents of a cardboard box. I crane to see what's in the box, risking letting my upper body dip into the pool of light coming from the doorway. But I still can't see properly. And then one of the blokes turns in my direction and says, 'You lost, honey?'

I freeze. Both of them are looking at me now. The game is suddenly very up.

'Uh, no, sorry, no,' I mutter as I step out of the shadows into the doorway proper. 'I was just wondering when you're opening.'

The second bloke, the one that didn't spot me, says, 'Yeah, whatever, sweetie, just get back to your hen night, we've got work to do.'

I frown. 'I'm not from a hen night,' I say, unnecessarily. 'I just wanted to know when you are opening. Your sign doesn't say.'

'Well, here you go.' The first man, the nicer one, takes something from the mysterious box and gives it to me. A small flyer, black printing on white paper. Under the gothic Schwartz logo is a graphic of a chain made of interlinked circle and arrow male symbols and a 'Grand Opening' date of a Friday a few weeks away.

I smile at him. 'Thanks.'

'No problem, darling. You tell all your little boyfriends about us now.'

* * *

Back inside Cruze I head up the stairs, feeling my cheeks flush and wondering perhaps if there might be one of those galleries that overlook the dance floor where I can watch all the goings on in anonymous comfort. But they don't, or at least if they do that's not where the staircase leads. It leads to a doorway. A guarded doorway.

Bright-pink velvet ropes cordon off the women-only section and are manned (a strangely appropriate term) by two extremely butch lesbians, who peer at me suspiciously, as if checking for any well-masked XY chromosomes before unhooking the rope and letting me into their realm.

It's darker up here than on the downstairs dance floor. The atmosphere is different too. Where downstairs was big and hot with testosterone and sweat, up here it's tight and cool and hard like a knife blade, bluey-black and strobe streaked. The women packed shoulder to shoulder on the dance floor are all short spiky hair and tight denim, heavy key chains and nose rings. A great number of them are exceptionally beautiful, moving with a jerky grace even the most sinuous men downstairs lack.

Around the edge of the room, most observers stand in couples, locked at elbow or at lip. Some stand frozen, watching the dancers. Others act entirely as if they are alone in the room. Naturally my eyes seek out the animated.

Backlit by the bright fluorescent light spilling out of the tiny bar, two baby butches clash lip rings and belt buckles as their tongues tumble in and out of each other; on a black leather sofa two high-heeled femmes endanger the upholstery as they rake each other's cheeks with perfect French manicures; in a dark corner a grey-haired bespectacled old hand snakes her arms around the waist of a Bambi-eyed ingénue. Everywhere I glance, girls meet girls in pretty symmetry and daring mismatches.

And there I am, right in the middle of a big, dumb male fantasy. Girl-on-girl action all over the place. And I look, of course I look. I get myself a cranberry juice and find a quiet corner and look for all I'm worth.

It's not my thing, not really. My thing is, in many ways, the exact opposite of girl on girl. But it's certainly not unpleasing to the eye – just not me. And it's not like I'm closed to it. No way. I'm not repressing anything. I'm pretty confident about that, I'm just not the repressing kind. But with me, as I've said, it's all about the look. If a woman looked right, I'd fancy her, no question, but it just so happens that every time I've ever met anyone with the right look they've been a big hairy bloke. Well, actually not hairy. Like my boy, smooth as a Greek statue. My boy! Christian! He'll be missing me by now. I must have been gone, what? Fifteen minutes? Not more than half an hour, surely?

I'm just about to head back, when I see a gorgeous-looking bloke on the other side of the steamy action, looking right at me. I almost do a double take, wondering how on earth he could have got past the officious bouncers, but before I even finish the thought process, he's walking towards me. And curiosity alone is enough to make me flash him a smile.

Which, it seems, is all the invitation he needs.

Next minute he's at my elbow. 'Can I buy you a drink?' he says, leaning very close to be heard over the throb, throb, throb.

I jangle the ice in my half-full glass. And he shrugs, then says, 'What's your name?'

'Imogen.'

'I'm Lawn.'

I frown, sure I must have misheard. 'Lawn? What, like mowing the lawn?'

'What?' He moves in closer as the track changes to something even more bassy.

'Did you say your name was Lawn?'

'Lorne,' he says, 'L. O. R. N. E.' And I strain to hear each letter.

'Oh, OK. Hi, Lorne.' I smile.

'Hello, Imogen. I saw you watching the floor. You want to dance?'

'Not really. I'm happy to watch.'

'Oh. Like that, is it?'

'Actually, yes. It is.'

Now Lorne is so close, and he's making the most of it by pressing his chest against my arm and his groin against my hip. I'm starting to notice one or two things that explain a lot. Like the fact that his throat is devoid of an Adam's apple. Like the way his voice, though deeper than mine, is still quite soft and refined. Like his mouth, small and soft. I have heard many people say, when it comes to boys and girls, that a mouth is a mouth, that a girl's mouth is a boy's mouth, but it isn't true. Mouths are more different than anything. Lorne's gender is confirmed, with a big tick in the box marked 'female', as soon as her lips meet mine.

But even so, it takes me a second to realise that this is not something I want to be happening. I gasp and splutter in a most ungainly way, pulling my head away as soon as I get my wits about me. 'Sorry, I . . .'

'Uh . . .'

We both look at each other, embarrassment bouncing back and forth between us. 'My boyfriend,' I say eventually, 'is downstairs.'

'Oh, will the Lord save me from fucking fag hags?'

Lorne looks genuinely pissed off for a second, and then she winks and vanishes into the heaving dance floor.

I stand on the spot for a little while, not sure what to do, and then yet again I think of Christian, and this time I actually do make a move.

I find the door and head back down to the ground-floor cavern and the Christian fan club, where my true love is laughing at a joke made by someone from his tight little doughnut of admirers, throwing back his head so he's all white teeth and white neck.

I'm buzzing for the rest of the night. The Lorne thing has freaked me out a bit. Christian notices my mood when the evening's done and I'm sitting on the bar, watching him, Dan and the club's staff do a variety of things that are all a mystery to me.

He walks over and strokes my back. 'You OK, babe. You look a bit zoned out.'

I make a face at him. 'I went up to the girlie section when I got bored. I pulled a gender bender.'

He laughs, rolling his eyes. 'Oh, you always have to go one better don't you.'

And it's then that I notice something. But Christian has already noticed it and so he's a split second ahead. 'What's this?' he says as he runs a finger over a foreign object, clearly visible, tucked in my bra. I grab for it too, but before I'm quite there he slips his finger and thumb under the elastic and yanks it out.

'Ow.' The what-ever-it-is is made of card and has jabby corners.

It's a business card. Christian squints and reads aloud. 'So Lorne, that'd be your gender bender then?'

'Uh, yeah.'

We look at each other. Christian's doing a strange unreadable face, his expression oddly placid under the flush of sweat and the slightly smearing mascara. I don't look away, and eventually he flashes his eyebrows at me and returns to his job of making tangled webs of dusty wires into sleek figure eights.

I take this as a punishment and am relatively pissed off.

An hour later, at home, we sit on the sofa with cups of tea. Christian is normally really horny after a high-pressure gig, but tonight he is shadowy and barely there. We drink our tea in monosyllables and then I let him take his sulk to bed.

I'm in half dark. We didn't switch the lights on when we came in, my habit, and drank our tea lit by the street lamps and moonlight. Street lamps, moonlight and the winking green glow of the laptop's stand-by. I walk over and fire it up.

While it chunters and whirrs, I walk over to the window. The sitting room doesn't overlook the courtyard, just the street. It's rained while we've been out, autumn at last, and the empty street shines wetly, like black PVC. The computer sounds its ethereal fanfare and reflected in the jet-black pane I see the screen suddenly light pale-blue, the on-screen skyscape beckoning me to another world. A better world. A virtual world. I turn. And sit. And double click.

Dark Knight is on me before I'm even sat down. Missing me, quizzing me, chastising me. He needs a sweetener, and I've got one ready. Pictures. Pretty, pretty pictures.

The one I choose is the one I knew I'd end up choosing. The one I'd all but decided on when I first saw them. It is of Christian topless looking over his shoulder moodily at the camera. He looks so beautiful in it and strangely unlike himself. Unlike himself and yet unmistakably him. Very slightly out of focus, his skin looks so flawless, pink blending into peach and then dusty rose in the hollow of his dimpled shoulder, invisibly fine body hair just a blurring fuzz, hazy and backlit, like an aura.

He looks eminently sulliable, and for one fleeting moment I almost check myself. Almost appreciate what I have long enough to reign myself in. But it is only for a moment.

In a flickering heartbeat my mouse moves, the cursor nuzzles onto the button marked SEND, my fingertip twitches, click, and everything changes.

The IM window flashes and I click. It pops up on the screen. <Wow>, he says, <you are one hot little pup.> And I grin quietly, in spite of myself.

I stare at the screen for about half a minute, just little me in my shabby sitting room. I've closed the curtains now, and the monitor is the only real light in the room, glowing like an alien thing, out of place and out of time, making it seem more important somehow, like the centre of everything, which, right now, it is.

I type: <Thanks>, and hit return, holding my breath.

I've been around. I know the etiquette of these things well enough. He needs to ask and he needs to ask now. Then the words: <Want to play?> flash up on the screen. I exhale. I have him.

My heart is beating so fast that my fingers shake on the keys. <Suer.> Bloody typo. <oops. I mean Sure.>

The pause that follows seems to last for ever. And then: <Then call me.>

I stare at the message and the string of eleven numbers that follow it.

4

She's about 25, long dark hair, sitting on the aisle seat so I can see her long legs. She's wearing light-blue jeans with the boots tucked in, just like she's just stepped out of 1987. Although, actually, that might be back in. I should keep up. One month I should buy *Elle* or *Marie Claire* instead of *Men's Health*. (Well, in truth, I don't so much buy *Men's Health* as read Christian's copy in the bath – and I don't so much read it as look at the pictures.)

She's nestled under the arm of her boyfriend, and he's sort of clean cut: big jaw, tautly ironed white T-shirt. They're not what I would have chosen, but it's salvageable. It's salvageable because she's got this look on her face that kind of says that – if my luck's in (and why wouldn't it be?) – she's actually going to suck his cock. Any minute . . .

I do like the cinema. It's so much more rewarding than the sofa plus the video shop. And that's because if the film's boring there's always another spectacle, always something else to watch. Here, there and everywhere, in the dark people act as if they are in private, which means only one thing for a depraved individual like me.

Just like 80s girl, I'm snuggled up to my boyfriend, but we're not in the back row, we're plumb right in the middle of the stalls. 'Best seats in the house', Christian calls them. He was an usher once – for about a week.

And it's been over a week since the fucking Fandango farrago. In fact, it's been a-whole-nother Fandango since the fucking Fandango farrago, and Christian's apology over throwing a hissy about Lorne and the bra-tucked card has long been accepted. And, of course, I took the opportunity to point out that I couldn't exactly help it if back-to-front transvestites planted their business cards on me. And he had to agree.

So, it seems, I was right about the fact that Christian starting up his own business with his homosexy pic co-star Dan is a really bad idea, because I certainly don't want him running his own show if it makes him a sulky stressed-out arse, who ends up in big moods (so unlike him) about tiny weird bits of stuff. And it doesn't get much weirder than the bra-card mystery (and, as a quick aside, I still can't figure out how Lorne managed that little reverse pickpocket manoeuvre).

But on the subject of crappy things that are currently at the forefront of my mind: this film is so dull. It was written up in the *Guardian* like it was some red-hot fuck fest, well soft-pink fuck fest, and it is so not. I know I might have slightly skewed expectations, but I know rubbish when I see it, especially rubbish that is trying to be sexy-rubbish in order to salvage itself from being rubbish-rubbish. And failing.

That's partly why I'm looking at them: the couple over in the back row. See, despite its overall dullness, the arty film is prettily lit, its only saving grace, really. So, although in the basic flat dark the couple would be shadowy, like pencil-sketched cobwebs, here they twinkle and shift in pretty colours as the scenes change. It's nice, sort of Christmassy – and, hey, it's only October!

And actually, I've changed my mind about this film in the last five seconds. I've had a total change of heart. This film might be a bit on the crap side, but it still has an awful lot going for it. Tons. There's the aforementioned pretty, sparkly lighting, and there's the fact that the cinema is emptyish, just dusted with people, because the arty film is not a huge draw. Not a huge draw and dull as can be, which might be pretty shitty for your average Mr and Ms Saturday Night at the Movies, but is just dandy for my purposes, because if you add it all together it means my chosen couple are delightfully lit, all but alone and bored stiff (ho ho). Perfect.

And predictable. I don't have to wait for a second more. Weightless, she slides onto his lap, straddling him and dipping her head into a wet velvet kiss. I shift in my seat, trying to get a better angle so I can see a little more than the back of her head. Straining and craning and at some risk of a crick, I manage to get an oblique view of her glistening tongue, making steady laps around his lip line.

Very nice.

She starts to kitten flick at his top lip, trying to get him to open up. He seems a little reluctant, maybe he's more aware of the people around them, or maybe he's just playing her – not quite as dumb as his rugger-bugger pose might suggest.

And I'm going with it, relaxing into the soft pace, as she responds to his reticence by shifting right up the gears, first to fifth, and sneaking off his lap and onto the snack-strewn carpet.

And that's great, because it means I can stop rubber necking to see soft lips and rough tongues, and just watch his big, lantern-jawed face. His face is all I need now she's on her knees and slowly sliding his cock into her mouth. So I just watch his face, head tipped back, mouth loose and stressless. I just watch.

As I squirm contentedly in my seat Christian nudges me. Slightly annoyed at the interruption, I glance at him and he grins, his face suddenly bright and toothy white as the big screen lights up with a shot of some big white sky. Spotlit. Glowing like an angel. My baby, he even has his own lighting effects.

'Enjoying it?' he's attempting to whisper, but it's loud enough to get him shushed from three rows back.

I wrinkle my nose. Not sure if he means the flick or my extra-curricular wandering eye.

'Want some assistance?' He makes that last word, 'assistance', sound so unbelievably rude, rolling the serpentine 's's around his mouth with a particularly filthy tone, and at the same time he raises his hand, fingers splayed wide, offering me his magic touch.

I check back. Boyfriend of 8os girl is lolling right back in his seat, delirious, boneless. So near.

'Yeah,' I whisper, a proper whisper, actually quiet. 'Be quick.'

And he gets it. He knows what I need. He doesn't tease or ghost. He finds my clit, all lubed and frictionless already, and pets it with his middle finger. Not crazed, not over-enthusiastic, because I couldn't take that right out of nothing, but clear and bright and definite.

I slide my hips forward and let my legs fall apart, imagining how my current viewing is doing exactly the same, opening his big thighs, so she can swallow all of him. I can picture exactly how she is taking him, angling his eager cock to the side, making sure that it glides against the hot moistness of the inside of her cheek. The endless soft pleasure, making him bite his tongue to keep from screaming – to keep from coming – to make it last for ever. But he can't, he can't, he's so near.

Oh God. And he's so not the only one.

Christian waits just long enough and then speeds up his dance on my clit, swooping and twirling. A gasp and a buck as jaw-boy in the back row starts to come, and I'm so close myself I barely need anything more. I look away from the couple as he keeps on thrusting and thrashing in a muffled discreet sort of way, and glance at Christian. He's got his pretty head bowed as he concentrates on what he's doing, biting his lip, hair falling into his eyes. I grab his wrist and speed him up. He looks so hot. He looks like his photo. The one I sent to Dark Knight. Oh God, Dark Knight.

And I'm coming. I'm coming to the image of Christian masturbating Dark Knight instead of me, his fist curled, tight and obedient, around Dark Knight's hot cock, and it's so very, very good.

And I sort of so wish it wasn't.

The pub over the road is so perfectly placed to catch the overspill from the cinema's own tiny bar that it is heaving with arty types and intellectuals in spectacles. (Well, they look like intellectuals to me.)

I secure a corner of a big scrubbed wooden table and, by some miracle, two stools, while Christian wanders over to the bar, whittling his way to the front with a suitably placed sharpened elbow. Hidden in the clanging din of voices, I rest my elbows on the table and my chin in my hands and watch him happily, still post-orgasm enough to feel warm and smug as he leans over the bar, looking so yummy in his I've-made-no-effort camel cords and black T-shirt.

Of course I know better. I know he always makes an effort. He fusses and whines in Gap and French Connection on his never-ending quest for perfectly cut tops and trousers that hang off his hips how he likes. He even thinks there's some kind of conspiracy against him just because he's a shade under average height. He acts like trouser lengths are there to spite him, but the truth, as I have tried and tried to explain, is all trousers are cut a bit long these days and a little extra fabric at the hem looks cool to me. I once joked that he should be glad of the extra bit to hide his stack heels, and he didn't talk to me for the rest of the afternoon.

Actually, though, he'd give his left bollock to be two inches taller. And I'm certain that that's running through his mind right now as he jostles amongst bigger boys at the bar. It really bugs him. It's not like he's got funny proportions or anything – he's scaled not squashed – but if I make a single crack about his being pocket sized, or the fact that I only have to sport an up do to be officially the taller one, and he pouts longer and harder than bloody Posh Spice.

Across the room, the barman approaches and Christian leans forward and stretches slightly, proffering a folded fiver, and my heart just sort of does this tiny flippy thing, which sometimes happens when I look at Christian doing something.

I watch Christian a lot. A lot, a lot. He kind of knows. He knows I do it; sometimes he even catches me doing it and just smiles. But he doesn't really know how much I do it. Because I do it all the time. Even though I live with him, sleep with him, eat with him and sit on the sofa watching GMTV with him, I still spy on him. I'm like a stalker, sort of, a kind of live-in one without the sneaking around part – except that's not true because I sneak around plenty.

I watch Christian when we're out mostly, just like I'm doing now. Sometimes when he's shopping for clothes I find a way to stand so that I can peek through the gap in the changing-room curtains and spy on him wriggling in and out of his chosen casuals. That's just wonderful. He still can't believe I never get bored when I accompany him on yet another anally retentive ultra-perfectionist shopping expedition!

Sometimes, and I mean very sometimes indeed – say, once every six months maybe (but not to a schedule or anything) – I follow him. Just that, plain and simple. I wait for him to leave the flat, give him a start and then I follow him. I suppose it's nothing that a suspicious girlfriend wouldn't do. It's not like I'm the only woman ever in history to sneak about in a headscarf and dark glasses peeking at her man unawares. But I'm not doing it to find out any of Christian's secrets. I'm just doing it because I enjoy watching him.

In fact, I realised a few weeks ago, pre-Dark Knight but only just, that what I'm doing online is watching Christian too. And it's the most furtive type of Christian-watch possible because not only does he not know I'm watching him, he doesn't even know he's there.

And it's funny, but I never really noticed how fucked up that seemed until right now.

Christian plonks down the drinks and then bends down to pick something off the floor. When he straightens up he's holding a small piece of paper. It's a flier for Schwartz – exactly like the one I've had in my trouser pocket since my extra-curricular activities during Fandango. Exactly like the one that appears to no longer be in my pocket.

'What's that?' I say. (Like I don't know!)

'Well, it looks like it fell out of your pocket. Good thing I grabbed it, babe, God knows what the good people of suburban South Manchester would have made of a respectable young lady like you having a flier for . . .' He makes a show of mock peering, leaning close as if the words were too small and too shocking to be made out. 'A dedicated gay BDSM nightclub.'

'Oh give it here.' I snatch it, leaving a torn corner in Christian's fist. 'I got it at Fandango anyway, well that night, so it's your fault; in fact that makes it yours, practically.'

He looks at me. I can feel I'm blushing a little bit, not wanting Christian to look close up at this particular part of my private little world.

But Christian keeps right on with the looking. And then he says, 'Do you want to go?'

'Where?'

'Here.' He points at the flyer and I feel idiotic. Doh!

'Oh. No. Can't.' I lean across the table and point to the small writing at the bottom, almost illegible in its super-embellished gothic font. I run my finger along the words: 'Strict Dress Code: Uniforms, Leather, Fetish, etc. No Jeans, No Trainers, No Tourists. GAY MEN ONLY.'

Christian smiles. 'Tch. Shame. Never mind, though, babe. I've got a real treat for you when we get home.' And the subject is dropped along with the flier itself, into an overflowing ashtray.

When we are at home, and after we've eaten an omelette from our knees in front of the telly, I get to find out what my treat is. Christian and Dan's fledgling company has taken a big step: their website is online. Which is certainly not a treat for me, in any language I understand. In fact, it's so far down the list of treats I would have picked for myself it's actually on another list all together. But I'm polite. I take a peek at the site.

Christian flicks and clicks, showing me the logoed banner, featuring cute head shots of him and Dan, and how there are neat pics of them sprinkled around from the shoot they did and a few of them 'on the job' at Fandango.

'D'you like it?' He looks over his shoulder with an excited little-boy grin and looking all of twelve. 'Dan did it.' His grin becomes a coy lip bite and shrug combo. 'So it's slightly censored.' A longish pause – beat, beat, beat. 'Or kind of.'

I can't help but return his infectious little look. I can tell he's dying to tell me about some risqué something or other. But I make him wait. Evilly, I change the subject.

'It's really good. Dan's not bad, is he?' I actually hate admitting that annoying wanker Dan is good at anything. He is though; the site's really swishy – striking and modern – without looking all 'designed'.

'Yeah.' Christian keeps on clicking, showing me pages of 'biog' and 'history' and 'corporate philosophy'. 'It's cool, isn't it?'

I lean over his shoulder and put my hand over his on the mouse, taking control so I can explore the site for myself. 'Yeah. Pretty.'

'You haven't even seen the best part.'

From the swivel chair Christian tips his head back, looking up at me standing behind him. His head is sort of upside down and sideways, but even at this angle I can tell he's still doing naughty-little-boy face.

'What?' I say, a two-syllable 'wha-at', sort of semi-stern.

Christian does a lip-bite grin thing and, taking back control of the mouse, clicks on the last button on the sidebar, marked 'downtime'. 'Dan gave me all the passwords and stuff so I could upload a few bits. And I couldn't resist.'

The downtime page loads slowly, probably due to our super-crappy budget-broadband, but eventually yet another rough-edged – yet glossy where it counts – page of text and graphics appears. Downtime is about what Christian and Dan get up to when they are not embroiled in the high-flying world of P and, indeed, R. It lists their hobbies and suchlike: Christian's, which are music, clubbing and looking good, apparently, and Dan's, the rather more pedestrian, chess, films and eating out. And after this and so much puff, scrolling down screen after screen, is the pic. That pic. William's masterpiece of quasi-porn that features the illustrious business partners in a post-coital snuggle.

I look at the pic for a little longer than I need to (because it's there) and then I look at Christian, whose mega-watt beamer would make the Cheshire cat look like a sour puss. I shake my head at him. 'Dan'll be pleased.'

'I know. I can't wait to see the look on his face. I wonder how often he checks the site.'

'What about your clients? Well, your potential clients. What are they going to make of this?'

'They'll be intrigued.' His voice is all squeaky. He is so clearly delighted with this. 'They'll be all, "are they or aren't they?" Like Torville and Dean and "Bolero".'

'Right,' I say in super-sceptical mode, because, well, just because.

'Oh, stop it. Like you wouldn't hire us if you saw that.'

'Oh, me, sure, in a heartbeat. But don't you think I might be kind of niche?'

Christian shrugs. 'Yeah, well, I like niches.' And he loops an arm round the back of my neck and pulls me down into a kiss, which is long and has very obvious motives. 'So,' he whispers when we break, all breathy, 'fancy an early night, or are you all spent from your cinema special?'

I think for a minute, and then decide to chance my arm. 'I'm pretty sated, but maybe you could get me in the mood.'

'Maybe I could,' says Christian.

When I was in my late teens I went to see one of those male strip shows, with some of my friends in the Upper

Sixth. It wasn't my idea. It was a birthday treat for someone else in our gang, who had just turned eighteen.

It was sort of The Chippendales, but not, one of those so-similar-they-might-as-well-be, rip-off acts.

All my friends pissed themselves laughing all the way through the show. And so did I. Except, well, except. See, I did find it funny. Who wouldn't find trousers with Velcroed seams and enormous oiled-up men, with bared super-muscly bums, très amusing? But, at the same time, this other part of me, the part I was just getting to know back then, found it the single hottest thing I had ever experienced.

Strip. Tease. And these days I don't have to put up with oily bum cheeks and oilier mullets to enjoy watching a sexy bloke get naked for me, because when I want striptease now, I can have my own filthy, sexy, twisted, little exhibitionist, writhing around to Suede as he sheds his clothes and strokes his cock.

In the bedroom, I tumble onto the mattress and snuggle into the bedclothes. Half buried under the duvet, I yank off my (once fashionably J.Lo-esque) pink tracksuit and fling it across the room, my bra and pants arcing after them, vaguely in the direction of the laundry basket. I pull the duvet up to my nose and kick my legs against the cotton. I'm buzzing suddenly, fizzy excitement rushing up and down my body, because I know what's coming.

Christian stands at the end of the bed. He's already nudged the CD player on and it's tootling out The Best of The Smiths (which no stripper on earth would choose, but which works perfectly for Christian, with his sort of grubby indie pixie-boy look).

After half a minute or so the track changes and

Christian starts to move his hips lightly, tilting his head and watching me through his over-grown fringe. His tongue darts out and snake flicks over the left corner of his top lip, a cute move that could be unconscious. And then the track kicks up a notch and so does he.

And how.

Christian takes hold of the collar of his T-shirt with both hands and suddenly rips the whole thing in half, straight down the middle of his chest.

I gasp, sucking in breath with shock. It's a move I've never seen before in the many, many stripteases Christian has done for me. A weird little rational part of my brain starts wondering when he planned this, when during our quiet evening he decided he was going to rip his T-shirt in half and made sure it were possible. (My money's on a quick snip through the collar with the kitchen scissors while he was making the omelettes.) But the rest of my brain, the vast majority of it, is screaming at this intellectual element to shut the fuck up, because Christian is suddenly half naked, bucking his hips and moaning, twisting his nipples with spit-slicked fingertips and about to move on to part two.

Thankfully majority rules, even in my fevered brain and I forget about Christian's questionable spontaneity, as I start to stroke my happy clit.

Christian's nipples are bright pink now, teased and tortured to hard peaks by his nasty fingers. He gives them both another harsh turn, crying out with pleasure at the same time. I cry out too. Moaning aloud and lifting my hips off the bed to meet my hand.

Christian's pretty face is so fucking sexy right now: eyes all sparkly with need; lips engorged and heavy, slightly parted; cheeks just a little red over his elegant cheekbones. I could look at his aroused face for ever. It's easily enough to make me come on its own, given long enough. But there's so much more than Christian's beautiful face on offer right now for my viewing pleasure. And I don't want to miss any of it.

Christian leaves his left hand tweaking one of his poor nipples, while he slides his right over his fabric-covered groin, tracing the outline of an obvious bulge. He caresses it slowly and moans. It's time.

Both hands are on his belt loops quickly, and then his trouser fly. He opens the top button and pauses, shucking his hips just a fraction so the waistband drops an inch or two, and a pretty tuft of high-gloss brown pubic hair springs free.

This is easily enough to make me stop fixating on Christian's face and move my attention to his lithe body. I gaze at him: his chest, angel smooth, but softly muscled and definitely male; his bright sore nipples, unmissably pinkly prominent; and the little whisper-fine line of down that traces a path from his belly button down to the eager little crop of shiny wiry hair, emerging from his half-open fly. The wave of comfortingly familiar pheromones breaks over me as I stroke myself, just looking and looking and looking.

Christian undoes the rest of his fly buttons quickly, pop-pop-pop, just like that. He lets his tan-coloured cords fall to the ground. He hardly ever wears underwear, and his erection leaps free, graceful and elegant; an even darker throbbing pink than his cooling nipples.

I sigh. So beautiful.

But the teasing can't last. We both know that there's a main attraction to be reached, and we're both working against the clock now.

Christian turns back around to face me and touches his elegant erection. A slow hand moving gently at first, but soon he's masturbating for me, steadying himself with his left hand on the foot of the bed.

I watch him lazily, loving every minute. I never tire of seeing this, even though I know every line of this show, which means I know very well, even if he's showing no signs of noticing, that he's only a few more strokes from coming.

'Christian,' I hiss, and that's the only thing I have to say. He knows. He knows me.

He almost dives the length of the bed as I fling back the duvet. A quick fumble and he's in me, moving fast, his arousal matching mine. He's fucking me like a teenage virgin. All frantic enthusiasm laced with desperate need and cut with a roughness that is almost clumsy.

'Was it good?' he pants, through the pounding. I only just hear him; I'm miles away, lost in the sensation of his smooth chest rubbing against my breasts, hot and slick, like his breath on my face and his hair in my eyes.

'Oh God, yes.' I moan, opening my legs wider and urging him deeper and deeper, squirming around to get the pressure right in the place I need it; trying to make his cock, his hip bones, his anything, replicate what my practised fingers were doing to my clit. I'm near, but the angle's a little off and my clit's attention is starting to wander...

Out of nowhere Dark Knight steps into my consciousness. Sexy and strangely recognisable for someone I have never seen. I try to push him away, wanting to come to my boy and his writhing this time, but my subconscious is persistent and I can't seem to shake him.

I cross my ankles, up as high as I can behind Christian's back. And he's at the perfect angle suddenly, but it's too little too late and even as I hit my spot I can feel Christian jerk and moan into his moments-too-soon orgasm.

* * *

64

If I were any good at hiding these things I so would, I'd at least try, but I'm not. Christian can read me like a Mr Man book. Still flushed and panting he lifts his head to look at me and I can see the question burning on his lips, but I know he's not going to ask, because he doesn't really need to. Instead he just says: 'Aww, shit.'

I hear myself say, 'It doesn't matter. I had my go at the cinema.' Because I really am that trite. And I know it does matter. It really does.

It matters because he tried. He put a lot of effort into getting me off. If this were only ever meant to be a quickie to send Christian off to sleep with a smile on his face that would have been fine. But it wasn't. Christian had a goal here and he missed. He went on stage, gave his all, but when it came down to it – no curtain call, no encore. I might as well have sat Christian down and told him that I don't fancy him any more for the same cold water over ego effect.

It's weird because I fancy the pants that he hardly ever wears off Christian, and a bit of work from him really should be enough to get me off. Even after an afternoon bonus. So it's weird – probably just one of those things.

'Shall I?' Christian says, unenthusiastically, offering me an unspoken choice of finishing-off techniques. But I smile and turn him down, because my bubble is so very burst.

Not long after, Christian goes out like a well-fucked light, but I'm not so lucky. Into the small hours I'm still staring at the shadow-shrouded ceiling. I rub up hopefully against Christian, who is all hot and smooth, wrapped in nothing but the snowy white sheet. In the familiar pool of light from the street lamp outside the window, he's as perfectly lit as ever. He's also perfectly sound asleep.

65

I fidget and roll over, thinking maybe if I twist and turn enough I might get Christian to stir and repeat his offer of a quick finish-off, but I give up when Christian gives a great big pig-like snort and rolls away from my coercions.

Next thing I know, I'm teetering on the edge between asleep and not. Drifting one way and then the other. And then I'm wide awake, but must have been asleep just before, because I was dreaming.

In my dream I was in a bedroom. It was a really cheesy 80s soft-rock, music-video bedroom with a huge four-poster bed and big gauzy sea-mist curtains that rolled around in a phantom breeze. The rest of the dream memory is hazy. I try to chase its tail round my brain, but it whips and slips away. But it was a sex dream. And it was about Dark Knight.

My eyes snap wide open in the dark. Christian's hot body is now snaked around mine, my head's still half in dreamland, and I only have one thought in my head. More. More Dark Knight.

I wriggle free of Christian's hold and climb out of bed. Shivering a little, I walk into the living room. The laptop's on. Bright-pink scrolling text with the simple message C&D Promotions is trailing across the screen. I graze the mouse and the screensaver vanishes, replaced with the C&D website and that picture of Christian and Dan.

It's still connected to the web, so all I have to do is launch the chat programme. And it's late, but I'm lucky. He's there.

I don't really know what to say, but that's OK because, as I've not so much as blipped his radar since the pic-sending incident of ten days ago, the first topic of conversation is my recent elusiveness and that'll do.

<You're getting cold feet, aren't you, pup?>

<Yeah> I reply. Thanking my lucky stars that he's gone

and given me an excuse for going AWOL right away. What a thoughtful top, he's saved me the trouble of trying to come up with something.

<That's OK, pup. I quite understand. You're new to this, aren't you?>

I'm not sure what to make of this, but I go with, <Yeah.>

<I know it's daunting, but we really should chat on the phone. It'll help you to relax, once you hear my voice.>

<OK> I type. Whatever. I'm not even paying attention really, just going with it and trying to work the conversation round to something sexy.

<We can just chat, nothing more. Well, if more develops then that's cool, but no pressure.>

<OK.>

<Well, you've got my number. Call me next Saturday.>

And he's gone, leaving me marooned in the aftermath of the world's worst ever cyber chat: nothing sexy discussed at all and a phone date I can't possibly make in the diary. Great. Add that to the evening I've had and it seems I have suddenly become the mistress of sexual disappointment. Double great.

I'm about to go back to bed, when I spot something in the desk tidy. It's Lorne's card, the one that she slipped into my bra on the night of Fandango. I pick it up. It's not a hugely informative card, nothing but a name and a mobile number. On one hand, the last thing I need is more complication, but on the other, as I've just set a date for calling Dark Knight anything further is surely just a drop in my ocean of confusion.

And she seemed quite nice.

I grab my handbag and dig around for my phone, when I find it I flip it open and switch to texting mode.

My thumb fumbles on the stupidly tiny keys, but I fight to get my message out, while auto text does its best to mangle my meanings at each new key press. At last I have: HI, WE MET AT CRUZE. IMOGEN. FANCY LUNCH TMW? And that seems OK, so I press send before I can reconsider.

Then I'm in text limbo. It's late, but it's Saturday and Lorne gave the impression of being a die-hard party animal. I can't decide whether to wait for a reply or go to bed. I stare at the phone in my hand for a minute or so, while I wait for my brain to make a decision. And then it bleeps the incoming message bleep, so loud in the silent living room I almost jump off the chair.

I press read. Heart banging, for some reason.

SURE. PERCY'S@1?

YEAH. OK. C U THERE.

5

By the time I emerge on Sunday morning Christian claims to have 'been up ages', which I seriously doubt, as it is only half eleven. My guess is he's been up fifteen minutes, max. So I poke my tongue out as a clever comeback, and join him on the sofa, where's he's watching some boring local political show.

And I don't think about Dark Knight, or Lorne, or last night's anti-climactic shag. In fact, I ignore my rather pressing to-think-about list and grab the remote instead, flicking through the channels mindlessly, and finally settle for the *Hollyoaks* omnibus and a Sunday-morning semi-coma.

A little while later, I persuade Christian to make me some coffee, and as he is walking back into the living room with a mug in each hand, he says casually, 'You know Mr Fox?'

'Uh-huh.' I reply affirmatively, because I certainly do know Mr Fox, if only in the obsessive stalker sense.

'Well, he had someone in his kitchen this morning. A man. Cute.'

'No!' I ignore the coffee Christian is offering and stare at him in shock and awe. 'Mr Fox never has overnighters,' I add with head-shaking conviction.

'Well, he must've done last night, because I saw them having breakfast.'

At this last revelation I take off like a rocket from the sofa, and tear into the kitchen – grabbing my fridge-top

69

binoculars en route – and skid to a halt by the window. I'm disappointed, though, even with magnification, Mr Fox's kitchen contains nothing but lonely white goods.

'He's gone now,' Christian says from the doorway, still holding a steaming mug in each hand. 'It was ages ago.'

I spin around. And I know I'm going OTT about this, but I can't help it. 'Why didn't you wake me?' I say, in a horribly whiny type of voice.

Christian shrugs. 'What makes you think I'd didn't try? Little Miss Girlfriend in a Coma?'

Stupid sleep! Stupid sex! Stupid sex dreams and late-night chat and texting! I missed Mr Fox's boy toy.

Gutted, I snort at the world and stalk out of the room, pausing to grab my mug of coffee and then give Christian's white cotton-covered crotch a half-playfully apologetic and half plain-old-pissed-off squeeze. Even when I am back on the sofa with my coffee, I can still hear him squeaking in pretend agony.

And I've only had one mouthful before I realise it's almost midday, and I have an appointment. I need to get a move on. Or, at the very least, get some clothes on.

The café Lorne suggested – Percy's – is not a place I would ever have chosen to meet someone, well not unless that someone was visually impaired. It's half in the gay village and half in the student stamping ground, and it tries to cater to both groups, thus failing in a weird no man's land mish-mash, which can only really be described as an acid-induced, cartoony, campy, freak show. The décor features cartoon pigs, cavorting around the walls, which, call me picky, I find vaguely disturbing when I'm tucking into a bacon buttie. Either Lorne really doesn't like me, or she has really terrible taste.

I find myself a secluded table (not that there are any secluded tables at fluorescent-strip friendly Percy's) and fiddle nervously with a ridiculously huge, ridiculously garish, laminated menu.

The menu/windbreak provides a nice little bit of cover, though, so I kill time by staring at a nice-looking man in the corner. He's wearing a soft, moss-green suit, which hangs on his small body, all drapey and lovely. His dark hair is a little over-long, like he's growing it long, or growing out of a much sharper cut. It falls over his ears, but I can still just about see little sideburns peeking out. Yum. I love sideburns, I don't know why, maybe it's a Mr Darcy thing (even though really I'm far more of a Heathcliff girl) but, God, a man with sideburns will always pique my interest even if the rest of him is ropey as hell.

I find myself wondering if Dark Knight has sideburns ... and my mind starts to wander as I stare at green-suit man and that's bad news. I'm not paying attention to where my eyes are resting, so when the man in my glazed stare line looks up, I don't twig in time to look away within a respectable interval. He catches my eye and smiles and, oh fuck, it's only bloody Lorne herself.

She jumps up and makes her way over to me, calling out 'Imogen, hi,' and beaming, all wide-spread arms and air kisses. After I have been suitably embraced, she sits down, kind of languidly, like she's made of play-dough (or does a lot of yoga), lounging back in the cheap moulded plastic and filling up more space that I would have thought her small body could. Her sparkly eyes are the same pretty moss green as her suit, rimmed with dark lashes and framed by dark brows. They are the kind of eyes that are hard to look away from.

'Hi,' I say, and smile.

'I'm glad you texted me,' Lorne says, picking up her menu and fiddling but not really looking at it. 'I was wondering about you.'

'Wondering about me? Wondering what about me?'

Lorne flashes her black eyebrows. 'Oh, just what a straight girl with a boyfriend was doing in the dyke section of Cruze eyeing up all the girls.'

'Oh, that.'

'Yep,' says Lorne, 'that.'

'Long story,' I say, and I'm about to elaborate when a waitress appears.

Without even consulting me Lorne shoos her away again with a blithe hand wave, and then looks down at her menu. 'Well,' she says from behind the big piece of laminated card, 'let me choose what I'm going to eat and then you can tell all while I eat it.'

A few minutes later, when the waitress returns, Lorne orders a jacket potato for me – as requested – and a mixed grill for herself. Lorne is fascinating and so endlessly watchable. She's quite domineering in a way, doing things like ordering the food, taking charge. What with that and the way she sits with her legs spread wide and her elbows on the table – filling up her space – and the way she subtly controls the conversation, she's almost more like a man than an actual man. Like a parody of a man.

The other thing about Lorne, something I can't believe I missed during our aborted Cruze face-suck, is the fact she is absolutely jaw-droppingly gorgeous. In fact she looks spookily like my own personal archetype of gorge: Christian. She's the same small compact size and has similar pouty lips and high cheekbones, oh, and the sideburns, of course. OK, her eyes are green to Christian's smoky dark brown and the hair's different – Lorne's is a little longer – but it's still pretty close. They could almost be twins.

One thing – she doesn't dress like Christian (i.e. like a gay man with a shopping addiction and a Gap charge-card) but I like the way she dresses, like a delicious fetishisation of all things masculine – all sharp lines and tailoring.

Mmm, suits. Christian used to wear a suit all the time when I first met him, but he doesn't bother any more, doesn't like to look like he's trying too hard, apparently. In fact, he hasn't got dressed up all sexy-smart for ages – not since that networking do.

And I can't start thinking about suited Christian without wondering whether Lorne's wearing as little under her suit as my own boy regularly does (and then I'm hoping desperately that my naughtiness isn't blindingly apparent on my face).

But I simply can't spend all afternoon eye-fucking Lorne and wondering where my heterosexuality just went. I came here for a Sunday confessional. And she's waiting.

First things first. She asked a question, so I explain about Cruze. And about Christian and about Fandango. About how I got bored and then I went over to see Dan and then ended up in the women's section, etc., etc. And I finish up where Christian finds the card in my bra and gets all uppity.

I sit back and wait for Lorne to speak. She swallows what she's eating (a grilled tomato) and then says, thickly, 'You know what puzzles me, though?'

'What?'

'Where'd Dan go? One minute he's there and then you're on your own.'

I frown, puzzled at this bizarre conversational tack. Surely this can't have been the most notable part of my epic tale.

'I dunno,' I say. 'He must have wandered off. It took me a while to get over to him. I had to cross the dance floor and it was pretty heaving. He probably went to the bar or something.'

'Maybe he got lucky. Maybe some hot guy dragged him into a corner.'

I almost spit out my iced tea at this. 'Dan! Ha! No fucking way!' I blurt, all staccato crazed with the shock! Horror! And when I stop laughing, I end up telling Lorne all about Dan's little character flaw and homosexy website pics, and even as I'm saying it, I'm realising that this is hardly evidence for Dan's uber-straight-i-tude, which Lorne points out (of course). But it's all good, because talking about those pics is the perfect opportunity to steer the conversation around to exactly where I want it.

'Actually, it's the pics I wanted to tell you about.'

Lorne raises a single eyebrow. 'They don't sound like my sort of thing, really.' And she punctuates this by looking right at my tits, as if I might not have got what she meant otherwise. Just in case I'd totally got the wrong idea and thought all the evidence I'd witnessed so far (the being dragged up as a man, the being in a gay club, the snogging of me) pointed to her being a red-blooded het-girl.

So I ignore the ogling, and soldier on. 'You see, there's this bloke and, well, he kind of thinks I'm a bloke.'

Lorne smirks at this, which is pretty understandable considering that Lorne (apparently) spends 24–7 in her boy drag.

But again, with the soldiering on. 'Yeah, well, it's online see. I've kind of let him think I'm a bloke because, well, he's gay and ...' and it all comes out, right up to the sticky question of Saturday's phone date. Yet again I find myself waiting expectantly for Lorne to say something in response.

She looks a little bit fazed. She's been staring at me for the last few minutes, while I've babbled on about

Dark Knight and Christian and cyber sex, ignoring her last few morsels of bacon and mushroom.

Eventually she coughs and then smiles and then laughs. 'Imogen, you nutter! I thought you were little-miss-straight. And here you are, queerer than queer. Hell, you're queerer than me.'

Wow. I'm not 100 per cent certain that this is a compliment, but I feel myself blush slightly anyway.

'And I don't see your problem,' Lorne continues. 'What's wrong with phone sex? Isn't that even better? Better than cyber, I mean.'

'Well, yeah, but how can I have phone sex with Dark Knight? He'll be able to tell from my voice.'

'Oh.' Lorne's excited face falls as the penny visibly drops. And then just as quickly, she seems to perk right back up again. 'Oh but, oh, that's simple, isn't it.'

'It is?'

'Well, yeah, get Christian to do it for you.'

With a stomach full of lunch and a head full of conflict-ing ideas, I walk down to the tram stop and think about Lorne's 'simple' idea. And realise that, really, it's the only option anyway. Well, the only option outside dropping the whole thing. And, that's not exactly been the glitter-ing uber success I'd hoped. Dropping Dark Knight clearly only works until I have a few mildly cross words with Christian or one wet dream and then I'm right back in his lap writing cheques my gender can't cash.

The only real drawback is the fact that Christian would never have phone sex with a stranger, just for my vicarious pleasure.

And that's the thing, though. Of course he would. He so would.

Because Christian has happily bought the whole, love me, love my kinks package. OK, there's stuff he doesn't know about, like my porn videos, but that's only because I choose to keep them secret. It's not like he'd freak out if he knew or anything – I'm pretty sure of that. He happily assists with Fox-watch and he picks leaves and grass out of my hair, about once a month, when I've been lurking in bushes. He even gives me reports on what the neighbours have been up to while my back's been turned, because, well, what can I say, he's cool with it. He's cool with me.

And that's how it is with Christian and me. And that's why we're lifers. In it for good. Together for ever. In fact we've already been together for ever, or seven years, which is as good as for ever, really.

I met Christian way back in the dark ages, when I was a baby of 22. I'd just burst out of Uni with a 2:1 in art history tight in my fist, and no clue what I wanted to do with it, or with my life.

Well, I had some vague idea about earning huge amounts of money so I could afford to live in a sumptuous Beckingham-Palace-style mansion staffed by horde of naked male models (or failing that, maybe doing something in marketing), but the bottom line was some kind of quick cash, to start making a dent in my debts. So I followed the well-worn groove from the graduation ceremony to the nearest temping agency and signed up for anything that paid.

And the agency actually came up trumps. Well, it was second-time lucky because the first thing they sent me on was a job as PA to the Chief Exec of a printing company, who didn't seem to like me very much. He got rid of me after a week because we 'didn't gel'. I got the distinct impression that the whole gelling problem was mostly due to me not being some big-titted blonde who enjoyed giggling at his pathetic jokes. Bitter? Moi?

But, actually, it worked out pretty well for me, because the second job the agency fixed me up with was as an Admin Assistant in the weirdly monikered Paranoid PR.

Ah – Paranoid, the fact that there were always at least five shiny aluminium scooters parked up in reception summed up their company ethos better than any of their cleverly worded 'visions'.

I liked it a lot at Paranoid. And they liked me. I mostly worked behind reception and, unlike the bastard printers, the super-unconventional Paranoid liked having 'a kooky-looking dreamer' on their front desk – or, at least, that's what one of the eerily young company directors told me one lunchtime in the pub.

And that was where Christian worked. In fact, he still does work there. He might be neglecting his day job horribly for the C&D Promotions moonlight-a-thon, but Paranoid is still his mortgage-paying bread and butter. I think he's something ending in manager now, but back then he was a plain old executive. Except he wasn't – plain, that is.

I didn't really get to know Christian when I started at Paranoid. I didn't really get to know any of the proper PR types. I was languishing in receptionist no man's land, even though my job title was Admin Assistant, and Christian and his account exec counterparts would just screech into reception in the morning and scoop up their post and whiz off to the open-plan office out back, where they did their high-powered thing. Occasionally I'd have a thrilling exchange with one of them along the lines of, 'Gen, is the boardroom free at 3?', or 'Gen, can you order more pink Post-its, there's only yellow'. That sort of thing, but really, to them, I was just another bit of esoteric-looking office furniture.

But it isn't like I minded, not really. Receptionist at Paranoid is still one of the best jobs I've ever had. I had two huge windows where I could watch the world slink by, a huge stack of glossies I could flick through and nothing particularly taxing to do. Perfect.

Now, for some reason, I, as receptionist, was entrusted with the huge responsibility of holding the stockroom key. Whenever any of the back-room bunnies wanted to burrow into the basement and rifle around in the warren of dangerously stacked cardboard boxes of promotional T-shirts and logoed biros, then they had to come and see me and sign out the key. Why this level of security was required for a stockroom full of freebies and tat was quite beyond me. But what did I know? I was just the Admin Assistant. Well, the Admin Assistant and the key holder.

And that really was the key to it all.

So there I am one otherwise dull and completely unnotable day, when Christian comes up and asks me for the key. Now, at this point, Christian and I are close-enough colleagues to say hello in the lift of a morning, but nothing special. But that's all about to change.

Christian has been gone for about half an hour and I'm flicking idly through *Go*, when all of his team trot through reception, clearly off on a lunch outing, a regular-enough feature – about half Paranoid's business happened in pubs and bars. Anyway, as the corporate promotions department file past, I hear a short blonde girl say, 'Where's Christian?' and her taller companion replies, 'Dunno.'

I'm about to tell them, he's in the stockroom, when I stop and instead of letting on I just sit tight and watch them all file out the door. I button it because a bell has suddenly started ringing in my head. And I like the tune it's playing an awful lot.

See, the previous evening I had been at the pub with a crowd of my old Uni mates. And one of the boys, a friend of a friend, completely sloshing with about six pints inside him, had started talking to me about some of the rather naughty things he likes to get up to at work, viz. secretly masturbating when he should be data inputting.

It was not a pleasant conversation in very many ways. Drunken boy was slurry and droney, with faintly pukey breath and kept putting his hand on my knee (although this could have been to stop himself tipping off his chair). But despite these horrors I stayed and listened, because I was horribly fascinated by his chosen topic of conversation. Drunken boy might have been making furtive masturbating sound a little unsavoury, but I was certain this raw info could be pure gold after my subconscious has spun it right.

'It's great,' he burbled, 'jacking on the clock. That's the beauty. You come like a steam train and you're being paid for it.'

'And you do this?'

'Everyone does it. Well, dunno about girls, but every bloke double-you-ay-double-yous.'

I frown at this last incomprehensible outburst.

'Wanks at work.'

And that conversation must still be floating around the back of my brain, because as I'm standing behind reception, wondering about the AWOL Christian, the penny drops.

My lovely little pretty boy wiggles off to the basement about twice a week, usually for about forty-five minutes at a time. Now, forty-five minutes isn't long, not really, but it's a long time to spend in the basement as frequently as that. The basement, after all, is a nasty place – dark and dingy, with a slightly odd musty smell, most people try and avoid it. And the really big news, the hold-the-front-page headline grabber, the thing that makes me really excited when I think it, is the fact that almost certainly no one at Paranoid knows quite how long Christian regularly spends in the basement but me.

Oh, on reception I hold all the best secrets, and that also includes the one about the existence of the spare basement key. (In case of emergencies.)

Not knowing I hold my entire future in my hands, I cry lunch, grab the boss's PA to mind reception and head for the lift, clutching the key to my magical kingdom. And trying not to mouth-breathe like some kind of psycho loon.

On my very first day at Paranoid I'd noticed Christian on my whistle-stop orientation tour of the offices, when I quickly ranked all my colleagues to be in terms of their easy-on-the-eye-ness. Christian had come first, second and third. And ever since I first spied him, Christian had been a pretty regular feature in my night-time fantasies. He was even a pretty crucial factor in shaping them, because although this was years before Mr Fox, or even my first pair of binoculars, way back then I still loved to fantasise about sneaking, stalking and spying on Christian in all kinds of situations, but most particularly, catching him stroking his own hard cock.

In one favourite fantasy I'm a stalker. I follow Christian home one night and watch his house, cloaked silent and invisible in the soft black night. When Christian goes to bed I climb a tree in his front garden, and safely nestled in the arms of its branches, I find I can see through open curtains into Christian's coolly spartan bedroom.

I squirm in the tree as he shucks off his clothes and settles onto the bed, conveniently eschewing the camouflage of the duvet, and stretching his smooth naked body like a cat, relaxed, but not quite ready to sleep just yet. A sly hand glides over his soft skin to his twitching cock and he takes it in a slick, warm fist . . .

As I wait for the lift in the tastefully decorated lobby, my heart turns over. Is my fantasy about to come true in the nasty basement?

Paranoid PR is based on one floor of a smallish tower block and the block's basement level is divided up into storerooms for the various tenants. It's a five-floor ride away. It seems to take about twenty million years.

When the lift doors finally swoosh open they reveal scuffed-up grey lino and the subtle change in air quality marks out the place as underground.

As I follow the twisty corridor lit by swinging bare bulbs, my heart is banging behind my throat. I nearly turn around and go back twice, almost but not quite convincing myself that what I'm doing is every kind of stupid. But when I reach the scuffed-up door marked 'Paranoid PR' it's locked. And suddenly I know I'm doing the right thing, because why would Christian lock himself in if all he's doing is a quick stock check?

Without even pausing to savour the moment, I stealthily unlock the door and ease it open, careful not to make a peep.

He's on the floor in the middle of the untidy room, lying back against a pile of shrink-wrapped T-shirts, shiny and slidey in their individual plastic bags. His jacket's off, folded and hanging over a filing cabinet. He's in rolled-up shirt sleeves and half-mast pin-striped trousers. His eyes are squeezed tight closed. There's a little flush in his cheeks and he's stroking himself slowly, completely given over to pleasure.

I steady myself on a rack of metal shelving. I'm only about ten feet away from Christian's auto-erotic tableau, but I feel pretty confident that I'm not going to set any frantic alarm bells ringing anytime soon. He's on another planet, which is good, because I'm rapidly heading into orbit myself.

Blast off.

My mouth is dry. My knees are weak. My knickers are significantly less clean than they were a minute ago. I'm suddenly a panting catalogue of arousal clichés. Christian stroking himself, oblivious and obvious is the most beautiful thing I have ever seen in my life. If it were a painting I would hang it on the wall (although I might take it down if people came round).

I like to think I fell in love with Christian right there. In fact, I often tell him so. It's not really true; I fell in love with spying, though.

Spying and taking risks.

Christian's hand starts to move faster, gliding easily over his shining, lube-slicked cock. His cock is very, very beautiful, olivey brown like his skin, with just a shading of deep pink at the tip. It matches his flushed cheeks exactly.

As the rhythm builds and builds I see him lean back, working his way deeper and deeper into the pile of bagged T-shirts, drowning in them. And I drown with him, lost in what I'm seeing, not even noticing the dinginess of the basement storeroom all around us, the sharpness of the metal upright I am holding too tightly, or even the noisiness of my own breathing – which is getting heavier and heavier.

Which might be why, just before he comes he opens his eyes, big and wide. He looks right at me and then disappears again as his orgasm overtakes him.

Oh. God.

* * *

I want to stay, watch his come-down, bask in the after-glow, even witness the clean-up. But I can't. He's seen me. And I scarper, knowing that Christian, in his half-undressed state can't exactly follow. Before he's even finished coming, I'm through the doors and half-way down the dirty corridor. As I'm waiting for the lift, all nervous foot tapping and under-breath muttering ('Come on, come on'), I hear the door open and his voice calling, 'Imogen?' But before he can reach me the grey metal doors slide open and I'm away.

Course, I can run but I can't hide, short of resigning on the spot, I can't actually avoid Christian indefinitely. But at least my reception desk offers me a little wall of protection from the mutual embarrassment to come.

As Christian walks in, I force myself to be suddenly engrossed in an email about the codes for the burglar alarm. But instead of just walking past and avoiding my eye, he stops, and leans on the desk.

I try and pretend I haven't noticed. Then he coughs politely, and I have to look up – he's holding up the basement key. As I take it from him a couple of his fingertips graze my hand. I meet his eyes and he smiles this big, knowing, meaningful smile.

Oh.

And three days later, when Christian heads for the basement, key in hand, I barely wait two minutes before I follow him.

It becomes a habit in less than a fortnight. Although I still wait a few minutes before I follow. Going down to the basement in the lift together for our mutual exhibitionist and voyeuristic jollies would seem weird – but at the same time it would also seem weird not to travel back up together. OK, so for the first few times I still whisk myself away while he's cleaning himself up, but soon I find myself dawdling, ambling down the corridors to the lift, hoping he'll catch up with me before it arrives.

The first few times we ride back up in the lift together we don't talk, just smirk if-they-only-knew smirks at each other, like naughty kids.

But on the fourth ride I say, 'It's better if you don't bend your left leg.'

'Huh?'

'If you bend your left leg it obscures my view of your, uh, you know.'

'Oh, right.' Not the best conversation we've ever had, but it's pretty momentous in its own little way.

The time after that I don't even leave the basement while he gets himself together, I just lean against the teetering metal shelves and watch him fumble his way back into his clothes.

'Was that OK?' he says, looking back over his shoulder at me as he shrugs on his suit jacket.

'Er, yeah,' I say, sort of looking away and a bit at the floor.

'Good,' he says. 'It's, um, it's much better when you're here.'

'Yeah,' I reply, all studied dispassion, but my heart gives a little leap and I find myself gazing right at him, a huge grin plastered across my face.

I see him swallow, so hard I can practically hear his Adam's apple banging against his tie knot. 'It's so hot, having you there, knowing you're watching. Don't know why.' And he doesn't drop my gaze while he says this.

I hold his gaze right back and say, 'Well, I always think it's best not to analyse things too much.'

Three days after this Christian comes up to my reception desk. 'Um, Imogen,' he says, his manner sort of half-way between full-on confident office-Christian and awkward semi-shy basement-Christian, 'do you want to come for a drink?'

So would Christian call Dark Knight for me? And pretend to be me pretending to be him? And let me listen in?
   Do exhibitionists fuck in the woods?

6

The following Thursday night, while Christian is out doing his money-grubbing thing at Fandango again, I spend the majority of my Home Alone time fretting about how near Saturday is, because I still haven't asked Christian to do me a certain little telephonic favour. After making the big decision to ask Christian to do the call to Dark Knight, I didn't reckon on the actual asking part being so hard, but then I didn't reckon on the fact that I am a gigantic cowardly pussy.

The get-Christian-to-do-it option is all well and good, but it involves actually telling Christian what I've been doing, from porno vids through to online adultery. And no matter how convinced I am that Christian is going to be fine with it all, that doesn't seem to make it any easier for the actual words to come out of my mouth.

At about 9ish, for a change of fretting venue, I go into the kitchen and put the kettle on for a cup of tea, praying we've got some biscuits in, because I really need the sugar. And while I'm in the kitchen I glance out of the window and notice that Mr Fox is in his. He's unshaven and half-naked in just a pair of artfully torn jeans, the gorgeous and biteable lower half of a latte-tanned buttock peeking through the distressed indigo. I continue to watch him idly while the kettle rasps to its crescendo. He's fiddling with a bottle of red, and I smile to myself, as I consider traipsing over to Mr Fox's flat and asking him to make the call to Dark Knight. It would almost be worth doing it just to see the look on his oh-so-studious face.

Mr Fox aside, in all seriousness though, I have no other option. No fall-back position. Who else could I ask? (Even if I had time, which I don't.) Dan, who is almost certainly the worst possible candidate? My boss Frank, who is also almost certainly the worst possible candidate? And that's it! Those are the only men I know! Well, apart from a few idiot blokes who work in my office and the men I know only because I spy on them (I know some of them pretty well, though). God, I need to get out more. Maybe I should go online, on one of those dating sites and meet some nice friendly open-minded chaps.

(However, that probably wouldn't work for my purposes, unless I go to a special site where you can meet nice friendly men who will agree to impersonate some kind of weird hybrid of oneself and one's boyfriend in order to carry out a freaked-out SM phone date with some highly dubious third party.

And I just can't even be bothered to type all of that into Google.)

So, upshot is, I have to ask Christian. Or I have to find a way to make myself ask Christian. And I decide, after some deliberation, there's really only one way I can do it: completely pissed.

Christian finally rolls in at 3 a.m. I'm so sozzled by this time I'm totally recumbent. With a whoop of greeting that betrays the fact that he has also had more than a drink or two, Christian takes a flying leap from the doorway onto the sofa and my prostrate form. Luckily I'm merry enough to be more or less anaesthetised to the floor-shaking impact of his misjudged belly-flop.

Lying full length on top of me, he observes me for a sec, in super-close-up, no doubt clocking my bleary eyes and wobbly movements.

'Baby,' he says, his voice kind of soft-loud, which is

Christian's pathetic version of a whisper, rendered even less like one by his own alcohol consumption. 'Baby, are you pissed?'

'Bit, maybe,' I say. And Christian goggles, understandably, because I don't really drink. I have my vices and alcohol just isn't one of them. Control freaks like me don't like to drink. Well, except when they have to ask their boyfriend to pretend to be them in some kind of homoerotic tragi-farce. Which, frankly, is the very definition of exceptional circumstances.

Christian leans in and pops a beery kiss on my lips. Normally I hate the taste of beer on his breath, but a few drinks always make me horny, and so I stretch up as he retreats from the kiss, and catch his mouth a full-on lusty smacker. Then, somehow, the frantic snogging that quickly ensues, causes Christian to fall completely off the sofa, taking me with him, and next moment we are rolling around on the floor, all panting hot breath and fabric-tugging hands.

It's not a shag really. It's more of a clumsy clothing-shedding fumble, which turns into penetration through sheer fluke. And it ends with Christian collapsing, unsated on top of me, laughing and spluttering, 'I can't. It's going soft.' It's possibly the worst wannabe-fuck that Christian and I have ever perpetrated together.

So we abort and in our drunken states we roll into bed. Alarms are not set. Clothes (the ones that survived the shag, at least) are not properly removed. Huge, reviving glasses of water are not drunk. And hangovers develop nicely.

We wake up late with thumping heads and bone-dry mouths. We have no choice. Sickies are pulled.

By lunchtime I'm working steadily on my rehydration with a second bottle of Vittel and Christian's doing likewise with a share-size bottle of Coke. We're both doped up on paracetamol and daytime telly, almost catatonic, side by side on the sofa. And it's Friday, just over 24 hours until I, or at least someone in this flat, is meant to call Dark Knight.

'You know,' says Christian in a distinctly gravelly voice, 'fifty per cent of all sick days are taken on Fridays.'

'Uh-huh.' I'm kind of distracted by the telly. Fern and Phil are giving the low-down on a horrifically watchable celeb-reality show, and currently updating us viewers about a budding romance between a pneumatic ex-soap star and an uber-tanned washed-up pop star. Both parties are very pretty. Despite my delicate state, I'm liking.

'Yeah. Cheeky buggers. Give people like us who really are ill on a Friday a bad name,' he says, recovering from the exertion of this exchange with a long pull on his Coke.

I laugh, and then squeal in crossness as Christian grabs the remote and flips over to MTV.

Then I laugh again, as Christian reels back from my squeal in agony, clutching his splitting skull. Heh. His hangover is worse than mine, which is a victory of sorts. I snatch the remote back and Fern and Phil return to the screen. I am triumphant.

After lunch I feel pretty much fully regenerated, having nipped to the greasy spoon round the corner and brought us both back a full English in a polystyrene box. Just what the doctor ordered. Christian is still looking slightly peaky, though, despite having consumed twice his body weight in Coca-Cola, and suddenly it feels easier to do my dirty little deed, with him all weak and kittenish.

So I do. 'Christian, I want to tell you something.' Just like that. No more faffing around.

'Huh?' Christian grunts. He's lying on the sofa under a protective duvet, which is strewn with the day's debris.

'Well, I want to show you something, really.'

'Does it involve me moving from this sofa?' Christian says.

'Uh, no.'

'Then show away.'

With my heart feeling weirdly dead and heavy in my chest, I walk to the wardrobe in the spare room and pull out *Private Punishment* and *Hidden Camera Studs*. Then I walk into the room, slide the latter into the video, and grab the remote.

Christian frowns. 'Did you just get that video from the spare room?' he says. It's not really a question, more just a what-the-fuck?

'Yeah, I keep a couple of videos in the wardrobe.'

Christian suddenly looks more animated than he has done all day. 'Oh my God! Are they of porn? They are, aren't they? They're of porn. God, Imogen, I didn't know you were into porn.'

'Well. It's not exactly porn,' I lie, almost dripping sheepishness on the carpet.

I press play. *Hidden Camera Studs* has no titles or credits. It's straight into the action, so there are a few moments of hissy snowstorm while some blank tape spools and then bang! It fills the screen. It's a locker room full of naked men, none of whom seem to be very focussed on getting changed. It's edge-to-edge big male nudity. I swallow hard.

We watch for maybe ten minutes. The locker-room scene becomes some very rough, very dirty sex in the back of a car, rendered almost incomprehensible by being filmed through the almost opaque, steamed-up back windscreen. It's weird watching with Christian, because he may be cool as fuck, but I can still be bashful about my particular choice of wank fodder. So I'm partly squirming with embarrassment, but the tape still turns me on as much as it ever did, so I'm partly squirming for another reason too. It's a very weird experience.

Eventually Christian says, 'Oh, I get it, baby. I see why you like this.'

I just wait. I don't say a word.

After about another minute of on-screen sweating and writhing he says, 'No, really, babe, it's fine.' He turns to me and shrugs. 'So you watch porn. Big deal.'

'Yeah, but . . .'

'You don't need to keep it secret, babe. I wouldn't hide my porn from you.' Which, I guess is true, except that Christian doesn't like porn. He's says it's predictable, too obvious. He doesn't appear to be lying either. I've never found a secret porn stash. And, believe me, I've looked. He is, I believe, unique among men in this respect, and therefore, possibly some kind of new species.

'Well, it's not really a secret. I just like to watch them on my own.' I feel myself get a little flushed.

'Aww, sweetie.' Christian snuggles close and gives me a hug. 'Whatever does it for you, babe, you know that. It makes you happy, so where's the harm? Victimless crime.'

'You mean that?'

'Sure.'

'Fancy a walk?' Because although I'm on a roll, stage two calls for neutral territory – with alcohol.

It's only a five-minute walk from the built-up urban jungle where we live into the relatively fresh open air of the fields down to the canal. And then about another easy twenty to a little pub called The Moorings. It's quite a popular spot, having got a reputation as a gastro-delight, serving the kind of mashed potato that could make even the most hardened atheist find God.

However, on a miserable autumn Friday afternoon it's quiet enough, so we sink into a cosy booth opposite brimming pints of rejuvenating hair of the dog.

And off I go. 'You know I like spying on people.'

'Yes.'

'Especially people having sex, men having sex, gay men. That's my super-kink.'

'Or men masturbating,' Christian adds, with a cheeky grin.

'Well, yeah, anyway you know that. Well, there's something else I like to do that's sort of similar but different.'

'Ooh,' says Christian in a tone of sort of semi-faux excitement, 'a new chapter in the book of my sexy girlfriend's deviant tendencies.'

Sometimes, I think the thing that Christian finds most attractive about me is the fact that I'm 'naughty' – like textbook naughty. It's not so much what I desire, as much as the fact that I act on those desires; the fact that I am ipso facto a naughty girl. Sure, there's a big old exhibitionist slut barely contained within Christian's not so mild-mannered exterior, so a voyeuristic girlfriend is a nice little bonus, but really, for him big-picture-wise it's all about his girl behaving badly. And he really does love it – bless him.

But strangely his enthusiasm for a new facet of my deviance doesn't make this any easier. In fact I feel rather cruel, with him panting like a puppy waiting for a new sordid tale, and me knowing what I really want is to steal his testosterone for my own evil purposes.

But I do it, nonetheless, if only because there is no

way out now. I tell him about Dark Knight. Then I tell him Dark Knight is gay and thinks I'm a man. Then I tell him that the man Dark Knight thinks I am is him (including the part about emailing the pic).

And then, finally, Christian says, 'Wow.'

'Is that a good wow? Or at least an OK wow?'

'I don't know. Er . . .' Christian grabs his three-quarters full pint and takes a long, long drink. 'I don't know.'

'Are you cross?'

Christian shrugs, then he shakes his head. 'No. Um, I wish you'd told me. I don't really like to think of you doing all this stuff in secret. But I don't mind. Or, I don't think I mind. It's not like you're having sex with this Black Knight or any of the others. It's just pretending. Right?'

'Dark Knight,' I correct, feeling stupid about correcting something so, well, stupid. 'And yeah, I'm not really having sex with him – well I can't, can I?'

'Yeah, right. So, you know, babe, it's fine. Bit out there, but then it's you.' And he reaches forward and ruffles my hair. 'And that's you, baby, big with the weird.' And his eyes, which have been glassy and a bit distant for a while, are back suddenly, sparkly bright.

I sigh with very audible relief. It's him. It's OK. We're OK.

Christian smiles at me, then picks up his glass and drains the rest of his pint.

'I think I'll have another half. Steady my nerves after all the shocking news from my shocking girl,' he says, in an evil little tone of voice. 'Want one?'

'Nah,' I say. And with another one of those weird shrugs that I can't quite make out, Christian heads off to the bar.

* * *

I'm staring idly out of the window at a tall thin mousta-chioed man, walking a red setter, when Christian slides back into his seat with his dinky little half pint.

'Imogen,' he says, 'can I ask you something?'

'Sure.'

'All this stuff you've told me today, why did you? Uh, why did you tell me, that is, or at least tell me now?'

'Oh,' I say, and then again, 'oh.' Because, idiot that I am, I almost forgot. In the weird shit-scary world of my true confessions I actually forgot the whole bloody point of why I was telling Christian all this stuff. Almost like, I was so relieved I got through the telling part, I forgot the actual asking part.

'Um, well,' I go on.

And oh God, oh God, oh-my-fucking-God. It's a pure top of the roller-coaster moment, I've ridden all the way up, slowly, slowly, and now I'm at the top, with only one way down, which is this one. 'He wants me to call him. He likes the picture – you know, the one of you – so much he doesn't want to talk online any more, he wants to talk on the phone.'

'Ah.' Christian half bites his lip. 'I see your problem.'

'Well, yeah, and the thing is, Christian, I really don't want to just drop him. I tried, actually, I really did try. I wasn't even going to send him the pic, even. But I can't stop thinking about him and –' I can't carry on looking Christian in the eye and so I drop my gaze to my hands, twisting frantically in my lap, '– I wondered if you might do it.'

'What?' It's not an angry what, it's more the kind of thing you say to someone who might as well be speaking a foreign language for all the sense they are making.

'Well, you know, pretend to be me, pretending to be you.'

'Imogen. Have you gone nuts?'

I look up. He looks a little bit amused. Only a tiny weeny bit, but the corners of his mouth are just ever so slightly turned up. So I play my trump card. 'Oh, come on, baby, you know as well as I do that I'm not the only one who likes a little bit of homoerotica.'

'And what's that supposed to mean?' Christian huffs, although I can tell he doesn't really mean it. He does mock affronted so well, especially with a lager-foam moustache.

'Oh, I don't know.' I begin to count off on my fingers, gazing airily around the heavily timbered room. 'The naughty gay-a-sexual pictures on your website; the fact that every, and I mean every, gay man you meet either hits on you or pulls me aside to tell me how you're clearly a big poof and I shouldn't be too upset about it because really you'll only be happy if you're true to yourself; the fact you've been beaten up by townie scumbags twice for being gay. I could go on.' I waggle my eyebrows and Christian smirks. 'Oh yes,' I add, as if it has just come to me, 'and your continued enthusiasm for being fucked up the arse.'

And then we both look at each other for quite a long time, saying nothing.

But I'm telling the truth. Christian has always liked to play around with his sexuality. As far as I know he's never had any kind of sexual encounter with another man. But, as he says, he wouldn't rule it out; the right man might come along one day. Just because he hasn't fancied any of the ones he's met so far, doesn't mean he's never going to fancy any of them – well, that's his line. And even though he's mostly into girls (if not totally exclusively) he sets off the Gaydar something rotten. And his reaction to this state of affairs is, mainly, to play up to the world's assumptions and find it all ridiculously funny.

Finally Christian breaks the silent stand off, 'I suppose you're right, baby,' he says, still smirking, 'I am pretty gay. I guess that makes you a man then.'

I reach across the table and hit him round the head, playfully, but only just.

'Oi!' Christian fends me off and then looks thoughtful. 'No, really, fair point, baby,' he says slowly, 'I suppose I should put my money where my mouth is – so to speak.'

I say nothing to that, just smile sweetly and hope, hope, hope.

'Well,' he continues, 'let's go home and I promise I'll think about it.'

Dammit, left in suspense. 'OK then. But he's expecting you and or me to call tomorrow night.'

Christian shakes his head. 'I'll think about it.'

We don't talk on the way home. Which is not really abnormal, we're both fine with the not talking thing, except, of course, this isn't plain old not talking, this is real, charged, not talking.

It continues right through the last bit of the afternoon, and even the daily discussion about what we are going to have for our supper (toast), feels heavy, weighted with the expectation thunder clouds hanging in the air.

At 8 p.m., exactly 24 hours before that all important call is due, Christian comes out of the bathroom – fully dressed but still all squeaky shower fresh – and says, 'OK, babe, I'll do it.'

Now, obviously I'm feeling pretty loved up and just plain grateful after this. So I decide to show my appreciation in a way Christian will really, well, appreciate. A little later that evening, I decide, quite simply, to give Christian the very best shag he's ever had.

Now, the thing about being a couple in a long-standing relationship is that in some ways it's quite hard to do best-ever-shags. There are precedents, for a start, and there isn't that sparky, shiny, breathless, stress-fuelled lust to peg it all on.

On the other hand, though, the good thing about the long haul is, when it comes to sex, I know his kinks and hot buttons inside out. The fact is, I know exactly where to press without even looking. In fact, when it comes to my Christian and screaming ecstasy, I can practically touch type!

So I decide to give Christian a really special treat. All of his eclectic kinks fulfilled in one extra-special, custom-designed and built, bespoke session. It's the least I can do really, because right now, nothing is too good for my baby.

So I count off his top five kinks one by one.

1. Exhibitionism

Obviously exhibitionism is one of Christian's biggest deals. It's the thing that brought us together, the exhibitionist and the voyeur, perfectly matched, like a little two-piece jigsaw puzzle. Of course, it's a bit harder to fulfil an exhibitionist than it is a voyeur – Christian just has to put on one of his trademark strip shows to press my biggest and reddest button, but to reciprocate is a little harder. Not impossible, though.

I take Christian by the hand and lead him into the bedroom. He follows obediently, a little shy smile on his face. I think he has a pretty good idea he's going to get some. He knows he's just scored some major Brownie points.

Once the door is closed I make sure I'm between him and the bed, so he can't see what I've got out of the secret sex-box. I only have to take care for a minute or two, because shortly it's not going to be a worry.

The blindfold is very simple: a navy cotton eye mask,

with a piece of elastic to hold it firmly in place. I seem to remember it was acquired on some aeroplane flight or other, and for the sole purpose of satisfying this particular predilection of Christian's. It's part of his exhibitionist kink somehow, he likes the fact I'm looking at him even more if he can't see me. Kind of makes sense, if you think about it with your head on one side and your eyes half closed (or, I guess, with a blindfold on).

I quickly slide the blindfold over Christian's honey-dark eyes before he twigs quite what I'm doing. When he realises it's the blindfold, though, I feel his knees sag a little as he exhales with a little moan – instantly aroused. Yum.

With one hand holding his to guide him, and the other on the small of his back, I lead him over to the bed and help him lie down on it. And that's when I grab the ropes.

2. Bondage

Christian likes to get tied up a little. Just lightweight stuff, for the most part. He likes a little scarf round his wrists, that sort of thing – just enough – but I checked up on the web and scarf-bondage can cause nerve damage or something, so I ordered some cute rope 'n' cuff type restraints from a kink-toys website. They're ever so nice, the ropes are purple velvet and they have little padded leather cuffs for the wrist. Very comfortable, yet totally secure. Oh so perfect for my boy.

It's funny, because although Christian likes bondage and stuff I don't really think of him as sexually submissive. Not, say, in the way his online alter ego is. This is just – well – just Christian stuff. He'd never cower and call me 'mistress' or anything like that; he just gets off on a little bit of bondage fun.

I carefully secure his wrists and fasten them to the bed posts. Christian giggles, very cutely. I have a matching pair for his ankles too, but I can't use them now because my plans necessitate a bit of wriggle room.

'Oh babe, that's so. Oh God.' He's excited. We haven't done any bondage for ages.

I step back, and pause a second for emphasis, just delaying the moment when I look up at him, and . . .

Oh wow, he looks stunning. He's naked from the waist up, with enough dusky skin on show to make me very happy indeed. His jeans are still on, but mostly unbuttoned, and his hard cock is only just contained. There's something very yummy about this stripped to the waist look – kind of dirty and wanton. And just that look on its own would be enough to make me lick my dry lips in anticipation. But add in the fact that he's blindfolded and tied down, squirming and panting, and it's a perfect kinky vision. This is meant to be his treat, but I am loving every minute. (Also, there's something incredibly sexy about seeing someone you love so very turned on. So beautiful. So arousing.)

3. Anal playtime (and a bit of talking dirty)
The ever popular strap-on's up next, and I slink into it, adjusting and buckling it on without even having to look. Christian knows this device as well as I do, and he knows all the tell-tale slight sounds it makes too. The leather on skin sounds and straps sliding home. I don't try and keep quiet, so he knows exactly what I'm doing, and I hear his already heavy breathing crank up to the really very turned on indeed setting, letting me know exactly how much he approves of my plans.

He so loves to be fucked. He likes to be face down, pushed deep and helpless into the pillows and nailed hard. But he also likes face to face, which is good, because that's the position I'm going for today – the romantic side of fucking one's boyfriend up the arse.

I push his legs apart with one knee as I climb up on the bed to kneel just below his aching thrusting groin. He opens his legs eagerly, displaying himself for me, wanton and wanting.

'Slut,' I whisper as I slide my eager fingers under the waistband of his jeans, feeling the blood-hot skin nestling underneath. My own arousal spikes, sudden and delicious.

'You look so hot, baby, so sexy,' I mutter as I fiddle with his trouser fastening and begin to remove them. 'In fact, I ought to invite all my friends around to see how fucking sexy you look right here. It's not like you could do anything about it if I did.'

He makes a noise, sort of like 'Nnnghhh.' I smile. Naughty boy. He so loves it. I love talking dirty to Christian. It's such a simple little thing, and he responds so prettily.

'Oh yes. They'd enjoy it, you whore. See you here like this, bound and blindfolded. Naked.' I've managed to wrangle his trousers right off by the time I say this, leaving him appropriately nude on the bed. 'They'd get so turned on looking at you. So hot, but I'm afraid they'd be disappointed in the end, because only I get to fuck you.'

And as I say that I push his legs wider apart, and he responds by pulling his knees close to his chest. A little shuffle forward and I'm right there, in perfect pole-position, with the head of my cock, nestling right in close, his skin liquid warmth against mine. A quick pause for lube, and I slide home – so easy – and he sighs – so satisfying.

But I don't give him any more than a quickie. I build up speed as quickly as I dare. But not too much, I don't want to have to scrape him of the ceiling just yet. And then I thrust deep into him hard and fast, just fast five times. Then I'm out, and before he can protest one of my fingers is on his lips as I whisper, 'Just wait and see.'

4. The best hand job in the world

Being the exhibitionist he is, Christian has always, always enjoyed being aroused in public places. Particularly aroused to completion. We're not the wild young things we were, and we don't do the wild young things we used to. But we still talk about them.

Christian's legs are resting back on the bed now, and I'm still crouched between them. My hands are bright and shiny with copious amounts of lubricant and I'm stroking his twitching cock very, very gently.

'Do you remember,' I say in a low voice, a naughty voice, a voice that hints at scandal and has to be careful the neighbours don't overhear, 'how I used to do this to you sometimes when we were out in public? Play with your cock like this, make you squirm in places where anyone could just look over and see you?'

'Uh-huh.' It's not fair to ask questions really, poor Christian is beyond the point of stringing a sentence together as I stroke him over and over. He's cast adrift, just a little bit of flotsam swirling around in the eddies and currents of my gentle, gentle touch.

We used to do it all sorts of places. In the car was good, with me driving, and him sitting next to me, mostly stroking himself, with me reaching over whenever I could and touching him too. The car was fabulous because it felt very exposed, but it was quite safe really. Even in broad daylight, no one ever looks at the people in other cars properly, not below chest height. Even parked at traffic lights, say, it was always quite safe. Well, almost always.

Trains were also good, so long as they had tables for cover and Christian was in the mood for keeping a straight face. If my nerve broke (or his, but it was usually mine), we could always nip to the loo for a quick finish. Very exciting, especially with that unique trainy rhythm to stroke along to.

We never do it now. We're too old for those kinds of high jinks. Now, we just talk about it.

I slide my frictionless fingers over his cock, shaping them into a soft dark well and pumping, still very gentle. He groans so deeply and so needily that my resolve almost cracks and I nearly give him the extra pressure he needs to come. But I don't. I manage to keep my eyes on the prize, and tease him just that little bit longer. Because I know, even if he doesn't, that this is the penultimate act of the show.

I take him right to his ragged, panting, begging edge. This is another advantage of knowing someone really, really well. It would surely be impossible to take a one-night stand to the very brink of orgasm and rein him back once, then twice, while they thrash around, incoherent with frustration and need. (With Christian though, every squeak, every moan is a little mark along a path I know very, very well. I know where to touch and for how long to make him come in hard jack-knifing spasms, or, as in this case, not come. Not yet.)

5. Pussy
Even I find it odd sometimes that a boy as reconstructed as Christian can still love pussy (yeah, and still call it pussy in a pinch), but he does. Christian is one of those men that love it to the point of crazed obsession. He will go down there for ages and relish every minute of it. I can't see what the great attraction is, but Christian insists it's wonderful, and he really isn't that good a liar.

And pussy is why I wanted him face up.

As quickly as I can, so as not to break the mood, I shed

my tracksuit bottoms, my knickers and my T-shirt and then I climb back on the bed, straddling Christian's hairless chest. He can tell I'm naked. He can feel my bare legs snug against his sides and my hot, happy cunt resting right between his nipples.

'Genny,' he says in the hoarse distant voice of a man who has been teased and denied to the point of near madness. 'Oh God, Genny, you're so wet, aren't you? I can tell.'

I laugh softly and dip one finger between my legs, bringing a tiny bit of moisture to his mouth and dabbing it on his bottom lip.

'Mm-hmm,' I murmur, 'it's all for you, my gorgeous baby, you know that.'

I watch his pink tongue flick out to lick at the little glistening patch on his lip. And as he does I swear I can feel his granite cock grow even harder.

I climb off then, because I want to try something. Something that, unbelievably, in all our hundreds of years together I have never tried. I turn around and climb back onto the bed and straddle him again, but this time facing the other way, facing down his compact body. My cunt is hovering above his face. I can tell he feels what I've done. His breath's gone all raggedy-fast. He knows I'm only a tongue flick away. He's breathing me.

Slowly, slowly I lower myself down onto his eager mouth. He licks me at once, so suddenly I almost pull back. But I don't. I make myself relax and let him stroke me, melting into his mouth.

And it's so good, so transporting, that I forget for a minute the part of the plan where I am meant to be leaning down and sucking on his cock.

Reluctant to do anything that isn't concentrating on Christian's soft tongue tracing pleasure swirls on my cunt, I force myself to return the favour. I have to stretch my neck a little, but only a little, and I try to remember to tell Christian what a good thing it is that he isn't taller as far as 69 is concerned.

I lick as he licks, matching his pattern as I run my tongue up and down his warm, wanting cock. It doesn't take long.

Of course Christian had a pretty comprehensive warm-up, which is why in a matter of three or four tongue caresses I'm having to work to hold him back from tipping over the edge. I sit up and stroke him idly with my hand, concentrating properly on the sparkling sensations between my own legs.

My stomach flips as an all-too-familiar fantasy pops into my head, but in the light of what's happened today it doesn't seem wrong to fantasise about Christian and Dark Knight, while we're together. In fact it seems highly appropriate. I imagine Christian tied down the way he is, straining his neck to take Dark Knight's cock in his mouth, swallowing it with all the gusto and eagerness that he exhibits towards my cunt.

And then I'm bucking hard, driving down onto Christian's face, riding him, mercilessly, not even caring how he's breathing. This it seems is no bad thing, though, because Christian suddenly comes in my hands, over and over, but I barely notice because I'm there myself and I'm tipping, tipping, tipping over the edge.

Later, after bonds have been loosened and sheets have been retucked Christian does indeed whisper in my ear that it was the best ever. And I snuggle down, smug with the satisfied glow of a job well done.

I'm almost but not quite asleep when my phone rings. I barely answer, being, as I am, in a sex-induced coma. But somehow my hand meanders from under the duvet

– autopilot. I hit answer without even looking and press the phone to my ear, muffling myself in the bedclothes to avoid disturbing my snoring angel of a boyfriend.

'Uh?' I say, by way of pleasant greeting.

'Imogen, babe, it's Lorne.'

'Hi, Lorne,' I murmur, keeping my eyes closed in an attempt to remain asleep throughout this conversation.

'Babe, I've come up with the best solution to your little problem. You're so right, Christian'll never go for it. But I'm at this new club, it's a women only S 'n' M thing. You'll love it, honey, get down here. Invite only, but if you drop my name . . .'

'Lorne,' I hiss, stopping her thoughtful but completely inappropriate offer mid-flow, 'it's OK, he said yes.'

'Christian?'

'Yes.'

'Is doing the call?'

'Yes.'

'Blimey.'

'I know.'

Then Lorne laughs, and as she does I can picture her throwing her tousled head back and crinkling up her pretty green eyes. 'You pair are such perverts.'

7

Next morning I email Dark Knight to confirm that I will indeed call him tonight. We ping-pong a few messages back and forth, and the time is fixed for 9 p.m. I glance at the clock in the corner of the screen. I still have nearly twelve hours to wait.

I spend the first two of these hours simultaneously panicking and coaching Christian. I show him the logs of all the chats I've had with Dark Knight (thanking God for the automatic saves in my chat program – I'd never have remembered to keep them all myself).

At my invitation, Christian settles on to the swivel chair at the computer desk and studies them diligently, well maybe not quite diligently, but he reads them and doesn't make wisecracks. Mostly.

'Pup! What's all this pup business?'

On the sofa across the room, I squirm with embarrassment. I'm finding this whole thing kind of squirmy. For all that I like spying on people going about their private business, having my own private business on show is not nice at all.

'Pup is me,' I explain, awkwardly, 'well you, well you and/or me.'

'Pup! Heh, I like it,' he says with a big grin and, satisfied, he turns his attention back to the screen.

'Yeah, I always thought it was sort of cute,' I mutter, half hiding my scarlet cheeks in a copy of the *Guardian* Guide.

Christian reads on, occasionally exhaling loudly, 'whew,' or chuckling cluckily to himself.

'I don't know, babe,' he says after a fashion, shaking his head, 'this Christian of yours is some character. It's a good job I did GCSE drama, that's all I can say.'

I have to laugh at this. It makes me feel a little better and my mood swing-o-meter jerks back over to the bright side. 'I wouldn't worry too much about it taxing your acting abilities, baby, I think you'll find you have quite a lot in common with our young pup,' I say, smiling.

'What, with this submissive, slutty gay boy?' Christian exclaims, all mock indignation. Then adds, 'Oh yeah, I see what you mean.'

My new improved, more relaxed state lasts through lunchtime, but I soon get all stressed again. I'm just not designed for this type of thing. And no matter how much Christian pats my shoulders and tells me to relax-because-it-will-be-fine, I'm still wearing a Grand Canyon-sized groove in the shag pile with my nervous pacing as I stride up and down, wishing I smoked and chewing the life out of an innocent Biro. I somehow manage to convince myself that my not-very-high-tech plans for conducting the phone call won't work. The plans, such that they are, are for Christian to talk to Dark Knight on the phone in the bedroom, while I listen in on the living-room cordless. Suddenly I am convinced that this will cause too much fuzziness on the line and Dark Knight will rumble us for sure.

Christian is justifiably scathing. He points out that Dark Knight, if he does notice anything, will only think it's a bad line and redial. (He also points out that I have Biro on my chin.) But in my current jangly state I can't deal with any kind of unknown quantity, and so I decide we need a dry run, and that means we need a stand-in for Dark Knight.

Immediately (and rather predictably) Christian suggests Dan.

I sigh. 'Yeah, right.'

'Oh go on, babe, Dan'd do it.'

'No he bloody wouldn't. You know he bloody wouldn't and he'd get his knickers in a big bloody twist about being asked to do it. You're only suggesting him because you want to see the look on his face when you explain what you're up to.' Dan baiting – the sport of kings!

'That is so not true. Well, OK, it is true, but you have to admit, babe, the look on his face would be fucking something.'

I guess Christian is trying to lighten the tone and cheer me up again. It's quite understandable – it worked before when I was bashful about my transcripts, but this isn't the same thing at all. I'm borderline hysterical at this moment and I really don't need some light stand-up comedy about how repressed Dan is.

'For fuck's sake, Christian,' I explode, 'please take this seriously.'

Christian stares at me – reverberating in the shock waves.

'Anyway,' I add, snappily, 'I know someone.' A horrible bitchy tone has crept into my voice. I don't mean to be mean, but I just can't help it. I feel so hot and bothered.

But there is some light at the end of this bad-temper tunnel, because there's only one candidate for the job of Dark Knight stunt-double really, or at least there's only one option that means I don't have to go through the horrific experience of explaining this situation to yet another living person. I grab my mobile and punch up the number of the only man/woman for the job: Lorne.

Thankfully, the phone is answered quickly. 'Hi,' says a voice that sounds like it is being scraped off a cave wall somewhere far, far away – I guess it was a good party.

Lorne sounds, well, like shit. 'You sound like shit,' I say, charmingly.

'Imogen, babe, hi.' And I can almost hear the swagger then, as Lorne springs to life, turning on the charm just for me. 'How is my favourite little Kinkerbell?'

And I feel myself smile. 'Well, it's funny you should say that.'

Lorne, in typical style, finds my new predicament faintly amusing, and she is more than happy to come round later and stand in as Dark Knight. I relax for a moment, satisfied that my current obstacle has been overcome. Lorne will be a nice diversion and, as an added bonus, I will get confirmation – once and for all – that she and Christian are not actually the same person.

Affirmative action, I decide, is the key to not being overwhelmed. I need to do something else productive, insofar as anything I can do right now is productive. I sit down at the dining table with a pad of lined A4 and a now very frayed Biro.

A little while later Christian saunters out of the kitchen, where he's been washing up/hiding, and watches me for a minute, his head cocked to one side.

'What are you doing?' he says, when I'm about half-way down the page.

'I'm making you some crib notes,' I say, not really looking up.

'Ooh.' Christian pulls up a chair next to me and starts to read over my shoulder. I stare at him in annoyance and curl my hand around what I am writing.

'What? They're notes for me. I'll have to read them sometime.'

I look up at him and he pouts comically. I feel so mean, then. He's the one doing me a favour. I so don't deserve him. I start to melt again. Don't know about mood swings, this is more like a mood see-saw.

'Sorry,' I say, 'here.' And I move back so he can see what I've written, pointing out the first instruction I've written at the top of the page. In my scrabbly spider-scrawl excuse for handwriting, it says: 'Call him Sir.'

'As much as you can,' I add out loud. 'He really likes it, it gets him going. And you want to get him going, because then he'll do all the work and all you'll have to do is grunt in the right places.' I smile shyly at Christian and he nods.

I run my finger down the page. Next I've put: 'He thinks you work in a shop, do not ['do not' is underlined] tell him the name of the shop or any other personal-type stuff – real or made up – no matter how much he digs for it. And he might well dig for it.'

'Right – so I keep it vague,' says Christian.

'The vaguest.'

Next comes: 'Be a cock tease, say stuff like, "We couldn't." "You wouldn't." "No, I would never let you do that." So he can be a bit forceful.'

Christian looks up from the page again and squints at me. 'God, babe, this is pretty comprehensive. How do you know all this? You haven't even been talking to him that long.'

'They're all the same though – doesn't take very long to suss them out,' I say, matter-of-factly.

Christian reads the next part aloud. '"You like bond-age" – right enough – "and spankings" – ooh, OK. Spank me, baby, heh.'

I flash a warning glare.

'OK, OK.' He reads on. '"You're not that experienced, although you've played online." Right, well that's all fine.' And Christian has to stop there because he's come to the end of what I've written.

But I haven't quite finished. 'There's something else you might need to know.'

'Sure, what?'

I pull a face, this is embarrassing. This is possibly the most embarrassing bit of all. 'Well, it probably won't come up, but just in case it does: You're uncut, nine inches.'

Christian does a jaw-drop face. 'Nine inches! Why did you make me nine inches?'

'Well, you know, it was a made-up character. I could say what I wanted and to be honest, flicking through the profiles, nine inches seemed sort of average.'

Christian seizes my arm in mock alarm. 'Christ, baby, tell me the truth here, is nine inches really "sort of average"?'

I shrug playfully and, as I do so, the doorbell rings.

Christian doesn't seem to have noticed that we have imminent company. He's still got that stunned, my-actual-penis-is-smaller-than-the-penis-belonging-to-the-online-version-of-me look plastered on his face. So I go over to the entry phone, cursing this unwanted intruder.

I lift the receiver and the little black and white telly screen lights up. I look at the blurry face on the doorstep in confusion for a couple of secs, before I realise that I am a brainless idiot and the person outside is Lorne. The same Lorne I invited over less than an hour ago.

It isn't until Lorne is sitting on the sofa drinking coffee (white, with one) that I remember about this being the first time I have seen her and Christian together. They do look quite alike, although not so I have to worry about mixing them up or anything.

Actually, seeing them together, I see the differences rather than the similarities, like the clothes, the hair, the subtle ways their faces are shaped and shaded. They're quite, quite different. But, in all honesty, I couldn't begin to decide which of them I find most physically attractive.

But I don't have time to waste on Victor/Victoria musing, not when there's a walk-through to, well, walk through. So I start to hustle, insisting that coffee can be drunk on the job, and get on with getting Lorne positioned in the spare bedroom. I hand her my mobile and explain briefly that Christian is going to call her in a mo and, for the purposes of this reconstruction, she is Dark Knight.

'What's Christian going to say? Is he going to be all "slave boy"?' Lorne asks, with a surprisingly hopeful eyebrow raise for someone who claims that boy-on-boy action (or boys full stop, for that matter) isn't her thing.

'I don't know. I don't think so.'

'Aww.' Lorne pouts, seeming miffed at being a mere understudy who doesn't get in on any of the real action.

'Um, well, maybe he will, I'll see if he can think of anything.' I close the door on poor Lorne, feeling guilty. Someone else I'm going to owe huge favours to, just to get a quick phone jolly out of Dark Knight.

Talking of owing huge favours, Christian's now lying on our bed flicking through a copy of *Heat* with the bedroom phone extension right next to him.

'Hey, baby.' I smile at him as he looks up, and hold out a torn piece of newspaper on which I have scrawled my mobile number. 'It's my moby number – didn't know if you knew it by heart.'

'Oh right, yeah. She's on your phone.'

'Yes.' I turn to leave, then pause a minute, shifting my weight from foot to foot. 'Christi,' I say, in a voice that wants something.

'What?'

'Um, if you don't mind, could you be a bit sexy?'

'Well, OK.' He frowns. 'But aren't you taking this a bit seriously – it's only a technical run-through, baby.'

'I know, but, well, Lorne's done me some favours about this and I think she'd sort of like it.'

He shrugs. 'Well, sure, if you like, but really, baby, I don't think she's going to be so interested in me being sexy.' And his expression says it all – Imogen and Lorne sitting in a tree . . .

Back in the living room, hyper-tensed on the sofa, I toy with the cordless phone. I have a flannel at the ready – for wrapping round the mouthpiece to stifle any give-away sounds. I really hope it works. When the call is happening live I am going to be very prone to give-away sounds.

A moment later, when I swallow, I press the call button and put the phone to my ear. I can hear a ringing tone.

Lorne answers.

'Hello, slut boy,' she growls, sounding really serious and quite sexy for a second or two. I actually have a little squirm.

'Hello,' Christian replies, sounding, frankly, as if he is about to piss himself laughing.

'You're my bitch, you know,' Lorne continues, sounding a little closer to giggling herself this time.

'I know,' Christian purrs, 'I'm yours. Tie me up. Beat me. Anything you want. You own me.'

And then Lorne guffaws so loudly I can hear her through the wall as well as on the phone. So I shout 'Cut' into the receiver and hope that that will do as a test run.

Back on the sofa Lorne proclaims the technical side acceptable. 'I didn't notice it being a bad line really. Maybe a little hissy but some people's phones are like that anyway. It's fine. He'll never notice. I swear.' And she waves a dismissive hand at me for extra reassurance.

Meanwhile the dummy call seems to have triggered something in Christian. He's clearly getting high with adrenaline. A mere hint of a questioning tone is enough to send him into a babbling promo pitch. 'It's selling, babe. It's just PR, and PR is so me. PR is me. All I've got to do is sell your Mr Dark Knight me. That I can do.'

The rest of the afternoon flashes by after Lorne leaves. Suddenly it's nearly time for the call, and never mind butterflies, I think I have fully grown grizzly bears in my stomach. I don't really want to eat supper, and I certainly don't want to cook, but I feel so growly inside I know I have to force something down, so I make myself a bowl of Shredded Wheat and sit at the table, moving it around with my spoon. Christian is in a similar prowly, restless state – and has been for the last hour or so. He comes out of the bathroom while I'm 'eating' and wraps his arms around my waist, circling the chair back. He smells all minty.

'Did you clean your teeth?'

'Um, yeah.'

I frown at him. 'It's only on the phone you know; you don't have to clean your teeth.'

Christian laughs. 'Yeah, he'll be on the phone. But you won't.'

And I feel instantly better and smile, quite touched. Christian leans down and over the chair, and I turn my head so he can kiss me with his fluoride fresh mouth.

'Baby,' I whisper, when we are done kissing, 'I want to ask you a favour.'

He rolls his eyes but says, 'Sure.'

'Well, when you're on the phone with Dark Knight he might ask you to do stuff, like sexy stuff. And, as you're on the phone, you could get away with not doing it, but I'd like it if you actually did it.'

'What sort of stuff?'

'Just, you know, stuff.'

And it's nine before I know it. I feel strangely calm as Christian heads for the bedroom, and I wander into the kitchen, cradling the cordless phone in my arms like a sleeping baby. Across the courtyard, badly drawn curtains and unpulled blinds make any number of strange yellow patterns spill from the windows. Strangely distracted, disjointed from the here and now, I find myself looking out into the night, wondering what happened to affair-discovery couple and glance over to their flat. The curtains are pulled in their living room and their bedroom is in darkness. It remains a mystery.

I'm about to check the goings on in Mr Fox's kitchen, when I remember the phone and press it to my ear. I can hear a soft familiar tone – somewhere a phone is ringing, somewhere Dark Knight's phone is ringing.

When he picks up, his voice is exactly like I imagined, like sharp sand mixed with honey. At least I think that's what I imagined; maybe it's just that when I hear it I feel as if that's how I imagined it. But it doesn't matter either way, because it's just amazing the way I am wet and panting the minute I hear his soft purr say, 'Pup?'

'Hello, sir,' says Christian, and I have to bite my lip, because my mouth was actually opening to say that myself. I remember the high-tech Imogen muffling device and pick it up from the counter top, bunching it round the mouthpiece, in case I slip up like that again.

'I didn't think you'd go through with it, pup, you've been leading me a little bit of a dance.'

'Have I, sir?' I can almost see Christian's cheeky eyebrow raise. And, all kitchen-lurking shyness forgotten already, I find I am wandering out of the dark and through into the living room.

'Oh, you know you have,' Dark Knight replies and I can hear his breath catch as he says it. Christian has got to him already.

'Hmm, maybe I do,' says Christian teasingly. And I can't help smiling at him. From the sofa I can see easily into the bedroom. Christian is in semi-darkness, almost silhouetted by the bedside lamp behind him. A bright yellowish glow outlines his head and shoulders, like an aura. He's lying on the bed on his stomach, knees bent, swinging ankles crossed in the air. He looks very relaxed – much more relaxed than I feel.

'What are you wearing, pup?' says Dark Knight, sounding now even more gravelly and rough than he did when he picked up.

'Oh, nothing special. Combats, brown T-shirt – from Gap, I think.' Christian, bless him, would see no reason to lie here. Me, I would have said something a little sexier, but it's not like I used to brag to Dark Knight that I was wearing nothing but baby oil and a dog tag, so it's cool.

'Any underwear, pup?'

Christian looks up at me, and I shake my head. 'No,' he says, 'no underwear, sir. I know you like that.'

'You little slut,' Dark Knight purrs, and then I hear him swallow before he says, 'Strip. Strip for me right now.'

'Yes sir.'

Christian carefully puts the phone down on the bed and kneels up. He pulls his T-shirt off smartly and then slides out of his combats with a sexy little hip wiggle. Nude, he picks up the phone and breathes, 'Done.'

'Done what?'

'I've done what you...' I'm holding my breath, but Christian tails off in the nick of time, checks himself and continues. 'Sorry. I mean, done sir. Sorry sir.'

Dark Knight chuckles softly down the line. 'Always the forgetful pup. So, you're naked for me now?'

'Yes sir.'

'Are you hard?'

I look at Christian's crotch. I can't see clearly in the shadowy dark, but I really think he is.

'Yeah, I mean, yes sir. I am,' Christian says roughly.

'Oh good. I'm so glad,' says Dark Knight. 'Touch it.'

Christian's hand snakes into his shadow-dark crotch, moving in soft strokes. He sighs as he does it all 'Ahh,' right down the phone – giving me goose-pimples.

'Not too much, though,' Dark Knight says softly. 'You don't get to get off that easy, pup. You know that.'

'Oh, but sir, I, I'm so close already...'

'Shush,' Dark Knight silences him, all easy command. 'You need to earn it. I'll let you come pup, don't worry, you just need to be a good boy for me first.'

'But sir, I...'

'I said shush, come on, pup. You can do better than that. I don't want to have to punish you first time.'

'OK sir, I'll try.'

'Good.' In the bedroom I see Christian wink at me. I am not quite sure how much he is faking and how much is real arousal and frustration. But, really, I'm not quite sure I even care. Whatever his motivation for the show he's putting on, it's bloody hot.

'I really liked your photo,' Dark Knight says softly. 'I don't often ask my pups if they'll do a call so early on, untested like this, but you were really something.'

'Thank you sir.'

'I'm so horny right now, thinking about that photo

you sent me, picturing you acting the obedient slut for me. I wish I were there with you right now. I bet you could do something about this rock-hard cock I've got.'

In the living room, I lick my lips.

'Oh yes sir,' Christian purrs. 'Oh sir, would you let me suck it? I'd love to get down on my knees for you. Would you let me take your hard cock in my mouth and suck you until you come? I want to do that so much sir.'

'Maybe.' Dark Knight's voice is so low and rough with arousal it's hard to make out. I wonder if he's masturbating. 'You're in your bedroom are you?'

'Yes sir.'

'I do want you to get on your knees for me, pup. I want you to kneel on the floor like a submissive little slut. Kneel by the bed and put the phone where you will be able to use it without having to hold it.'

'Yes sir.'

Christian slips off the bed onto the floor. With this change of position I can see him better in the low light of the bedside lamp. His golden skin is glowing, burning bright, and he is hard, I can see it now in perfect profile. He kneels on the floor like he is going to say his prayers. Placing the phone on the bed, he bows his head to the mouthpiece and says, 'OK.'

And Dark Knight moans. It's very brief and very soft, but unmistakably there, just a little sound before he speaks. 'Ah good, so you're on your knees for me, good boy, good bitch. Put your hands behind your back.'

'Yes sir.' Christian places his arms rigidly behind himself, as if they were held fast in imaginary bondage.

'Are you still hard?'

'Oh God, so hard sir. There's, there's a little pre-come on the tip, sir.'

'I bet you wish you could touch yourself.'

'Oh God yes. I mean yes. Yes sir.'

I'm not sure when I started, but my hand is in my knickers right now, fast and true, and I realise, as I hear Christian's breathless frustration, that there is no way I can hold back from coming right now. Two more quick strokes and I'm jamming my free hand into my mouth to stop my cries betraying me.

I come quickly, squirming on the sofa, but I don't allow myself any relaxing comedown. I'm pressing the phone back to my ear, while the aftershocks are still rippling through me, not wanting to miss a single thing.

Back in the thick of the action, Christian is saying, 'Oh please sir, please let me touch it, just a little. I promise I'll do anything you ask.'

'Anything?'

'Yes sir, anything.'

'OK pup, here's the deal. I'll let you come now, but in return I'm going to want a little something from you. Is it a deal?'

'Yes sir, anything.'

'You come for me now and then I'll email you with a little task. Just something to show you're serious. And if you get that right then we can move up a level. If I like what I see, then this coming Friday, you meet me and you'll play with me for real. What do you say?'

'OK sir,' says Christian, almost sobbing with desperation. He's either really aroused by Dark Knight's dominance, or he's pretty good at pretending to be.

'Good, now come for me.'

Christian moves his hand, as his cock basically bucks into his touch. Suddenly I see how very, very hard he is and I moan aloud at the beauty of it. He strokes his cock a few times, eager and quick and I find my own, still half-aroused clit with my fingers. I'm coming up to meet him, and Dark Knight's voice on the phone is all husky snarl about dirty-slut-boys and wanting-it-hard. I'm cramming my knuckles into my mouth, but there's no need, because Christian's cry is so loud it drowns out everything, including me, bucking and writhing yet again on the sofa.

And when I regain consciousness, I sort of remember something. Something I think Dark Knight said before we all exploded into orgasm. Something impossible. Did he just ask Christian for a date?

Everything after that is a blur – a strangely calming drift downwards in fractured montage. I drift into the bedroom as Christian hangs up the phone and we both climb into the bed.

We hold each other, not speaking, not thinking for ages. I watch the ceiling. Even though it is just white artex, something about my prolonged staring seems to make it turn multicoloured, in a hallucinogenic daydream sort of a way. I watch and watch and then I realise something, something big, something profoundly important.

I'm hungry.

I nuzzle closer into Christian, working my face into his hair until I find his ear. When my lips are all but brushing it, I whisper, 'Want to go and get chips?'

It's not even that late, a little before midnight, even though, somehow, it feels like a million years since either of us set foot in the real world. Twined around each other and buried in overcoats, we trek to the local chip shop. It's not far, in the cute little area that was once the village green when this was a village, before it was swallowed up and became a suburb of Greater Manchester. The pubs are still tipping out and the chip shop queue is longish – out the door. We take our places at the end, stamping our feet to keep out the winter that is only a few weeks away.

The chip-shop queue we are in is full of typically trendy types, all wearing ultra-cool sportswear. The suburb where we live is quite a fashionable area now. We were lucky and bought our flat before it became so hot and sexy. Of course, Christian likes to think he was a cool trend spotter, but in reality it was just dull old chance.

As I stare at the cool urbanites waiting for fishcakes and batter scraps, my eye is caught by a couple of gay girls near the front. They're unusual looking – kind of beyond butch – slim and shaven headed, pictures of lithe androgyny. I find myself staring; half registering their pretty symbiotic ballet and half wondering about Lorne.

Lorne is attracted to me. This would appear to be the obvious conclusion from, well, mostly from her trying to snog my face off, but also Christian's comments and her notable attentiveness to me and her willingness to waste her time on my hare-brained schemes.

So, the question right now is, am I attracted to her? Or, at least, if things were different, i.e. if I wasn't so overwhelmed by what my boyfriend had just done out of love for me (not to mention the simple fact that I have a boyfriend at all), would I be attracted to her?

Until I'd met Lorne I'd always thought of myself as 100 per cent bullet-proof straight, but Lorne changed all that – well, kind of.

Actually I don't know if fancying Lorne would make me bi or straight or what – after all, she looks pretty much like a man. Christian might like his no-labels stance, but I've always been very proud of knowing what goes where, when it comes to my sexuality.

'Christi,' I say softly, not wanting any eavesdroppers in the queue to tune in to me. 'Do you think Lorne has a penis?'

'Sure, babe, she's probably got one in a box like yours,' he replies, in a voice which seems disturbingly loud, but in reality probably isn't.

I don't ask anything else. But I can't help wondering. My mind starts forming a dreamy randomish plan, a plan based on Frank and his web cams in the loos at work. If I could borrow one of those web cams I could plant it at home and wait for Lorne to use our bathroom.

And that's when I remember something else from that conversation with Frank that day, and I realise with a jolt, why I so need that web cam. And I realise that this isn't over, I'm not just going to delete Christian's profile and drop off Dark Knight's radar now we've done our dirty phone call. Oh no, I'm going to rise to his challenge. If he wants to meet his pup in person, he can jolly well bring it on.

So when we are walking back home, burning our mouths and fingertips on the too-hot chips, I say, 'Let's do it, baby.'

'What, right here?' Christian laughs, his mouth clogged with potato.

'No, I don't mean that. I mean let's do what Dark Knight asked you. Complete his email task – whatever that is – and go on the date. All that.'

Christian laughs. 'Somehow, I thought you'd want that.'

'But will you do it?'

'Sure, you know I will. But, well, I'm not sure how we can?'

'Oh, we can.'

And back in the flat I fire up the laptop, keen to see if Dark Knight has emailed as promised. I check the web-mail account I made for online Christian, and sure enough, a new message is already winking away:

From: Dark Knight
To: Sub Christian
Subject: Tonight

Hello pup

So nice to talk to you in person, you sounded
wonderful. I promised you some e-domination, and
here is your task – nice and simple for my little
virgin.

I want to see you naked. I've seen your face and
you've stripped for me, but I didn't get to see that :(
So how about a show? The hotter the better.

DK

I smirk at the screen. Is that all? Naked photos.

I dash off a quick reply, full of promises about how I
need to borrow a digital camera from work and cheeky
questions about preferred poses, thwack the send button
like I'm scoring a winning goal and glide off to bed, ten
feet tall.

Then, finally, I fold up into Christian's hot arms like a
little piece of origami. I'm so tired and sated I barely
even notice the way my smooth bare skin is sinking into
his smooth bare skin, melding us together like Siamese
twins. He sighs, long and deep, and buries his face in my
hair, breathing it in.

'Genny,' he says, the word just shaped on his breath.

'Christi,' I say back, so in the moment.

'I love you.'

'I love you, too,' I murmur, on the very edge of
oblivion.

'I meant to tell you,' Christian goes on, his voice
honeyed, heavy with sleep, 'I'm sure I've heard his voice

somewhere before, Dark Knight's that is. I recognise it, but I just can't place . . .'

His sentence vanishes into the dark.

And I'm wide awake.

8

Sometimes I just have to meet Christian for lunch out of pure desperation. I send up a smoke signal, in the form of a plaintive text message, and he appears, riding over the hill to whisk me away from Elaine or Frank or whatever else it is that is making me try and slash my wrists with a broken CD-ROM.

Mondays, in particular, can be such a painful desert for the soul, especially after a pure oasis-of-bliss weekend – like the one I've just had. And today it just so happens that Christian is positively gagging for a pair of blue-black jeans that he saw in *Arena Homme Plus*, so it's a-Arndale-Centring we will go.

Now I'm really rather pleased about this, because while there are good ways to spend a lunch hour and there are great ways to spend a lunch hour, the ultimate way to spend a lunch hour really has to be hanging around the changing rooms of Jigsaw for Men.

So hang around I do, while Christian tries on pair after pair of seemingly identical trousers – all identically tight – which I'm certainly not complaining about; in fact, it's all I can do not to literally jump for joy.

It's fairly quiet in the shop, which is good – no officious assistants worrying about the nonchalant way I'm wandering in and out of the thrilling male changing area, pretending to be bringing Christian cute little tops to try with his jeans, while I check out all the eye candy on the shop floor and hope that some of the cuter prospects will decide to try a few things on in the curtained-off chambers of delight.

Christian's just about to wriggle into the third or fourth of the tight little numbers he grabbed off the rails. I know this for sure because I was the one who pulled his curtain behind him, so it's gaping just right – just enough for me to lean back against the wall in the changing rooms' corridor and let my eyes dance over the place where his caramel crème skin meets his snowy-white underpants (yes, underpants today – a must for trying on new trousers).

Saturday night's phone conversation is still playing over and over in my mind on an endless loop, like some infectious pop song – but much more enjoyable! So, as Christian bends over, I can't help imagining Dark Knight's black silky voice talking of spankings, and punishment, and muffled cries for mercy going unheeded, and I have to stifle a moan. Well, I almost stifle it.

In the cubicle Christian looks up, spotting me through the deliberate gap in the curtain. He smiles and rolls his eyes, before looking away again, glancing down to fiddle with his fly.

And that's when I notice something out of the corner of my eye (because sometimes it really is like a sixth sense). I only see a vague shadow of something, a masked shape, a fleeting movement – just a hint, but just enough. And I'm drawn instantly, like a very perverted moth to a very kinky flame.

There's someone up to something that isn't fashion based, in the final cubicle right down the end of the little row. In fact, and this is the key factor, I'm pretty sure that the someone is, in fact, two someones.

I slink down the aisle, super-silent where it counts, and slip into one of the last cubicles on the opposite side of the corridor from my quarry. I draw the curtain closed behind me, quick and quiet.

A furtive exploration of different viewing angles easily reveals the one in which I can best see through the chink in my curtain and the little gap in theirs – right into a secret den.

And oh, sixth sense indeed – I am so very right.

Two blond men: entwined in blissful pursuit and blissfully unaware of me. One is half standing/half leaning, propped against the warm, honey-beige painted wall with open mouth and open fly. The other is pressed up hard against him, with a hand snaking into his partner's trousers, as he crushes their mouths together – fast and hot and slow and cool. Their long denim-covered thighs are pressed together, the more dominant man bearing down on his submitting counterpart, forcing him harder and harder against the wall behind them, and parting his compliant legs with one hard limb. It's a very, very pretty kiss, and I watch it for a long while, as their mouths melt and slide around on each other like strawberry ice cream on a blistering hot day.

And after a for ever of artful teasing and muffled pleading, top guy pulls out of the kiss, laughing into the bruised mouth and flirting with the darting tongue, that tries to chase and recapture his lips, but just isn't fast enough.

And in a moment Mr In-Charge is sinking to his knees and I'm thinking – excellent, a blow job. But he's thinking something else, which quickly becomes clear, when he reaches up and grabs his partner by the waistband, forcefully turning him around.

The standing guy is facing the wall now, and he braces himself against it – quite visibly shaking with need – as his kneeling partner helps him out of his already unfastened jeans. He's not wearing any underwear, which I'm getting so used to as a look, so I barely raise an eyebrow.

Kneeling man looks around, a quick furtive glance to check they're alone. I hold my breath, praying I'm well-enough hidden in the fold of slate-blue cotton around me, and that there are no strange angles in this hall of mirrors that are going to betray me when I least expect it. I get lucky, it appears. Kneeler finishes his surveillance sweep unawares, and turns back to his partner and the beautiful tight globes of his waiting arse.

Then I watch, dazed and bemused, as a pair of smooth buttocks are lovingly parted and a warm wet mouth – and a warm rough tongue – meltingly caress a dark little anus.

The man, the standing man, the one receiving this delicious mouth work, is so very blatantly turned on. I can clearly see his taut T-shirt stretched over his equally taut nipples, which are so hard that, instead of being a normal kind of ruby-cherry colour, they are almost white – pinched and painful.

Slowly, a languorous, lascivious rimming master class unfolds before my wide-stretched eyes. Knees buckle, and are quickly helped by supportive arms, before they give way. Lips part, and are quickly stoppered by hasty knuckles, before they cry out. Firm fists close around firm cocks. Moistened fingertips slide into moistened knickers.

I'm leaning against the wall in my own cubicle, and out of the corner of my eye I can see myself reflected in the full-length mirror, cheeks flushed, eyes alight. In the mirror in the men's cubicle I can see their reflection too, another angle on their tableau of expertly measured erotic friction.

I slide my middle finger back and forth over my hot

and bothered clit. As the gentle tongue strokes get deeper and the mutual masturbation rises and rises to a muffled crescendo, I find my sweet and perfect rhythm and join them at the peak ... and we all go over the top together.

And I'm barely even coming down when I find Christian at my elbow, a branded carrier bag swinging from his arm and a knowing grin plastered across his face. Silently he takes my hand and leads me, still dazed, out of the shop and onto an escalator and into the strange open calmness of the Food Court.

Sitting and picking at a baked potato, after Christian has been fully informed of just what Imogen saw, I see someone looking at me, spying behind a pair of incongruous shades. I'm not certain at first and I have to look away and back three times before I'm convinced. We're being watched.

I should have known this would happen.

Dark Knight had as good as told me that he would be on the lookout for his pup, particularly in shopping centres. I had assumed he would go for the expansive Trafford Centre on the outskirts of the city, but why not somewhere more central? Why not here? And why not now? If Saturday night had made as much of an impression on him as it had on me, well, it makes perfect sense that he'd be sitting in the Arndale Centre Food Court, dark glasses in place, scanning the crowds for his pup. His pup, who he'd recognise without any trouble at all. Shit.

Although he doesn't look quite how I expected. It's hard to tell with him being sat down, but he seems quite small framed – slight, even. All the same, he's oddly familiar. Too familiar, in fact. I squint, look again, and then sigh audibly as I realise I am a stupid tit and this

'Dark Knight' I'm so convinced about is in fact just bloody Lorne. Stupid sex-addled brain. Stupid Dark Knight obsession.

Lorne appears to clock me at the same moment I recognise her, and rises from her seat, dropping a scrumpled newspaper on the table and striding over, whooping her hellos from far too far away.

Much air kissing ensues, before she slumps into a convenient seat and beams at us both. 'So, don't keep me in suspense, kids,' she enthuses, 'how did it go?'

And Christian clears his throat, clearly itching to tell the tale of his night of triumph.

Lorne is suitably impressed by the blow-by-blow account she gets from Christian, who even slips off his chair at one point to re-create (fully clothed) the horny boy at prayer pose which he delighted both me and Dark Knight with on Saturday night. I just sit back and watch, slightly bashfully, letting Christian take the spotlight and thoroughly enjoying the action replay.

At the end of the story a wide-eyed Lorne says breathily, 'So, are you going to go through with it?'

'The naked photograph?' Christian teases.

'The meeting.' Lorne pouts, reciprocating the tease with a playful slap of Christian's upper arm.

'Owie,' Christian feigns, rubbing his bicep and giving Lorne a that-hurt face.

I roll my eyes, watching the naughty twins. They'd be so hot together ... And the minute I think that thought I have to grab it, bundle it into the boot of a car, drive for one hundred miles and crash the car into a lake at the very bottom of my subconscious, because I so, so, so do not need to start going there.

As I resurface from that little train of thought Christian is saying, 'Oh yeah. We can't stop now. The meeting is go.'

'Wow,' says Lorne, 'but how are you going to be there, Imogen? I mean, there's no point unless you get to watch. Right?' She looks a little quizzical as she says this, as if, while talking, she starts wondering whether this is the actual case.

'Yes,' I say, quickly. Too quickly. A kind of look-we're-not-fucking-swingers-or-anything type of quickly, that has protests-too-much practically dripping off it. I slow down, and add, 'I have a plan.'

I don't tell Lorne my plan. I haven't even told Christian yet. I don't want to jinx it. And it all rests on this afternoon's little mission and a conversation I don't really want to think about too much.

As we leave the Food Court I spot someone else looking at us. I hardly notice, really, my mind elsewhere. But I do notice his jacket. He's not wearing it, it's slung over the seat, crumpled and skew-whiff, but I still make out the striking back print of a silver tiger, sparkling on the black leather.

I've seen it somewhere before.

I kiss Christian goodbye outside the imposing door of Paranoid PR. It's not the same building I used to work in. In fact Paranoid has moved offices three times since those days – keeping up with fashion, I expect. This latest, and spectacularly ugly, building is one of those old industrial ones, an ex-mill or something. It makes the old Paranoid that I once knew look rather charming.

I peep in through the drawbridge and see a rather goofy-looking girl sat on reception, flicking through a glossy, reigning over her small domain of desk, sofa and coffee machine. As Christian walks in, she looks up and smiles sweetly. And I smile too, adrift for a short moment in wistful nostalgia.

I follow the cobbles round a couple of corners to the skinny tower block full of dot-coms and telemarketers where EYE-SPY is housed. I'm planning to talk to Frank this afternoon – he's normally in on Monday afternoons (not Monday mornings, though – they're only for drones like me).

Despite this, though, I'm dragging my feet, dreading the escalator haul back up to the seventh floor and an endless afternoon. The trouble with being bored at work for me, I think, is that I end up doing extra fun things out of hours to make my life more interesting, but that's a double-edged sword because it just makes my work seem even more boring by comparison. If I'd just bought myself a limp sandwich from the little place on the corner then at least the trek back to my desk wouldn't feel like such a heartbreaking wrench. And I'm pondering this as I wait for the lift in the shabby foyer.

As I'm musing and foot tapping a man comes in through the double doors. He looks sort of familiar – which makes sense, he clearly works in my building – so I nod an acknowledgement as he walks past. He returns my nod, but with a slightly bemused expression that gives away that he doesn't really know who I am.

It's not until he's disappeared into one of the ground-floor offices and the lift is chiming its arrival that I realise he's one of the men from the Jigsaw changing rooms.

Elaine looks up briefly as I collapse into my chair with a huge world-ending sigh, and listlessly open Microsoft Outlook, hoping that maybe some kind-hearted stranger will have emailed me some porn, or at least an amusing

JPEG. But no such luck, nothing but a dodgy-looking attachment stuck on an email that is dubiously entitled 'Re: Your document'.

'Nice lunch?' Elaine says, slightly sarcastically, probably a reference to the fact I've been gone for about two hours.

I smirk over my monitor at her. 'Not bad. Christian bought some new trousers.'

'Oh,' she says, being nonchalant, but when I said his name I swear I saw her pupils dilate a bit.

'Mmm, they're nice, bit tight though.'

Elaine nods and returns to whatever it is she is doing without another word. Damn, looks like she's not going to rise to it today. Not fair.

I delete my Inbox's boring virus-loaded contents then allow myself a glimpse at Frank's office. He's in, I can see him through the frosted window, but it looks as though he is on the phone.

I fuss about with my in-tray for a bit, not wanting to get properly embroiled in anything before I broach Frank. This, I'm rather afraid, is the big one, well not as big as confessing all to Christian, or maybe even Lorne, but it's still a big, big step. So I wait. And I hate to wait.

It's not long before Frank's off the phone. And, learning my lesson about procrastination, I jump up and knock on his office door.

Once inside his domain, my mouth is dry and my hands are slick.

'Ah, Imogen. I wanted to talk to you, you must be psychic.'

'Oh, right. I wanted to talk to you too, um ...'

'Justin's leaving,' Frank goes on, apparently not noticing the fact I have just spoken at all. 'He came to see me at the end of last week. He's got a new job, buyer for, uh, somewhere ...' Frank tails off briefly and then suddenly seems to regain his thread. 'I was wondering if you'd be interested in acting up in his role, with an appropriate pay rise, of course. And, well, equal opps and all that, we'll have to advertise his post properly in due course, but, you know, I really hope you'll apply for it, Imogen.'

At this my emotions go all weird. I was already all sicky-nervous and now, with this news, I should feel happy – elated, even – but I just feel odd. In fact I feel like I want to vomit. Justin is (or was) the Product and Promotions Coordinator. He's hardly ever in the office because he's always out at trade fairs or chatting up wholesalers. He's not really my sort of person. He's loud. And I don't mean noisy-loud, I mean loud-loud. Christian is noisy, Justin is loud, with suits that shout and a car that screams. In short, he's a wanker, but that doesn't alter the fact that his job is pretty cool, or was, I suppose, as it isn't his job any more.

'So?' Frank says, obviously a bit perplexed by my complete non-reaction to his big news.

'Uh, yes, yes that would be fab,' I stammer.

'Well, good. I'm pleased to be able to offer you something more, Imogen. You're an excellent member of the team and you know the merchandise inside out.'

'Thanks.'

'So what did you want to talk to me about?'

I stall for a bit, um-erring, and then I say, 'You know that web cam, the one you tested out in the ladies' loo.'

Frank frowns. 'Yes.'

'Well, you said something about a new model. A miniature version – I just wondered if they'd sent through a prototype.'

'Oh.' And suddenly Frank looks startled and a little but bemused. 'OK, sure, I didn't expect you to start this soon. I was thinking maybe next week. But, why not, if you really want to get down and dirty with the merchandise, let's go and have a look in the cupboard.'

Wow. That went well.

I follow Frank out of the office and down a short corridor to the big walk-in stockroom, commonly referred to as 'the cupboard'. It doesn't hold all our stock – fulfilling the actual orders is all outsourced – but we have examples of most things here for marketing, plus stuff that gets sent to us, samples and prototypes etc., etc.

Frank is already rummaging around in the far corner. 'I've got all sorts of stuff back here from the last delivery,' he says over his shoulder.

I gaze around the room. The cupboard is a horrific mess. God only knows what's hidden in here. No one ever takes the time to clear it out properly, even though it's always put down as one of our annual objectives every time we redo our three-year plan (which is about every six months – for some unknown reason).

'Here it is, here it is.' Frank jumps up waving something in the air. The something is so tiny it's completely concealed in his meaty fist, which is promising. 'Miniature wireless web cam,' he chuckles, cradling it in his palm, as he stumbles over half-empty boxes of gadgets towards me. 'Little lapel mount and everything. Only a prototype, mind, a sample. Don't reckon I'll stock them, too pricey for our punters.' He turns the little piece of engineering over in his hand, thoughtful and almost misty eyed. 'Although – strictly speaking – that's your call now.'

I shift my weight from foot to foot. 'Frank, could I borrow this, take it home?'

Frank looks thoughtfully at me, while my mind races. I can see him wondering what I want it for almost as clearly as if it was written on his face. There is very little in this world as cringe-inducing as having to admit that Frank and I have a lot in common, but it's this commonality I'm appealing to right now. I hope he'll feel lenient, as I know exactly what kind of perve Frank is and I can only imagine what the camera's rental price might be.

'I don't know about that. It's a pretty pricey piece of kit, three grand or so. I don't think I could really let you do that. I know it was a sample and everything, but it'll still be on the stock take and if anything happens then the auditors ...'

While he's talking I'm gazing around the room, and while I'm gazing I get a flash of inspiration. 'Frank,' I interrupt quickly, stopping him in mid-flow with nothing more than pure desperation. I need that piece of kit and I'm willing to do almost anything to get it. My eyes flick around the dirty stockroom once more.

'Frank –' I swallow hard '– if you let me borrow it I'll come in tomorrow afternoon and tidy the stockroom.'

Frank gapes. I can tell he's rather taken aback. 'What? Imogen, are you serious?'

'Oh yeah. Deadly serious.'

So the next afternoon, one of my precious Mr Fox Tuesday afternoons, I'm not where I should be: which is lying on my bed with my best binoculars watching Mr Fox lying on his. Instead, I'm sweeping and sorting and piling and filing, and generally scrambling about in the dust and the dirt. But it's worth it. It's worth it ten million times over when I get home that night and after several futile hours reading instructions badly (and just plain wrongly) translated from the Japanese, I hide the tiny camera on Christian's jacket, link it up remotely to our laptop, and see my own grainy face filling the screen in jerky, silent black and white. It's the worst picture in the world, and, in another sense, the bloody best.

As if that wasn't exciting enough, Tuesday night is photo night. And Christian has snagged William, his photographer mate, to do the honours.

Of course we hardly need a professional photographer to take a quick nudie snap of Christian, but Christian, bless, does like to do things properly. So not only do we have a professional photographer, we have one who has turned up with a lighting rig and a silver umbrella, and we also have to have a bloody meeting: 7 p.m. round our dining table, me, Christian, William and a rather indecent proposal.

William isn't how I expected. I had imaged a tall, effete chap with chiselled features and over-gesturing hands. I suppose Dan's bizarre homophobic reaction to him led me to picture some kind of gay photographer stereotype. The reality, however, is a short squat man, with a cropped beard and crooked teeth, not exactly ugly, but then not exactly anything. He's nice though – kind of funny.

After Christian's given a brief run-through of what we are after, i.e. found a very long-winded way of saying naked pictures, William grins and runs his tongue around inside his left cheek.

'Well, that all seems fine,' he says softly. 'Might I ask what these pictures are for?'

Christian flashes me a panic-stricken glance. He clearly doesn't relish the idea of telling William about his new-found career as a gay-sex surrogate for his penis-lacking girlfriend. But he doesn't need to, I can field this one.

'They're for me,' I say, smiling a little shyly, because

who wouldn't smile shyly when confessing to wanting red-hot porn pictures of their own boyfriend.

'Oh,' says William, turning his chair slightly more towards mine, to form a Christian-excluding huddle. 'Well, in that case you better tell me exactly what you want.'

'What about me?' says Christian, obviously feeling a little bit left out.

William gives him a dismissive flick of the head. 'Oh, I need to talk to the art director now, honey, not the model. Why don't you wriggle over there and get into your robe.'

William gives me a very naughty smile and I chuckle back, as Christian huffs off to the sofa.

'Now,' says William, leaning very close across the corner of the table, 'did you have any particular poses in mind?'

And when he says that I realise that yes, actually, I do. I know exactly what pose I want. 'Wait right there,' I say, as I get up from the table and dash past Christian, who is sulkily removing his clothes over by the sofa, and make for the bedroom.

In the drawer of my bedside table I keep a stash of pictures. Mostly ones I have ripped from magazines – just a pretty parade of images that have caught my eye for one reason or another.

Right now, in my rush to find the one I want, I simply pull the entire drawer out and empty it onto the bed. Suddenly the duvet is strewn with pornish confetti. Well, technically not porn, not actual close-ups of big dripping cocks or anything like that. More erotica really, cute boys in moody clothes and moody poses that are way hotter than any close-ups of anatomy could ever be.

With a perennial favourite in my hand I head back to the living room.

Christian is perched on the sofa in his bathrobe. 'Oh God,' he says when he sees me, 'what have you got?'

I just wink and take the piccie to show William.

It's of a gorgeous guy, one of my favourite male celebrities, and one of a truly mouth-watering set of pictures. But this is my favourite, and this is the one I want Christian to re-create, in every detail, except where the current subject is artfully semi-clothed, my Christian'll be completely nude.

It's really surprising how long these things can take. William takes ages, fiddling with lights and angles and God knows what. Poor Christian is trying to be a big brave boy, but he can't be comfortable, kneeling on the bed with one outstretched arm gripping the headboard and his head turned so he's looking over his shoulder.

But I'm in bad voyeuristic girl heaven. The pose is mouth watering, and so much hotter with acres of bite-able naked skin on show. More flesh, and in the flesh, yum yum.

I try and be helpful, offering therapeutic cups of tea and biccies, but even with my ensuring adequate refreshment, it still takes nearly an hour before dressing gowns are shed and shutters start to whirr. William really seems to come into his own then, heaping praise on Christian, how hot he is, how good he looks, how he should stick his arse out just a little bit more. And it really works! All of a sudden, under William's tutelage, Christian becomes a glamour model and I feel like a very spare part.

He squirms and writhes on the bed, which has been stripped of our nice lilac duvet, under William's instruction, and re-dressed with some pale-blue and white striped sheets and a blue blanket (God knows where he found them). It looks good though, the crisp blue and white clinical-cool sets off Christian's dark skin, making him look like some kind of mouth-watering exotic treat, which he is, of course – and that's without even beginning on the delectableness of the pose and the way it features his cute little arse as the star of the show.

This being the age of the train, and all that, it's all done on digital. So once the snapping is done (much quicker than the arty arranging), it's just a matter of a quick fiddle with the laptop and suddenly Christian's oh so candid-camera shots are there in all their breathtaking glory. And, I swear, they are one hundred times better than the crumpled magazine page they were based on.

With the satisfaction of a job well done, William finally gets ready to go. He gathers up all the paraphernalia that is strewn around our bedroom, zipping it all into a black vinyl case that can't possibly be big enough to hold it all.

The ever chivalrous Christian offers him a hand down to his car, and the two of them disappear into the echoey clang of the stairwell. As I settle myself down at the computer I hear William ask, 'So how is the lovely Dan?'

I take a sip of my rather lukewarm tea, and compose a quick cute little email to Dark Knight, attaching the very prettiest of the pics. I'm just about to let it slide into the cyber when Christian reappears and stops me.

'Hey, is that for Dark Knight?'

'Yeah.'

'Well, hold up a minute. I've thought of an idea for our meet up. I've thought of the perfect place.'

'Oh really. Where?'

'Schwartz.'

I try not to spit out the mouthful of tea I've just taken. With some effort and concentration I manage to swallow and then say, in a weird strangly voice, 'Schwartz? Why Schwartz?'

'Well, you know that flyer you had before? It said the

opening night was this Saturday, and I remembered that and thought bingo! Gay nightclub – perfect. Kinky gay nightclub – even more perfect. And my best girl wants to see inside. It's just too, well, too perfect.' He pauses, long enough to beam at me. 'So, remember Timothy, who got me the Fandango gig?'

'Kind of,' I say, which is a lie, because I have no clue who Timothy is.

'Well, I rang him to see if he could get me on the guest list, I figured he'd know the guys from Schwartz, and guess what?'

'What?'

'Well, the Saturday night is just the plebby opener, there's a ticket-only VIP guest night on the Friday and guess who's got a pair of tickets?'

'No!'

'That's right, one for me and one for Mr Dark Knight. Good old Timothy.'

'Uh, wow. Good old Timothy.' I can't help but agree.

And wow is the word really, but my God I'm spitting jealous feathers that I'm not going to get to go to the top-secret ultra-exclusive Schwartz invite night, but when I explain this to Christian he smiles a big smile and says, 'But, baby, you do get to go, as me.'

I could talk about this all night, but it's late, and we have to stop planning for our Friday-night jaunt sometime. As it's a school night and it's just turned midnight, and neither of us wants to turn into pumpkins, we decide to wind up any more discussion in bed. Sort of. In actual fact, once we're snuggled things feel different, the dark seems to take over and although I have questions, my lips move slowly, weighted with sleepiness.

'Baby,' I whisper in the dark, 'I know I probably shouldn't ask this, but why are you doing all this? OK, you agreed to the call, and I can sort of get my head around that, but all this, the photos and Schwartz. I don't get it.'

Christian chuckles, super-soft. 'Well, I suppose the phone was like, for you, you know, because you wanted it and, like an idiot, I sort of like making you happy. But then, well, then I really enjoyed it. I suppose I enjoyed you watching me. It was ...'

He trails off and snuggles closer. 'It was as good as back at Paranoid, down in the basement. I've always kind of missed that. You, watching me.'

'But I watch you all the time.'

'Yeah, but this felt different. You, watching me. Me, putting on a show, but not. I really get off on it. I really got off on you watching me with Dark Knight. And the thing is, baby. I just so get off on you watching me do this kind of stuff. And it doesn't matter what I'm doing or where – wanking in a dirty basement, or going for it full-on with Dark Knight. It just does it for me. You know how that can be.'

'Yeah,' I mutter, 'yeah, I do.'

Because I really do.

9

It's Thursday night already, and what an excellent week it has been. To say Dark Knight loved the Crouching Christian, Hidden Nothing pictures is a massive understatement – he practically proposed when he saw them. Although, because sometimes he's not the most articulate rampant cyber dominant in the world, especially when faced with this level of tongue-tying eye candy, his praise was mostly restricted to the words, 'You are one hot pup', repeated in various combinations.

I've been talking to Dark Knight on Instant Messaging loads, with Christian in the passenger seat. In fact he's watched us chat so much now that he can just take over and play the part of cyber Christian, without me prompting at all. And that's pretty handy, because we've decided against any kind of two-way radio connection for the date. EYE-SPY has got loads of potential gizmos we could use, but they'd all mean wiring Christian up even more and if the date gets intimate, and I certainly hope it does, we've got nowhere to hide. So Christian's going bare except for the camera. And it'll be a silent movie, but I don't mind, as sometimes the pictures are more than enough.

As it's Thursday, it's Fandango night, so while Christian is off with Dan making sure things glide baby-oil smoothly in club land, I'm just across the road doing a bit of a recce of Schwartz.

The place hasn't changed much since my abortive attempt to get a look at it a few weeks ago, excepting one small addition to the tatty grey banner on the façade. It now sports an orange sash, draped across it like it's Miss United Kingdom, and proclaiming 'Grand Opening: This Saturday'. It's still an imposing building, though perhaps not so much of a sky-blotting monolith as I had once thought.

I pull a super-slinky credit-card-sized digital camera from my pocket (already, the EYE-SPY stockroom has become my personal playground) and snap the entrance and the front of the building. Then I sneak round the side, in the hope of finding another way in. The side street is tiny, a narrow run of cobbles that is barely the width of a single car. With the high buildings on either side, it's pitch dark, apart from a metal fire escape, which manages to catch a few bare licks of moonlight. I creep a little further in the all-muffling dark and then I see my goal, a back entrance.

It's set well back into the wall, in a deep recess and almost invisible; in fact I swear I spotted it more by intuition than eyesight. But there it is. A door.

I creep over, give it a tentative push and it swings open. There's no way I can turn my back on an opportunity like this. I go inside.

Schwartz is as dark and quiet as the tiny side street. There doesn't seem to be anyone here. I'm in a short corridor, totally dark except for a tiny bit of moonlight, which is seeping in from somewhere – just enough to see by – as I creep towards some double doors. I glide through them and suddenly there I am, in the *Marie Celeste* of fetish nightclubs, all alone on a quiet lonely dance floor.

It's seems quite small. Or at least this dance floor is smaller than the main dance floor in either Cruze or the Schwartz of my video, and it's made to look even smaller by the huge stage area, crowded with super-sized bond-age furniture.

Yum.

The wooden posts and stocks and frames that jostle for position, like an enchanted forest of very kinky trees, all have glinting metal attachments. In some cases clearly showing exactly how a poor victim would be strapped to each one, in others just bamboozling me.

High posts dangle shackles for wrists and some have rigidly fixed collars for necks or weirdly medieval cages for heads, suggesting at once some tortured slave boy, dragged upright, held tight and helpless, his toes barely scraping the floor. There are two pillories. One is the story-book archetype – ideal for crowds with rotten fruit to pelt – designed to hold a standing victim in wrist and neck stocks. The other subtly perverts tradition, suggest-ing a far more sexual motive for the wooden frame, by capturing the victim in the same style, but bent over or kneeling, so his face would be at waist height – ideal for all manner of uses. Almost hidden by the heavy black drapes at the back of the stage, an ominous X-shaped frame lurks upstage – a St Andrew's cross – with mana-cles at each of its four corners, hinting at yet more thrilling scenes, as my fevered brain threatens to go into overload. There are also strange triangular frames and other outlandish shapes that none of my pornish or online antics have briefed me for. It's a wonderland, in every way.

I so need to visit this nightclub, when it's up and running and I have grown a penis.

I stare at the laden stage for a little longer, feeling rather giddy, not sure which delicious item to commit to memory first. And then I feel a little weight in my pocket, and remember that memory doesn't even come into it, I can make a permanent record. I pull out the camera and start to snap away, smiling as I remember that my spying mission necessitated this special model that works in ultra-low lighting conditions.

I spot a cage, somewhere near the back of the stage. It's very small. To fit inside, an occupant would have to be on his hands and knees with his legs hitched up tight under his body. Very uncomfortable. I take a snap.

And I can't help it. I pause in my picture taking long enough to imagine a cute blond slave boy, hands cuffed behind him, collared and leashed and with a big red rubber ball stretching and stoppering his mouth. I imagine him being led across this very dance floor by a deliciously muscular master. The master drags his reluctant charge over to the cage and opens the door. The slave stalls, shaking his head violently at the prospect of being forced into this cramped space, but the master just laughs. He grabs the slave roughly by the neck and forces him into his prison, slamming the door after him with a resonant clang.

But then I suddenly snap out of my fantasy, all senses in prickly overdrive, because the clanging cage door in my mind blurs into something else. Something real. Voices, laughter.

I press myself into the dark wall next to the double doors I entered by, almost becoming one with the stucco, listening hard. Three, maybe even four, voices are in boisterous conversation, and heading this way.

My whole body goes bow-string taut as a door opens far across the dance floor, and a rectangle of golden light appears on the polished tiles. There in the open door are four silhouetted figures. Figures with dusters and mops and plastic carry trays of aerosol cans. Bloody cleaners.

As the cleaners march on in, oblivious to me, they carry on their semi-conversation, which seems to be nothing more than a mixture of loud whoops and laughing catcalls. One of them has a small radio, which is playing a tinny sort of pop or rap or something, and he sets it down on the middle of the dance floor, with a cry of 'Hey, it's the disco!' and bops around. After a moment or two of grooving, he calls out 'Jasper! –' not missing a single beat as he grooves his slinky hips '– can't you find a light switch or something. I can hardly see myself think in here.'

Lights! Oh fuck. I press myself even further against the wall and hold my breath – like any of that is going to make me actually invisible.

'Yeah, hang on,' calls back another of the cleaners, Jasper I assume, who has disappeared into the dark. 'They're on the decks, I think. I don't know if it'll help much though.'

A switch is thrown and the dance floor is suddenly lit, but only slightly. The few orangey spots that have come on are enough to show what's what and stop the cleaners from bumping into the walls, but that's about it. I'm still well cloaked.

'Fuck. Is that it?' says the dancing cleaner, who has stopped dancing for a moment.

'Yep,' says Jasper, appearing from somewhere at the back of the room.

'Well, if we miss some spots they can hardly blame us.'

The other two cleaners, who have been loitering by the far door, saunter onto the dance floor and join Jasper and the dancer. I can see them all more clearly now, the middle of the dance floor being the best-lit spot. They're all young boys, about nineteen or twenty. Jasper is standing right under one of the orange spotlights and I can see him quite well. He's a little geeky looking, with yellowy blond hair and thick black-rimmed specs. The dancer is also relatively well lit. He's a good-looking little thing, just my type with floppy dark hair and a classical face, positively boy-band material. Yum. The other two are harder to make out. They are wearing baggy jeans and T-shirts like their companions, but their faces are too hidden in shadows to see the details.

'Well,' says one of the shadow twins, 'I vote we skip it. I mean, how can we clean in the fucking dark? It's stupid.'

'Well, maybe we should just run a duster around a bit . . .' says the dancer, trailing off as his mouth falls open. 'Oh fuck me, look at that stuff.'

Of course, he's pointing at the stage.

With more whoops, more yells and quite a few shrieks of 'Oh my God', the boys hit the stage and swarm all over the bondage equipment. Call it that sixth sense again, but I ease the camera back out of my pocket, where I shoved it when I was disturbed, and hold it tight in my hand.

'Jesus,' says one of the shadow twins, 'this stuff is fucking perverted.'

The dancer sighs loudly. 'Yes, Cameron, this is a fetish club, remember.'

'Well, I know that,' says Cameron, fiddling with one of the manacles on the huge St Andrew's cross like it is something from another planet, 'but I thought that was just leather trousers and piercings. I didn't think they'd have all this stuff.'

'Like it then, do you?' says the other, still unnamed, shadow twin. 'Does it turn you on?' And he grabs Cameron round the waist in a playful hug. A very familiar type of playful hug. I can't help wondering if they're a couple, and if that's the case I hope very much that Cameron has been rendered hopelessly rigid by the equipment and the only option is for them to make full use of it in front of snap-happy moi.

And I'm a-wishin' and a-hopin' away in my dark little lair when things suddenly take a turn for the excellent. But not quite in the way I expected.

Cameron laughs. 'Nah, that's OK. I'd like to see you in it, though. All helpless and at my mercy. Fancy it?'

'Yes,' I mouth silently in the dark, willing unnamed cleaner to make the right choice.

'I've got a better idea,' says the dancer, with an evil little lilt to his voice. 'Oh Jas-per.'

Jasper looks up from where he is running his hand along the top of the larger pillory. 'Mmm,' says Jasper, sounding dreamy and far away, 'what?'

The dancer walks slowly across the stage to Jasper, his hips jerking from side to side in a sexy stylised prowl, slink-slink-slink.

Jasper looks up and sighs. 'What do you want?' he says sounding part forceful and part resigned.

The shadow twins, Cameron and his still unnamed possible boyfriend, are also on the move. They don't have the grace of the dancer, but they're closing in on Jasper from the right and left. And as those two position themselves at either end of the pillory, the dancer reaches it too, facing Jasper across its mirror-bright polished wood.

Jasper looks at the dancer, and then at the other two flanking him like predators. 'What?' he says again, sounding very unsure.

The dancer taps a finger against the wood and then, with a slow smile that spreads out across his face like ripples on a pond, he opens the pillory up. The top cross-piece comes in half, pivoting up like a greedy maw, and leaving three perfect semi-circular cradles in the wood – two for wrists and one for a neck. Even from across the dance floor I can see how beautifully made they are: luscious dark wood surrounds the holes, which are softly padded with red velvet cushioning. Chocolate cherry.

And suddenly Jasper has no choice but to inspect them at close quarters, because, as the dancer pulls the top piece up, the shadow twins move in and shove Jasper roughly into position, so his head and wrists are cradled in upholstered luxury.

And poor Jasper yells and shouts blue bloody murder as the dancer rams the top half of the pillory back on, trapping his frantic victim.

'Shut up, Jasper,' the dancer yells, 'you know there's no one else here.'

One of the shadow twins, possibly Cameron, but I can't remember which of them is which now, ducks off and returns quickly to slip a flash of yellow into the dancer's hand.

The dancer grins. 'Good idea,' he mutters, before stopping Jasper's mouth with the fluffy duster.

Then the nameless shadow twin passes the dancer something else. It's a reel of tape, which the dancer quickly uses to secure the duster in place, before stepping back to admire his handiwork. I admire it too. In fact I record it for posterity. Snap.

Jasper is still struggling against his wooden prison. Frustratingly, his flapping hands are trapped just inches from the catch that secures the two halves of the pillory. He jerks around, but it's clearly hopeless: the contraption he's locked into is built to contain struggles just like these, and it doesn't even creak.

The dancer looks a bit lost suddenly, not sure what to do with his prize now he's won it, and then the awkward silence is split by one of the shadow twins shouting, 'Oh my God. Yes.' And everyone (including me) turns to see what's causing these raptures. Even Jasper twists against the tight grip of his bondage to see.

The shadow twin is crouching over a box, which is low on the stage, and hard for me to make out, but I can sort of tell that it's a long lacquered shape, glinting midnight sleek in the dark. And shadow twin is holding something that he has plucked from the box up in the air. It's a small round paddle, shaped like a table-tennis bat, but meant for a very different game indeed.

The dancer looks a bit wary. 'I don't know,' he says slowly, but the shadow twins aren't interested in his concerns at all, and are already dancing around with the paddle and taunting the helpless Jasper. And I can't resist the pretty show. Snap.

'Come on,' says one of the twins, wheedling playfully, 'let's give him a few licks, he sure deserves it, always skiving off on the job.'

Jasper yells some muffled negatives into his duster gag and wriggles frantically.

The dancer purses his lips for a moment. 'Hmm, OK, I suppose he does need a few little whacks.' And he snatches the paddle, and slips around behind the pillory to where Jasper's vulnerable little arse is jutting out like a birthday present.

I'm pressed hard against the wall, feeling pretty vulnerable myself. The floorshow is hot, hot, hot, but I can't quite relax and enjoy it because, even with the subdued lighting, I know if any one of them really looked in my direction I'm lost. I daren't risk losing my concentration by sneaking a hand under my knicker elastic. Much as I'd like to when the dancer gives Jasper's arse a volley of playful swipes.

So I keep on snapping, but I watch the actual scene with a kind of detachedness, but I know in my heart that it's not a wasted opportunity. Sometimes watching is like this. At the time it doesn't quite come off. Circumstances aren't quite right. But it doesn't matter because it's all money in the bank for some other rainy day. Jasper, Dancer et al. will return, dragged out of my memory bank to provide a little extra spice when I need it. In this particular case, probably with the added value of a photo slideshow on my laptop.

When the howling Jasper has been punished enough, the shadow twins make their exit, something about wanting to catch the last hour of Fandango. I freeze as they lope out, but I still go unnoticed in the shadows.

The dancer walks back round to the front of the pillory and gazes into Jasper's glassy eyes.

'Oh God,' Dancer moans suddenly, leaning forward and covering Jasper's face in eager kisses, somehow talking at the same time. 'Oh God,' he goes on, between licks and nips, 'it was so fucking hot locking you down with those two. You struggled like a bitch. God ... so hot.' And he fumbles with the tape until he can pull the duster out of Jasper's mouth, plastering his own lips there instead, and devouring them in a greedy snog.

As soon as he gets a chance to speak, Jasper hisses, his voice heavy and blatant, 'Oh God, Pete, please bring me off right now. That was, ah, so good. I'm so fucking hard. I'm so hard it fucking hurts. Please, Pete.'

Pete chuckles very quietly, mussing Jasper's hair with loving hands. 'Oh, well that's a bit of a shame,' he teases, 'because I'm not feeling in a very charitable mood right now.'

'Don't.' Pause, swallow. 'Don't tease, you fucking bastard,' Jasper says, in a very dirty tone of voice.

'Uh-uh,' Pete ticks him off. 'Be nice – you don't want me to leave you in there for the muscle boys to find in the morning, do you?'

'Promises, promises,' Jasper replies. And they both laugh. And then start to snog deliciously again, stubble and saliva burning like sandpaper, on peach pretty young skin. Snap.

But Pete must be feeling charitable really, despite his swagger, because while they lock lips, he reaches down and finds Jasper's bucking hips and straining fly, flicking it open with one-handed ease to find that desperate Jasper is very pleased to see him.

The rough kiss rolls on and on and Jasper writhes in Pete's hand, twisting in the wooden frame, achingly close. And then, just inches from coming, Jasper opens his eyes and looks right at me. His mouth opens, just a little, and I'm sure he's about to blow my cover, but too late, he's coming in Pete's hand. And I scarper, reeling from an attack of full-on déjà vu for that basement in Paranoid and Christian writhing on those plastic bags and spotting me just before he comes.

I slide out of the narrow side street and round the front of Schwartz proper, trying to get my bearings and figure out where Cruze is from here.

As I'm looking up and down the street I see a very good-looking man standing, looking up at Schwartz. I know I've seen him somewhere before and as I stare I realise where: it's Mr Fox. The very same Mr Fox I spy on every Tuesday afternoon, well, every Tuesday except for when I'm having to clear out the stupid work stockroom.

And it's weird seeing Mr Fox like this, in the real world, like being back at school and seeing a teacher out shopping. As I continue to lurk by the mouth of the side street, Mr Fox finishes his looking at the exterior of Schwartz and walks off down the street, turning his back to me.

And as he does so I see that on the back of his jacket is a huge glittering silver tiger.

* * *

'So Mr Fox is the man from the Food Court!' I say animatedly to Christian in the VIP bar of Cruze as Fandango winds down around us. I've been explaining the evening's revelations (but not the sexy cleaners part) as if they were the results of a secret post-mortem on Princess Diana, and Christian is yet to be impressed.

'But if Mr Fox was the guy in the Food Court, why didn't you recognise him then?'

'I only really saw the back of him then and from miles away. But look, don't you see? Mr Fox is on to me. He's decided to stalk me right back.'

'What, just because he was at the Food Court in the Arndale Centre, i.e. the main shopping centre in the city where he lives?'

'And outside Schwartz just now.'

'Well, forgive me, baby, if I sound a bit harsh here, but why the hell wouldn't Mr Fox, a gay man, be out and about in the gay village? Furthermore why wouldn't Mr Fox, a big gay pervert, be eyeing up the frontage of a new gay pervery club on the Thursday night before it opens?' He takes a big slug of his G and T in a very Q.E.D. sort of a way.

'Well, it all seems a bit odd to me,' I say weakly, wishing I had a drink to punctuate my clever points too. (If I had any clever points.)

'Oh baby, you've just got the jitters about tomorrow.' Christian puts his arm around me gently. 'Just relax, everything'll be fine.'

Back at home, I'm making a quick cup of tea before bed. I glance out of the kitchen window and notice Mr Fox is home too. He's standing in his own kitchen, waiting for his kettle to boil. I find myself feeling nostalgic for the days when a sight of Mr Fox making tea would make my heart do a little schoolgirlish leap and

I'd peep at him through the binoculars while he dunked his tea bag. But now Mr Fox just makes me wary and strange. Does he know about me? How much does he know? I stare out the windows that face mine and find myself filled with suspicion, instead of plain old lovely curiosity.

Christian takes his tea straight to bed, but I decide to check my email first, and for some reason I fire up my IM program too. Dark Knight's little window pops up on my screen instantly.

<Hello pup. I was hoping you'd be on tonight. Are you excited?>

Er, yes. <God sir, yes sir, I am. I can't wait.> Which is all totally true.

<Actually, pup, I was thinking, you're very trusting.>

<Am I, sir?>

<Well, yes, you don't know what I look like, do you?>

<No sir, but I've read your profile, you sound pretty good to me.> Dark Knight must sound good in his profile or I would never have started this. I forget exactly what it said, though; possibly that he had dark hair and that he was tall – I seem to remember tall.

The truth is Dark Knight is, in my imagination, a huge imposing muscled master, à la my porn films, and it has never actually crossed my mind that he might not live up to that in the flesh. Until now.

<Well, you never know with cyber, people bend the truth in their profiles> Dark Knight replies. <That's why I wanted your photo and to speak to you. There are far too many wind-up merchants and time-wasters out there. You can't be too careful.>

Hidden safely behind the screen, I gulp. <Yeah> I reply, weakly.

<So, shall I send you a picture of me?>

<OK, sure.>

I don't want to have to look at his picture live, so I beg tiredness and ask for an email, then log off quickly. Then I go and make more tea. But the email from Dark Knight that is sitting in my inbox when I return isn't a photo, it's a little list.

To: Sub Christian
From: Dark Knight
Subject: Tomorrow Night

Dear Christian

I thought I'd better clarify the sort of behaviour I expect at Schwartz. I know you can be a forgetful little pup, but I don't want to hear any excuses.

You are my pup and my property, for the evening you belong to me. I give orders, you obey.

As soon as you see me you will come straight to me and stand directly in front of me, lowering your gaze.

You will call me sir.

You will not wear any underwear of any kind.

Dark Knight

P.S. Do you have a safe word?

I bite my lip and stare at the screen, shivering with excitement as the pretty, pretty words sink into my brain – he is so wonderful and commanding. I fire back a quick email with a safe word – elephant – not very original, but it's late.

Still no sign of the photo, but it's bedtime and I decide it can wait until morning.

* * *

After a night tossing and turning, while Christian inexplicably snores merrily away beside me, I wake to a new complication.

Christian often works from home Fridays, which really means he does a little bit of his proper job first thing, and then pisses about doing his moonlighting naughtiness for the rest of the day. However, I haven't even finished my Shreddies when he's swearing at the laptop.

'Aww fuck it! Genny, did you use this last night?'

'Uh, yeah. What's wrong?' I get up from the table, carrying my bowl and spoon, and wander over to see. But I see precisely nothing, the screen is completely blank.

'I'm not sure. I think the power cable's bust. Look, the light's not on.' Christian taps his fingernail against the little place where a green light should be winking its readiness.

'Well it was fine last night.' Stupid dodgy cable.

And with no power cable our laptop is now officially fucked: the battery died over a year ago and without a working cable there is no way to get electricity into the thing that is now no longer a computer and more an expensive doorstop.

'Fuck,' says Christian. 'I'll have to go into the office now.'

Which means he'll have to do proper work.

And all this also means no Dark Knight photo for me, well, not until I get to work anyway.

Except that doesn't happen, because work is so crazy right now. My mind is so not on my work it isn't true. Despite my current out of hours life, I'm actually working my arse off during the day – my work–life balance has gone to shit. And I really need all my energies directed at managing the stupid muddle Justin has left.

So I'm struggling like mad trying to get on top of my new job (Frank stopped mentoring me after two days) and it just doesn't help how buzzy and scared I feel about the evening's event. Keeping my mind on the job is a constant struggle. Stupid Frank, fancy handing me this promotion this week of all weeks. Doesn't he realise I'm up to my eyes arranging for my boyfriend to have his first date with my online lover? Well, obviously he doesn't realise that, unless he is psychic, or even more of a psycho stalker than I've given him credit for.

I'm stuck in the cupboard all day again, checking the stock we actually have against what we should have, and compiling a mile-long list of things that are strangely missing (with a separate appendix for the things that I happen to know are in my flat). I don't get near my desk, let alone my computer all day. Just after lunch (a limp sandwich eaten perched on top of a pile of *What Camcorder?* magazines), Christian texts me to say he has managed to get a new cable and is off home, so I decide the Dark Knight picture can wait, and soldier on with my list of AWOL gadgetry until home time.

After a whole day spent in the choky-pokey stockroom I almost run from the tram station to Maple Court, flying down the road, high on adrenaline and anticipation. When I bang through the door, Christian looks up and smiles at me, clearly delighted by my flushed cheeks and excited glow. All the stockroom dust that I felt was coating me when I left work seems to have blown away in the sharp evening air, and every last work-related thought along with it. This stuff I'm doing might be morally dubious in so many ways, but it's one hell of a stress buster.

'Oh God, Gen, you look amazing,' Christian says, breathy soft, 'want to maybe go to bed instead?'

I laugh. 'Actually, no.'

And then I just stand still right where I am, and look at him. It's like he's my big hero, my champion, making his noble sacrifice to keep his lady happy, and I feel all shivery just thinking about it.

Then I shrug and say, 'Well, maybe, just for a cuddle then.'

An hour later, I'm surveying my handiwork with barely concealed pride. Camera nestled in fringe aside, I've styled Christian myself. Not caring for anything clever or different I've led with my groin and put him in leather trousers and a leather body harness. He protested that every other boy in the club would be dressed just the same, but I just pouted and reminded him that this was my project, and I was having it my way. But I let him smudge a bit of black kohl under his eyes, just because.

And it's not until then, not until we've done all our checks and goodbye kisses and I've even shown him the print-out of Dark Knight's emailed instructions that I remember the Dark Knight photo.

Christian tells me to forget it, he's got to go. He stops by the hall mirror and pouts into it.

'After all, he'll recognise me.'

And before I even have a second to tell him that it won't take long to download the pic, he's gone, out the door with one last kiss plopped on top of my head. I shout at his back that I'll text him a description and he shouts something back, but he's too far down the stairs and whatever it is doesn't reach me.

I sit down at the computer and type my password into the website which houses cyber-Christian's email account. And there, sure enough, is a message from Dark Knight with an oversized cartoon paperclip showing that it has an attachment: the pic.

It takes several long seconds to open and I tap my fingers on the table top, partly impatient, partly nervous.

And then the image flashes up onto the screen. In big living colour. It's Dark Knight. He's right there, sitting on a dark red sofa, shirtless. And I needn't have worried because he's very, very good looking.

He's also Mr Fox.

10

As promised, I text Christian a description: DK = MR FUCKING FOX. But he doesn't reply.

Next I bash at the computer keyboard frantically until I get the picture from the web cam up on the monitor. But all I can see is the inside of a tram carriage – there's no sign of Christian checking his phone. Maybe he has no signal.

I keep watching, until eventually the tram judders to a halt, and the camera jolts and wobbles even more, as Christian stands up and alights.

And, strangely enthralled, I start to forget about the Mr Fox revelation as I stare at the screen. And the longer I peer through the magic window, the more I'm hypnotised by the little twinkling image it contains. I'm like Alice peeking down the rabbit hole into wonderland.

So Dark Knight is Mr Fox, well, that's not so sinister really, more like a weird coincidence than anything. It's not exactly evidence that Mr Fox is stalking me (or that he's cackling away Wicked Witch of the West style, while plotting my downfall through e-porn and mistaken identities).

Meanwhile, my Christian is walking through the dark wet streets, so the web-cam picture I'm wallowing in is just shiny streets at the moment, dark glossy cobbles like best quality chocolate – at least 70 per cent cocoa solids.

The picture quality is not actually all that good – kind of grainy and jumpy like a flick book – which I'm mostly

OK with. Visually motivated as I am, I'm not one of those people who are suckers for big screens and crystal-sharp clarity. I like a bit of blur and murky durky sometimes. I see it as the chink I need to stick in the crowbar of my imagination. The best pictures are inside my head, anyway.

I continue to stare at the screen, until something properly big and epic happens, like a moment from a film. Christian angles his body and the camera tilts up, rain splatters on the little lens, blurring everything, for a moment, into a fractured prism pattern of split colours. And then it clears, as Christian – bright spark – realises what must have happened and wipes the lens quickly, showing me what he is looking up at. It's the raggedy grey fabric sign for Schwartz, with the bright-orange opening-night sash hanging across it, all casual and slightly skew-whif. We have arrived!

Christian makes his entrance. The steps and lobby are familiar – of course – from my first visit, but other than that it's like a whole new world. In fact, it's really rather reminiscent of my *Hidden Camera Studs* vid, with the shaky first-person camera and the furtive atmosphere. And, actually, I don't think I'm really making the connection that Christian is wearing the camera any more. With my boy's eye view of this thrilling exotica, I feel like I'm wearing it. Or even that there is no camera and it's really me going into Schwartz. It's like I'm inhabiting Christian's body – really playing the part.

Christian/me/the camera greets the door staff perkily and flashes a black embossed invite. The yummy lump of beefcake on the door waves him on in, blissfully unaware of my presence in the back seat.

Now this is really something! I'm drifting through the glittering curtain that separates the lobby area of

Schwartz from the full-on pervy heaven of the club proper, and into my personal previously unseen footage.

Christian stands in a wide corridor. It's clinicalish, white-painted, with some groupings of metallic tables and chairs scattered about. There are several doors off the corridor and a sweeping metal staircase, leading down from a lobby above. Christian moves his head around in slow sweeps, probably for my benefit. There are a few groups and couples lounging on the furniture, some very handsome, some cuties, some average, some rough, all worth looking at, because all of them are dressed in outfits that are either tight or short or just mouth-wateringly kinky.

His slow pan stops on a couple of youngish men. One has close-cropped dark hair and a heavy shading of stubble across his chin. The other, taller and leaner, has a spiky blue Mohican. They're pasted into a corner, pressing their naked chests together and grinding their shiny leather crotches, as they kiss and fondle. It takes me a while to notice, but blue Mohican, who is being driven harder and harder into the corner by the rough embrace of his partner, has his wrists handcuffed together behind his back. Yum.

After lingering on this couple (who he must just know are going to do it for me) for a short while, Christian heads up the stairs and through a door on the balcony.

Upstairs, Christian is in a sort of lounge. A lounge bar, I guess, as there is a huge bar-counter running the length of the opulent room. And it's very loungey indeed in here, all red and plush and sweet and rich, kind of like the inside of a strawberry. The actual bar itself is huge, dripping gold and crystal like something from *Footballers' Wives*. I love it. And I love it even more when Christian, with a quick head tilt, points something rather extra special out. A little bit of added value.

On the far wall, opposite the bar, in a long thin line are a row of cages. And in about half of them is a prisoner – a semi-naked male prisoner – standing and looking out helplessly at the world.

Unfortunately I am restricted to viewing this excitement through Christian's eyes and before I have enough of the caged studs, he's turned to look back at the bar.

'No, Christian,' I shout out loud at the screen. 'The cages, I want to see the cages.' And I bang my fist on the edge of the table.

Then, as if by magic – or, more likely, as if he was only fucking with me – Christian turns back around and walks over to the wall of cages.

Close up, the cages look pretty sturdy, not just showpieces that would actually be a doddle to get out of if the occupants so wished. They're not locked, just bolted, but the bolt is outside and completely unreachable for the poor prisoner. I actually find this even more sexy than I would a heavily padlocked cage. With the bolt set up, any passer-by could set the occupant free if he so wished, but if no one shows any mercy the poor prisoner is helpless.

As Christian bends close to inspect them, I discover that on the front of each cage is a black slate which can be written on with chalk. The one Christian is looking at says:

PRISONER: Malachi's Boy
SENTENCE: 2 hours
RELEASE: 10 p.m.
IMPRISONED BY: Malachi

Christian looks up at the cage's occupant. A tall blond man in his mid-thirties looks back at him. He's all in black PVC from ankle to neck and he raises his eyebrows at Christian resignedly. The camera bobs, probably Christian giving a sympathetic nod, and then the view swivels back to the bar.

And as it does I spot Mr Fox in the crush.

And I catch my breath.

Then suddenly, like some kind of unbelievably sexy whirlwind, Mr Fox is right there, right next to Christian, and I'm straining to lip read. I spot the unmistakable word 'pup', and I know that that's got to be enough to clear up any doubts Christian might be having about the identity of Dark Knight.

For the next five or so minutes, I don't think I breathe once.

Mr Fox, looking beautiful – and taller than I thought he was – is in tight greyish jeans and a white T-shirt that is close cut enough to show all his elegantly toned swimmer's muscles. Beautiful. He slips his hand easily into Christian's and leads him away through the steamy strawberry bar.

They stroll through some double doors and into another long white-painted corridor and suddenly Mr Fox slams Christian up against the wall and kisses him, vicious and hot, becoming nothing but a blur on the screen.

And I'm so turned on by this sudden demonstration of lust that I'm practically rocking in my seat.

I continue to writhe and squirm around as I enjoy the slightly surreal sight of Mr Fox snogging my boyfriend (although it is only clear by extrapolation and context that that is what they are doing as all I can really see is a blurry orange shape filling the screen). Yet again I thank my lucky stars for my extra vivid imagination.

Then their heads fall apart and Mr Fox drags Christian to one of the identical plain white doors that line the corridor and kicks it open.

It's just what I was expecting. Because the room inside is not unlike the room that the master takes his slave to in *Hidden Camera Studs*. It's small and sparse but for a single hard chair and a small lidded box.

Mr Fox manoeuvres Christian so he is sitting in the chair, dripping with apprehension. Then, just as I am convinced I am going to actually levitate off my seat with excitement, Mr Fox's hand suddenly fills the screen. I'm confused for a second, and then I get it. I watch, helpless, as Mr Fox grabs the camera from Christian's lapel and the screen suddenly dies.

And so do I.

I stare at the fizzing grey static.

I panic. Desperate to contact Christian, I try all the avenues open to me. I call Christian's mobile twenty million times and leave a variety of messages, from the concerned ('Baby, check in will you'), to the hysterical ('Babe, it's me again, I saw Mr Fox smash the camera. Are you OK? Call me back OK, it's just past eleven. If I don't hear in half an hour I'll come down . . .'), to the hyper-real ('Baby, I'm on my way. Don't let him hurt you and if that's you listening Dark Knight I'll fucking smash your fucking face in if you've so much as tweaked his nipple').

And it's when I send this last message that I hear it. I've been pacing the floor like a mad thing, wandering from room to room. I send that last message in the bedroom and as I hang up the phone I hear the tell-tale beep-beep of a mobile receiving voice mail.

Christian's phone is lying on the dressing table.

This is where I realise I'm going to have to mount a full-on rescue mission.

I grab my big coat and set off, wondering how late the trams run on a Friday night at this time of year.

* * *

Once outside Schwartz I am met with a slow headshake and a resolute: 'It's a private party.'

'But my boyfriend's in there and I think he might not be OK . . .' Oh God, I can't exactly tell them why I think he's not OK can I, so I end with the rather feeble, 'Christian Omar, he does the PR for Fandango.'

'Look, love,' says the bouncer, not unsympathetically, 'I don't care if he's Christian bloody Slater, you're not going in there. It's invite only, and it's men only, so unless you can produce both an invite and a penis, nothing doing.'

I'm about to break into another desperate, 'but you don't understand', when a voice at my elbow says, 'Want me to have a look for him?'

I turn around to see a Boy Scout smiling at me. I'm about to protest that I don't think this is a very appropriate task for a bob-a-job, when I realise the Boy Scout is, in fact, Lorne wearing a costume that I'm not sure I want to think about in too much detail, but I smile back and nod, relieved.

Twenty minutes and one of Percy's' finest milky coffees later, Boy Scout Lorne appears at my table and slumps into the chair opposite me with not so much as a 'Dib dib dib'.

'Oh,' I say, my heart crumbling in dread slow-mo.

Lorne shakes her head. 'No sign. I did what you said, private rooms upstairs, off the bar. Nothing. I barged in on quite a few interesting scenes, but none of them had your Christian in them.'

'And he's definitely not in there?'

'Can't say that for sure. The place is huge, and heaving. But I looked and looked.'

'Oh.' I feel a bit tearful, more from frustration than anything. I can't think what else to do.

Lorne grabs my hand. 'Look, darling, it'll be OK. So he

wasn't where you said, he's probably in there somewhere. I'll go back and look. I saw him earlier.'

My ears pick right up at this. 'What?'

'Yeah, I was in there a couple of hours ago and I saw
him, only briefly, didn't get a chance to go over – I was
kind of busy.'

'Oh. OK.'

'I'll go back; some friends of mine are in there anyway.
I'll find him, sweetie, you go home.'

But I don't want to go home. I end up huddled on a
bench in my favourite park. Couples of all denomina-
tions pass me by, but they don't even blip my radar, let
alone persuade me to follow them in case they stop off
for some pressed-up-against-a-tree-trunk action. I pull
my coat tight around me, trying to find some comfort in
faux sheepskin.

Anything could have happened to Christian. Perhaps
Dark Knight is a front for a ring of white slavers! Perhaps
Christian was bundled out the back of Schwartz into a
sinister van and whisked away to a life of cruel servi-
tude. (I tell myself off then, for finding that thought
more than a little sexy.)

Actually, I know it isn't that. Well, I suppose I don't
really know. I don't know for certain, or anything. But I
do know that that is a pretty far-fetched scenario. I have
another possible-case scenario. And that is far more
likely, and far more worrying.

Christian has always been pretty fluid and laid back
about his sexuality. Which I've always chalked up as a
positive, especially when this began. I am fully aware of
how (not very) far I would have got with this plan if I
was dating Mr Average Unreconstructed.

And Christian always says it the same way: he's never
been attracted to a man, but maybe he hasn't met the
right man. And so I have to ask, what if Dark Knight is

the right man? What if Dark Knight is the right man and I bloody well introduced them. Not only that, I fucking oiled the fucking wheels. It's too ironic. I am absolutely convinced that Christian, right now, couldn't care less that Dark Knight tossed the camera. They're still there. They're still snuggled in their private room up to all sorts of stuff that would be a-OK if I was getting to watch – but is so very not OK if I'm not.

This is the trouble with getting hot for gay boys. In fact, one of the main things that attracted me to Christian was his feyness. And I've fallen hard for far more 100 per cent gay guys than I want to remember, right from number one – my first-ever boyfriend.

He was called Andrew. He had slightly too tight trousers and wore smudgy black eyeliner and, God, he was sexy. But, in retrospect, I'm sure one of the main reasons he caught my eye in the first place was because there were so many rumours flying round the school that he was gay. Not that I realised it back then. I thought pretty Andrew had just piqued my interest because of his nice eyes and cute smile.

I wanted Andrew, though, whatever the real reason. And so I hunted down my quarry. Poor little Andrew didn't stand a chance – I can be quite a go-getting sort of girl when I want to be.

So we started dating, and even shared several cute little chaste kisses in our three-week romance, until the day he tearfully told me the rumours were true and he had a monumental crush on this guy called Darren, who was something of a school stud and quite definitely the boy most unlikely to consider Andrew date material. A perfect adolescent melodrama ensued and Andrew sort of broke my heart in a puppy-love kind of a way (as well as his own over dumb old Darren, who was so not worth it).

But there was a bonus a few years later, when Andrew and I were both home from university one summer. I was a little voyeur in training by then, and I managed – using some rather clumsy methods – to orchestrate things so I was hiding in the wardrobe in his parents' bedroom when he was entangled with his new boyfriend on their bed. In fact, after that I managed to get in on lots of action with my Andrew-shaped passport. I did the whole gay-nightclubs-fag-hag thing. In fact, I still do sometimes, when Andrew and I are both visiting our parents. I persuade him to take me to a club or two, and he has never quite twigged my motives, which is good actually, because he's no laid-back Christian type – I reckon it would really freak him out. It's possible he thinks I am still in love with him. Once, while drunk, he told me that I was the only girl he'd consider if there were some kind of right-wing revolution and it was heterosexuality or death. (Apparently neither I nor Christian gets a say in the matter.)

But, reactionary revolution aside, Andrew is in the past and Christian is the present and the future (or at least he was the future up until tonight).

Stupidly, I had really thought that with Christian I could have it all – the best of both worlds. So, instead of being content to have a perfect, cute, slightly camp boy, who still loves to press his tongue up against my cunt and cuddle up with me under a warm duvet, I had to make him into my ideal gay man to perve on too. How could I possibly have thought that my perfect Christian wasn't enough as he was? It's all my fault. I thought I could have a straight boyfriend and still get to hide out and watch him get off with some big beefy bloke. Looks like I thought wrong.

And in the freezing cold park freezing cold tears drip down my face.

I'm still sniffing and snuffling, when my phone tweets. I pull it out of my pocket and stare at the screen. Lorne has texted me.

NO SIGN OF C. MEET UP?

I can't face any more Boy Scout Lorne. So I lie. GONE HOME. C U 2MORO?

And, as I have claimed to be tucked up in bed, I decide I might as well head there now.

I stand up, slow and creaky in the cold – like a statue come to life – and turn to head down the path towards the tram station. A few frozen footsteps later, my phone tweets again.

I COULD COME TO YOURS.

I feel quite guilty, and part of me knows company would be good right now, but I turn her down. SO TIRED. SORRY. 2MORO.

There isn't even time for the kettle to boil between me getting home and the door banging to announce Christian's entrance. My heart stops.

He bounds across the living room towards me, looking strangely normal. Not like a man who is about to announce his engagement to Dark Knight, or who has just escaped a gang of ruthless slave masters, or anything else. He looks completely normal – well as normal as someone dressed in a leather body harness with matching trousers can look.

He drowns me in a big bear hug and then, face buried in my hair, says, 'God, babe, I am so fucking sorry about the camera. Are you going to be in the shit?'

I twist round so I can look up at him. 'Huh?'

'The camera? Dark Knight smashed it; you did see that, right? It did work? The camera?'

'Oh, uh, yeah.'

Christian frowns. 'Babe, are you OK?'

'Yeah, I'm fine. I just ... why didn't you take your phone?'

'What?' Christian looks confused – just for a sec. 'Oh. My phone.'

I nod.

Christian takes a step back and holds out his arms. 'Babe, you dressed me. No bloody decent pockets. I mean, have you seen how tight these trousers are?'

And I have to smirk, because obviously I have seen that. 'But, well, what about keeping in touch?'

'I didn't think it would matter. Not with you having Christian-cam. I never reckoned on the camera getting trashed. Sorry, babe.'

I frown. 'Why did Dark Knight smash the camera? What happened?'

'I think he thought it was a bit of glitter or some shit in my hair. He was being all masterful, I think. You know how he is. He didn't know it was a camera until it was doing the backstroke in my G and T. He was really sorry.'

'Did he ask why you were wearing it?'

'Oh yeah, course he did. I just said it was for work, you know, bit of data capture, reportage, stats.'

'And he was OK with that?'

'Seemed like it. He didn't care. That place is full of CCTV anyway. Security and that. He was far more worried that he'd bust such a pricey piece of kit. It was fine. But anyway, once there was no filming going on I knew there was no point in doing the do, so I told Dark Knight I had to go and sort out about the broken camera and exited sharpish.'

And I have to laugh. Partly it's relief, but mostly it's the way Christian tells it, all cartoony big gestures and crazy eye rolls, like he is presenting kids' telly, well, kids' telly in some perverted alternative universe.

But then I stop. 'Hang on, if you didn't do anything with Dark Knight then where have you been?'

'Nowhere, well, you know, bit of schmoozing and stuff. All the Fandango crowd were there checking out the kinky competition.'

And that's when I start to feel tears roll down my cheeks again.

Christian's face crumples when he sees them. 'Babe,' he says quickly, taking hold of me with both hands, 'babe, what is it? What's the matter?'

'Oh God, I was so worried about you. I thought something awful might have happened.'

'What? Really? No, sweetie, no, nothing bad happened. I just assumed you'd realise I was doing a bit of business. You knew it was the VIP night and everything.'

'Oh. Yeah, OK.' But I feel sort of stupid and not really very OK. Christian holds me while I cry out the horribleness of my night of fretting in the freezing cold park.

'So you didn't know it was Mr Fox until he was right there?' I say softly.

Christian smiles. 'Not really. Well, when he came up to me I thought he was just going to say hi, because we've chatted once or twice about stuff in the building, maintenance and shit, but then as soon as he started talking to me and his manner was all, all, you know, dominant, I realised where I knew Dark Knight's voice from, and ta-dar. It was double lucky too, because I'm pretty sure he didn't recognise me as his neighbour, which means he won't pop round, clock you and get all bamboozled.'

'Oh.'

'It was easy, babe. Apart from the camera thing it all went like a charm. At no point did our hero stop and say, hang on a minute it's not you I've been talking to at all is it? It's your kinky voyeuristic girlfriend.'

'Oh,' I say again, my voice now all soft and thick with more teetering tears.

'Don't, Genny.' Christian makes a sympathetic face and pulls me into a hug. 'I know it didn't do what you wanted, but don't be upset. Everything's OK.'

'Except the camera,' I mutter into his bare shoulder.

'True. Are you going to be in the shit about that?'

'Maybe. But if I am I'll just have to blackmail Frank or something,' I say in a voice that is laughing and crying at the same time.

But mixed in with all my relief something is bugging me. It's Christian's line that he was just hanging out with the Fandango crowd after he left Dark Knight. It just doesn't ring true. If he was just quaffing in the bar with a big gang of mates, wouldn't Lorne have spotted him?

I must have a sleep debt to repay. I don't wake up the next morning until way past midday. But when I finally regain consciousness, I am greeted by a bright sunny Christian holding a bright sunny plate of bacon and eggs.

'I've made you a cheer-up breakfast,' he announces, popping it down on my lap before I have even got my eyes open properly.

'Thanks, baby,' I say, struggling to sit up without spilling grease on the duvet. 'But you didn't need to. It was all my fault.'

'Nah-ah,' says Christian with a comedy finger wave. 'I said I'd do you a show-and-tell with Dark Knight and so I will. We just need to get in touch with him, rearrange stuff, feed him some excuse or other – I'll say I got embroiled in business and couldn't tell them what I was really doing there. Easy peasy.'

Boggling at this pronouncement, I swallow a morsel of bacon and smack my lips. 'Hmm, well, it would be nice but ... well, are you sure you haven't burnt your bridges?'

'Nah, I got him wrapped around my little finger.'

When Christian says that I actually feel a little jealous pang. I used to be the one who had Dark Knight firmly in my pocket. Now I've handed him over to Christian. Not fair, stupid gender.

In fact, I'm like Lady Macbeth, in a way.

But before I can leap from the bed screaming 'unsex me now', Christian tells me, rather sadly, that he is going to have to head off to work. Apparently that bit of networking he did last night has landed him a bit of promotional work at Schwartz's big official opening do tonight.

'And I've kind of got to be there early.' Christian wrinkles his nose in displeasure. 'Sorry.'

I shrug. I am disappointed sure, but work is work.

Later, very late afternoon in fact, with breakfast eaten and shower taken, I wander into the living room and flop onto the sofa in the silent flat. The Saturday papers are deadly dull and even the shiny items in the magazines I scooped from work (the *International Journal of Covert Hardware*) can't whet my jaded appetite this afternoon. I'm in the mood for watching something, not porn, I haven't been in a porn mood for a while, but definitely something hot and sweet.

I settle for watching *Velvet Goldmine*, a film that, although not exactly a roaring critical success, has some undoubted high points, and not just the two male leads elegantly kissing. Well, truth be told the appeal is mostly that, but that's exactly what I want right now. Not heavy sweaty deep-throat-hard-cock action. Just two pretty boys, in pretty clothes, kissing sweetly. Really, I have such simple tastes – well, some of the time I do.

But I don't even get to the kissing scene, because the phone rings. And I pick up to find Lorne, who is checking up on me. And I have to shamefacedly admit that Christian was home when I arrived last night and is safe, sound and unsullied. And what an absolute cow I am that I didn't even bother to text poor old Lorne and tell her to call off the search. I know I had other things on my mind, but even so. Guilt, guilt, guilt. I'm having a full-on remorse attack, which, I suppose, is why I'm rather more open than I would normally be when she starts trotting out a party invite.

'It'll be a great party, kind of like Schwartz, but mixed. You'll love it, darling. It's in a private house and it'll be packed with fascinating sights. Plus I have something I need to talk to you about, about last night.'

'OK, OK,' I say, resigned to agreeing to any request Lorne makes, although, really, this doesn't sound half bad. 'You don't need to sell it to me any more. I'll be there.'

Lorne starts to reel off an address, but I interrupt her. 'Text it me.'

'Sure, see you there. Oh, and, there isn't a dress code as such, but something exotic would be very much appreciated.'

I can almost hear the wink.

Not that I have anything exotic to wear to a kinky house party. Not that I have anything exotic to wear to any kind of house party. My attire, generally, is quite conservative, consisting of tracksuits, T-shirts, jeans, that kind of stuff, and with good reason. I find it often pays yummy dividends not to stand out too much.

But, not wanting to be defeatist, I go and root around in my wardrobe for exotic. I dig out my pink tracksuit, it's probably the most fun thing I own, but as I tug it out of its place on the shelf I spot a real gem and think again. OK it's not a big old cowgirl fancy-dress outfit – or other such spectacular – but it is a pair of semi-cute Chinese print slippers that I had forgotten I had.

I smile as I turn them over in my hands. I used to wear them all the time when I was a student. A brilliant second-hand find, I had instantly fallen in love with the bright turquoise silky fabric and the cute silver embroidery of pagodas and willow trees and other things that are vaguely Oriental.

Once I get them on my feet, though, I'm not so certain of their perfect brilliance. They're backless and have sort of weird curled-up pointy toes. I walk the length of the bedroom and back, and they're not very comfortable, or even very stable. But they are the most exotic thing in my wardrobe.

I check the time. It's just gone seven. So I have a couple of hours to kill before I hit the party trail. I slide into my exotic slippers, along with a fresh T-shirt and jeans, and even add some make-up before slinking back into the living room, to finish watching my video.

When the tape clicks to a halt and starts its whirring rewind, I stretch. Nearly time to go. But I'm well sated by pretty-boy action and my flat's all cosy and outside is so cold. I linger a while, watching the news. But eventually that I-am-such-a-cow guilt takes over and I haul myself into the bedroom and touch up my mascara. Lorne has been so sweet to me, and I have been consistently useless, preoccupied and mean.

Surely going to her party is the least I can do?

11

The address Lorne gave me is rather upmarket; certainly a district that is way beyond the mortgage-ability of me and Christian. But I have, at least, visited those snooty suburbs in the not-so-distant past so I know what to expect: acres of wide pavements, lined with 30s semis that are all black and white facades and manicured lawns (with kinky sex parties going on behind the immaculate nets).

I catch the bus across town and then clack around the neat streets in my badly thought-out shoes, until I find the right house. It seems so placid and leafy-suburban compared with my fevered imaginings of Lorne's party antics. In fact it's so quiet and calm that I shake my head and have to get my phone out and check the texted address more than once.

It's freezing, an early frost hangs threateningly in the air and the bottle of red I'm carrying seems to be made of ice-slippery glass and is making my fingers all achy and numb.

As I crunch up the drive, I start to worry about the wine, a rushed after-thought from the offie near the bus stop. Is wine OK? I don't really drink and I don't really go to sex parties, so it's all a bit of a stab in the dark, frankly. I mean, just what beverage should one be bringing to a sex party these days? Or, to be specific, just what beverage should one be bringing to a sex 'n' bondage party after an invite from a drag king? Wine is probably right out – I should probably be bringing satsuma-flavoured lubricant or something.

I stamp my frozen feet on the doorstep as I ring the doorbell. The poshish house I'm standing in front of is exactly like its Siamese twin, and the pair of them are exactly like every other pair in this long thin cul-de-sac (and exactly unlike the House of the Rising Sun I was half expecting). The lights are on and faint pop music (possibly by Blue) tinkles in the starry air, but the house seems so very normal. Or at least it does until the door opens.

Because, although the door is opened by a man, well, kind of, in another sense the door is also opened by a strange green goat-like thing, for the man is entirely green from the waist up, face, hair and all. He even has horns, little green ones sticking up through his equally green hair. Lower down, legs etc., he's more basic goaty. He has fuzzy brown and green goat legs and little hooves. The goaty leg things are not entirely convincing, more BBC costume department than big-budget CGI, but it's pretty disconcerting nonetheless.

'Well, hello there, Mr Tumnus!'

I don't actually say that.

What I actually say is this: 'Hi, uh, I'm a friend of Lorne's. She ...' She? He? What's the correct etiquette here? Talk about Stranger in a Strange Land. 'Uh, she, is he here?'

Tumnus grins and when he does he looks rather less freaky. 'Imogen?'

'Yeah, hi.' So Tumnus is expecting me. OK, I assure myself, this is not too strange. Not run-away screaming strange. Not yet.

'Imogen, it's me.'

I stare at Tumnus's green face for a moment and then, fuckity-fuck, I realise I am looking at the green grease-paint smeared face of Lorne herself. 'Oh God,' I splutter, 'you might have told me you were done up as Goaty the goat boy.'

Lorne laughs at this, or at my semi-confused semi-terror. 'I'm the Green Man, silly, Pagan god of all sorts of cool stuff. Green Man: Lorne. Get it; it's a joke on my name. Like Lawn. L.A.W.N.'

'Yeah, yeah, I get it.' I'm starting to think that Lorne is rather annoying. But she's drunk and drunk people always annoy me, with their weird slurry voices and wobbly worlds.

The bonhomie still bubbling over, Lorne grabs my wine and ushers me through a small hallway, stopping about five hundred times to exchange whoops and bum pinches with the fancily dressed people milling and spilling out of the downstairs rooms.

By the time I am in the kitchen my cheeks are flushed red with the temperature change, and Lorne's tight grip on my elbow in this claustrophobic space is starting to make me really jumpy. There are actually only about five people in the kitchen itself, but it's a small galley affair, so that makes it pretty packed.

As Lorne introduces me I don't even bother to attempt to remember names. The two women in there both look a bit like they are modelling for cheap soft-porn mags, all stringy leather bras and stringy blonde highlights. The men, who are both fat, and not in a chunky sexy masterful way, but in an I'm-so-not-bothering sort of a way, goggle at me. They make me feel like I am all out of place because I'm not conforming to the leather bra/ blonde highlights dress code that this kitchen clearly has. Fancy Oriental slippers, it seems, earn no kudos here.

And it gets worse. I've not been feeling uncomfortable in the kitchen more than a minute, when one of the women drops to the floor and starts to fellate one of the fat men. I try not to sigh. And I love a blow job normally, too. Oh yes, a furtively spied-on blow job is definitely in my top five. But here? Now? Super-boring.

Just then another man, who is wearing a sort of purple all-over suit thing with a zip at the mouth, wanders in. This makes the kitchen far too full in my opinion, and so, as Lorne is distracted greeting Mr all-over-bodysuit, I slip out the door and clack away down the stripped boards.

I escape to the beige-painted lounge, where things are much less intimidating. A huge wide-screen telly is showing some rather unsubtle-looking porn, while a lot of people are sprawled around on white-leather sofas. Most of them are in states of semi-undress, which makes me wonder, frankly, about the cleaning-up situation. If I could afford white leather sofas I certainly wouldn't let a load of half-nude strangers loll about on them.

I could worry about this for longer but I don't, because I quickly notice the room's main attraction, which is far more interesting than concerns about upholstery hygiene. Far, far more interesting.

In the middle of the off-white carpet is a big black leather bag, which is squirming manically, jerking around like . . . well, like someone is inside it, frankly.

And all the eyes in the room are focussed on it. Which is great, because it means no one in the crowded room has given me even a first glance let alone a second one, just how I like it. I relax against the tastefully neutral paintwork for a moment, and I watch. It actually takes a second for the penny to drop about what I'm watching. But when I realise it's so obvious I have to smile.

It's pretty cool. It's escapology.

With my eyes fixed on the squirming sack, I slip further into the room until I am properly a member of the audience. Then, feeling bolder by the moment, I take a final step and perch on the arm of the largest sofa. A thin bald man budges up a little on the seat to give me elbow room and I relax. This is OK.

The flapping and writhing of the bag gets more and more frantic. I can't help thinking that it would be a more exciting spectacle for me if I knew who was inside it and exactly how they were restrained. But I make the best of it. With no data I imagine a best-case scenario. Maybe it's an uber-cute little brunette nineteen-year-old, all shorn body hair and tiny tight little shorts. I picture him thrashing around hot and flushed in the stifling leather, surrounded by the overpowering smell of it and knowing, just knowing, a whole crowd of people were just staring at his futile attempts to escape. Yum.

All of a sudden I'm wet (and I can't quite silence that voice at the back of mind, still concerned about the upholstery).

Then, out of nowhere, a buzzer suddenly goes off, making me jump. A very pretty, very rounded woman dressed as a nurse (if nurses were wipe-clean), shouts, 'Thirty secs!' And the crowd laugh and catcall. The squirming bag squirms harder and so do I.

'Twenty seconds.' This is greeted by even louder laughs and shouts and even more frantic squirming from the bag.

'Ten seconds.' Again everything cranks up.

And then someone shouts: 'Ten!'

'Nine!'

'Eight!'

The bag is going mad. The room is at fever pitch. I'm on the edge of my seat.

'Five!'

He isn't going to make it.

'Three!'

'Two!'

'ONE!'

The crowd go insane. The bag stops writhing and stills. I'm not breathing. The plastic nurse walks forward and begins to unbuckle and unstrap, pulling away swatches of leather until a small blonde woman in handcuffs and leg irons is revealed, panting and flushed.

Yet more whooping and cat calling and then a chant starts up of: 'Punishment! Punishment!'

I smirk and roll my eyes a little as the wipe-clean nurse pulls out a floppy-looking cane, and the girl from the bag bends (a little too eagerly) over the sofa arm.

This party is still a little bit kinky-by-numbers for my tastes, but I try not to be churlish, as six playful strokes are counted out. OK, cute young woman in a bondage 'n' caning scenario doesn't quite do it for me the way a cute young man would. But it's no biggie. And I figure, after a quick glance around the room, that there's enough eye candy here and there for me to get my best-case jollies sooner or later. All I have to do is stick around and find out who's getting bagged up next.

Which is what is being discussed right now.

Which is where it all goes horribly wrong.

'So who do we want to see?' That's the nurse again; who I'm now clear is running this little show.

'Well,' says the skinny bald man next to me, 'how about my new friend here?' And to my absolute horror, he gestures towards me.

In response there are a lot of murmurs, both dissent and agreement. I feel suddenly very sick and shake my head, first in stunned disbelief and then, as I realise that disbelief is getting me nowhere, in vigorous negative.

But no one seems to notice (or care) about my consent issues, because I'm quickly being pulled to my feet, and the wipe-clean nurse is holding my elbow gently, as she leads me into the centre of the room, and whispering, 'It's just a game, honey, nothing to worry about. You might even enjoy it.'

Every face in the room is on me. And I hate that. And suddenly I find myself wishing Christian were here. Because I know Christian would save me. He'd bound across the shag pile with bouncy conviction and claim that sack and centre stage, like some kind of warped superhero.

But there's no Christian here. And there's no way I'm thrashing around like a landed fish for the entertainment of this bunch of perverts. There's only one way out – assertiveness.

'I said "No!"' I shout, wrenching my arm out of the nurse's grip and twisting away from her with all the force I can muster. The twittering room goes horribly silent. But I don't let this, or their stunned faces, stop me making my escape. I spin round and head straight for the door, hurdling a couple of pairs of legs on the way out, not looking back and ignoring the very distinct mutter of 'Bitch' that follows me out of the room.

Back in the hall the house feels small and crowded. It makes me feel kind of exposed. I have to push past people to get anywhere and I know for sure that this is not a place I am meant to be. My normal don't-notice-me outfit (jeans, T-shirt) makes me conspicuous here in fancy-dress-ville, and I hate being conspicuous.

The music is bassier than when I arrived, all throb-throb, but still not loud enough to hide in, and the air is too hot and smells of old smoke and under-dressed people. I would have left right then, if I hadn't suddenly seen him – just a leg and half a leather-clad bum at the top of the stairs and rounding a corner – but after six months of weekly Tuesday afternoon dates I think I'd know him anywhere. And luckily anywhere happens to include a sex party in a suburban-semi that could be straight out of the pages of a *Daily Mail* exposé (really, I'm expecting to bump into a defrocked vicar at any moment). Mr Fox is here, therefore Dark Knight is here.

I don't even think. I follow. I head straight up the stairs, after the mysterious leg. I stumble and fumble a bit because half-way up a girl dressed as Alice in Wonderland is snogging a girl dressed as Xena Warrior Princess (at least that's my interpretation of their costumes), but eventually I make it to the upstairs and a landing with three closed doors. Oh.

I freeze, paralysed by indecision. In fact I seem to stand there, on that landing, dithering for an age. Luckily no one comes up the stairs or out of any of the doors and the snogging couple on the stairs have other things on their minds, so I can dither at my leisure.

Eventually, behind the door to my left, a toilet flushes, it swings open and a man who is not Mr Fox comes out. He holds the door for me to go in – assuming I'm waiting – and so I do. It would seem rude not to.

I sit on the loo and have a wee, because it's there, and also to steel my resolve. When I come out, I decide, I am going to stride down the short hallway and open the second of the two remaining doors, the one I calculate leads to the master bedroom. That'll be where Mr Fox is lurking. Got to be.

The door I've chosen opens silently, swinging wide on well-oiled hinges. The person standing in the room beyond isn't Mr Fox. It's a woman – resplendent in red rubber from neck to ankle. She's a very tall, very made-up, very dressed-up woman. She's the type of woman that may well, actually, not be a woman at all, once all the trappings are removed. And next to her, kneeling sweetly on the floor, is a heart-stoppingly beautiful dark-haired young man, almost exactly like the one I had imagined thrashing around inside the bag downstairs.

I hesitate on the threshold, because this does seem rather like a private affair.

But then the woman smiles at me and holds out her hand, proffering it benignly. My God, she's tall. 'Well, hello, my dear,' she says in a slow wavering voice. 'Would you care to join us?'

I look up at the woman and then down at the man and, although she is terrifying, he is more than beautiful enough to counter-balance that. The decision is made in a snap. Even Mr Fox bubbles away into a forgotten part of my brain for a while, as I'm totally hypnotised by a bit of prettiness. I take the huge woman's even more (proportionally) huge hand and say, 'Er, yes, OK.'

The room I step into is nice, just a normal sort of suburban bedroom really, marooned somewhere between Laura Ashley and IKEA, but pretty and practical and strangely familiar. The woman, who is still holding my hand, leads me over to a brightly floral armchair. I sit down, which only exacerbates the height differential between the enormous woman and little me.

'I'm the countess,' says the woman, her voice sounding like trees creaking in the wind. 'And this is my pussy boy.' She gestures vaguely in the direction of the beautiful creature on the floor.

He is so exquisite. I can see perfect dark blue eyes, shaded by long dark lashes and dark cherry lips, bitten in apprehension. He's wearing a strange purple-latex bodysuit, which has long sleeves and a high neck, but which leaves his legs bare. Yuk. I quickly mentally undress him and put him in a pair of tight white underpants and a simple little black collar. Yum, much better.

'So,' I say, almost, straining to make eye contact with the towering countess, 'what are you up to in here?'

'Well,' says the countess, and her strangely wavering voice is making me think of Lady Bracknell, as she judders through each sentence. 'Pussy boy here has been a bad, bad little slut and so I've decided to fit him with a chastity belt.'

'Oh,' I say.

Oh, I say! Suddenly I'm saucer eyed with wonder and delight. This little cutie? All frustrated, hard and helpless, in a chastity belt? Yes, please.

The countess holds out a spindly looking item in her long shell-pink fingernails. It's a sort of series of linked rings, creating a little penis-sized tunnel, with some bigger rings towards the base. I'm not sure why the idea of a gorgeous guy like her pussy boy being locked into this cruel device is turning me one quite so much, but it is. It really, really is.

I'm yet to really discover how I fit into this procedure. I seem to recall her mentioning the word 'assistant' when she plonked the chastity belt in my hand. So I stand dumbly by, holding it, while the countess gives pussy boy a bit of a telling off. Apparently she caught him playing with himself, when she came home early one day, and this is most definitely out of bounds, by the rules of their relationship. Uh-oh, naughty pussy.

I keep right on watching as she strips off his purple bodysuit, leaving him nude and clearly aroused. His thick, pretty cock is so hard that it's tight and firm against his flat stomach. As she marches him over to the bed, I notice that it is bondage ready, fitted with manacles at each of its four corners.

With a shove and a sneer, pussy boy is thrown onto the eiderdown and stretched out in all directions, spread-eagled naked on his back, helpless, hard and knee-weakeningly beautiful. I try not to pant.

'Now, pussy,' says the countess, looming over her victim like a deliciously threatening panto villain, 'I have been considering allowing you one last orgasm before I strap this little device on to your cock for ever.' She gestures to the bundles of rings in my hand that form a little penis prison. 'What do you say?'

Pussy moans softly. 'Oh please, my countess. I know I don't deserve it, but please. Just one last time before you lock me up.' It's the first time he's spoken and his voice is wonderful, soft and lilting – some kind of Celtic accent I can't quite place.

'I'm just not sure.' The countess plants an elegant finger on her cheek in thought. 'What do you think?' she says. And I almost look around for someone else in the room before I twig that she is talking to me.

'Uh,' I say, 'well, yeah, maybe. I suppose.' Which is such a dazzlingly succinct answer that I'm sure she'll be asking me to join in her bedroom fun again.

'Hmm, I'm still not sure. Do you have a coin?'

Again she's talking to me, so I dig in the pocket of my jeans and find the change I got when I bought the wine. Crumpled up in the offie receipt are a few coppers and a fifty pence. I cross her palm with silver.

'So,' says the countess, looking down at her tightly stretched slave boy. 'Heads or tails?'

'T-tails,' stammers pussy, and his cock jumps. Clearly he's painfully aware of how much could be resting on the flip of this coin.

The countess slaps the coin down on the back of her left hand, quickly covering it with her right one. I catch my breath as she peeks at it and then smiles enigmatically.

'OK then, pussy. Here we go.'

She sits elegantly on the edge of the bed, by pussy's waist, and steeples her fingers, tapping the indexes against her slick red lips. Pussy is panting and rocking as he watches her, and then she suddenly reaches out, grabs his hard, hard cock and begins to pump it, in a vague uninterested sort of a way.

I, on the other hand, am anything but vague and uninterested when it comes to watching this little hottie getting made to feel all the hotter. As his mistress's movements get firmer and faster he starts to squirm around in his bondage, so utterly turned on by having no control.

The movements go on and on. The countess even lifts her left hand and inspects her manicure before giving an exaggerated yawn.

Then she looks over at me and smiles. 'You like him?'

I glance up at the slave's face: he's panting hard and can't be far off coming. 'Uh, yes, he's very pretty.'

'I suppose he is. I'd let you have a go.' She nods at the hand working the now frantically jerking penis. 'But you don't know him like I do, and I need to read the signs so I can, uh –' And she suddenly lets go of the slave's cock.

He twists frantically and cries out in tormented frustration. Clearly she let him go just as he was about to orgasm. 'Sorry, pussy, but the coin was heads,' she says, with a soft smile. 'Now, where's that chastity belt?'

Pussy lets out an agonised scream, that quickly turns into a pathetic whimper, as I hand the belt over.

It takes a while to get him firmly locked into the contraption, as it relies on locking a flaccid penis down between the wearer's legs, and pussy's penis isn't really in the mood for pointing south. The countess swears loudly as she grapples – even though the state of pussy's cock really is all her own fault – and finally snaps the padlock on the device shut, with a laugh of triumph.

Then pussy is set free from his manacles, with his penis well and truly locked down. The device is quite impressive, he clearly could no more get an erection than I could. He stands up, dejectedly, hanging his head.

'Now, pussy my sweet,' says the countess, stalking her way across the room towards an oversized oak wardrobe, 'time for your punishment.'

Pussy's mouth drops open a little at this, as does mine. We are both confused. I thought the chastity belt was the punishment for his wrongdoing. But neither of us says anything, of course. The countess is far too daunting for either of us to question her fairness. And we both slam our mouths shut very fast when she flings open the wardrobe doors to reveal, where most people would hang clothes and tuck away jumpers, tens if not hundreds of whips, crops and canes.

'Fuck,' I say, and, although I say it quietly, the countess looks round.

'Oh no, dear,' she says, with a slightly comical expression, 'I never fuck him.' She reaches up and takes hold of a long thin cane. 'In fact, this is the closest he ever gets to anything like that.'

Poor pussy.

Then she looks away from me and over to pussy, her eyes flashing white lightning. Pussy trembles, but I can see his cock twitch a little in its crystal prison. I think the countess notices that too, because her creamy lipsticked smile spreads like treacle across her face before she says, 'Bend over, pussy boy.'

There is a single dining-room chair in the centre of the room, which is clearly what pussy is meant to bend over. He does so slowly, either trying to put off the moment or savouring the anticipation. I glance at the countess, expecting her to be glowering impatiently at pussy dragging his heels, but she is, in fact, smiling indulgently.

Pussy stands behind the chair and grasps the high back, bending over it elegantly, like a gymnast, until his head is almost resting on the seat. Then, he repositions his arms so his hands are gripping the legs to steady himself. He's ready. His bare arse is stuck right up in the air, soft and creamy, like ice cream – Mr Whippy. I smirk a little at my private joke, but not that much, because I can see his chest rising and falling with each heavy breath and I'm totally transfixed.

The countess takes up her position with her crop, and very suddenly snaps it down across pussy's helpless flesh. He screams and bucks a little, but his hands don't leave the seat of the chair – he holds his position obediently.

I lick my lips at the beautiful sight, watching intently as the countess raises the cane again over pussy's flesh, which is now bisected by a screaming streak of red soreness. The countess strikes again. Crack. Pussy yelps and I jiggle my excited hips. The crop is raised again and again. Crack, crack.

And suddenly an odd thought wanders into my head out of nowhere. I find myself wondering what exactly is going on here, not in the relationship – I can figure that one out – but in the location. Why on earth have the countess and pussy come here, to the sex party, and then locked themselves away in this room to do these things that they could be doing at home. It makes no sense.

And then, just as pussy yowls from his fifth stroke of the cane, I realise why this room is familiar, and I start casting around for the camera.

I saw this room downstairs, when I was in the living room, checking out the amateur Houdini act. That wasn't random porno on the wide-screen entertainment centre. That was this room. That was this.

And there it is, a great big CCTV job mounted above the door. Really bloody obvious, except I was far too bamboozled by the gorgeous pussy to notice.

I don't really relish the thought of all those weirdos I ran out on seeing me standing here goggling at the floorshow. So I make a garbled excuse to the countess, who clearly has other things on her mind and doesn't really register, and I'm out of there.

Then I'm back on the stairs. And back where I started. I re-evaluate the situation.

Setting aside the possibility that while I've been assisting the countess and pussy boy Mr Fox has buggered off, he has to be behind the third and last door on the landing. And because I'm damned if I'm going back downstairs without finding him after all I've been through, I wrench it open and find myself blinking in semi-darkness.

And he's right there.

Sitting on a single bed, alone, lit only by light from a portable television, is Mr Fox. My Dark Knight. He's holding something in both hands and watching the screen intently.

I wait in the doorway for a second, unsure quite how to greet him. After all, I have a lot of options. Do I go with 'Hi, I've been watching you through binoculars for several months and your cock is spectacular', or perhaps 'How did that S and M with my boyfriend go last night? He seems unwilling to really tell me'?

Mr Fox puts the joy pad aside and squints at me.

I chew my lip. 'Hi, uh, sorry.'

'That's OK,' he says, and seems weirdly ordinary. 'Want to play?'

I gulp, feeling all déjà vu at that line, but he's pointing to the joy pad. I shrug.

'There's Tekken.'

I shake my head, wishing I were some kind of Play-Station geek girl so I could thrash Mr Fox at Tekken, because some weird part of me very desperately wants him to like me and think I'm cool. I rummage around in the back of my brain to find something fascinating to say. And eventually come up with: 'I really wish I hadn't worn these shoes.'

Mr Fox looks at my shoes and then smiles. 'I know you, don't I?'

Oh-my-God. Oh-my-God.

'You live in Maple Court, right,' he says, all light friendly charm. 'I've seen you around.'

Half of me sags with relief, the other half is still on tenterhooks that his next sentence is going to be 'with your boyfriend'. But it isn't. He doesn't say anything else. So I say, 'Yes, Imogen Taylor, number twenty-seven.'

Mr Fox extends a hand and I step into the room to shake it as he says, 'Derek Ryan, number eleven.'

Derek!

Dark Knight is called Derek! Mr Fox is called Derek! Derek. Weird.

Taking the introduction as an invitation, I walk over and sit down next to Derek on the bed. I glance briefly at the screen of the little portable telly. It looks like he's been playing one of those terrifying zombie games as, on the paused screen, a limbless bloody creature is writh-ing around, half hidden by mist. 'Ew,' I say, half to myself and I hear Derek chuckle.

'So how did you get invited to this shambles?' Derek says lightly. And I'm so glad to hear that he thinks this party is on the crappy side. I was slightly worried that finding him on the guest list of something like this would ruin all my fantasies about him, both as Dark Knight and as Mr Fox.

'Um, Lorne invited me. Do you know her?'

'Course.'

Wow. Lorne knows Derek.

Derek goes on, 'And now you mention it that really makes sense. You are so Lorne's type.'

'Really? Shame she's not mine.' This is actually sort of a lie. Lorne is my type. If she were a guy she would totally be my type, but I still can't quite get my head round the gender-bender thing.

'Yeah, well, sadly for her, her type is predominantly straight girls. That is the tragedy of Lorne. I sometimes think that's her main motivator for going for the whole gender-reassignment thingy: to get straight girls.'

'Oh.' And, although that's a bit of a crappy thing to say, I feel quite safe in the knowledge that there really was nothing else I could have said to that.

'Sorry. I probably shouldn't have said that. But anyway, nice to see you. Any friend of Lorne's and all that. In fact it's good to see Lorne did invite someone, because she promised she was going to round up a crowd of interesting types last night and then I get here and find this bunch of Readers' Wives and sex tourists. The little bugger promised me she'd track down some likely types for me at Schwartz but she got too pissed as per usual.'

I can't resist it. 'Schwartz, is that that club?' I say, my heart banging.

'The new SM club in the village? Yeah. It's nice, actually. Kind of swishy. I was going to go there tonight too – some kind of fancy opening-night special. But, like an idiot, I chose to come here instead. No prizes for guessing where all the hot little bucks are this evening. Fuck it.' The last couple of words are muttered. He seems genuinely sad. I feel a bit sorry for him.

'Never mind. Some of us can't go to Schwartz at all.'

'True. Yeah.' And then Derek looks a little oddly at me. 'But why would you want to go though? It's all gay.'

I feel myself blush a bit and I'm glad of the darkness. Derek won't spot my red cheeks when the only light is the flickering image of a dismembered zombie. 'Well, it's sexy isn't it?' My voice sounds weird. I sound like I'm five.

Derek laughs. A little loud burst that stops as soon as it starts. 'Well, I never, so there's more than one pervert in Maple Court. And I thought it was the most respectable place.'

I ponder this statement for a moment, wondering why Derek has labelled me a pervert only now, when surely my very presence at this wonderful do would have been enough to file me under distinctly kinky. I mean, has he seen downstairs: the people tied up in sacks and the leather-bikini crowd?

And that's without starting on the countess and her pussy next door.

'Well,' I say after a bit of a lull, 'is it good? Schwartz, I mean.'

'Yeah, I'd say, with the right company. Definitely.'

'I see.' And I can feel myself sliding into the dark as I speak. Something inside me remembers a very significant fact: I know this guy; I know what he likes and dislikes. And I know something very important right now. He loves to talk about himself. All I need to do is draw him out a little. I lean back against the scrumpled pillows, nodding occasionally, just enough to coax him, and listen.

'I met this cute little pup there. It was kind of a date. He was gorgeous, as cute as a model but not all "Look at me. Look at me."' And he pulls out his top as he says this.

I laugh.

He laughs too, then switches his face to serious and says, 'But you know how pretty boys can be.'

'Yeah, yeah. I know pretty boys.' And, oh God, this is very weird, but I like him. I don't just lust for him. Now I've met him, I actually really like him too.

'And he was a very cheeky little sub too. I'd been talking to him online for a while and once I got him on the phone and I knew he had the naughty brain to back up his naughty look. But in the flesh he was something special. I wanted to see him again tonight actually, but he wouldn't play. I'm always too pushy, that's my trouble. In too deep. Probably looked desperate, probably blown it.' He bites his lip. 'It's tough being a dom you know, you have to be all cool and aloof. Not easy when you get a hot prospect like Christian.'

And when he says the name, even though there was no doubt at all who he was talking about, my breath catches, just for a second.

Derek stops talking and smiles as if in reminiscence. I wait for him to go on with his story, feeling pretty confident he will share his fond memories any moment. But then my mobile squawks like an intruder in the charged air between us and I almost jump off the bed in surprise.

'Sorry,' I mutter, grabbing it from my pocket, meaning to turn it off, just dump whoever it is into voicemail. But as I'm about to do just that I see that it's Christian calling. The irony alarm goes off in my head along with that big red what-the-fuck-do-you-think-you-are-doing light, which is flashing for the hundredth time since I entered this party.

And I realise that I really do want to talk to my baby.

Hoping against hope I don't seem like an ultra-rude

fucker, I mutter, 'Sorry, got to take this.' And press 'Answer'.

'Hi, babe,' I say. And I pray that Derek won't be able to hear Christian's voice and recognise it or anything like that.

'Genny, where are you? It's one o'clock in the morning.' His normally loud voice seems tiny and far away.

'I'm at a party. I thought you'd be out until late.'

'Nah, I didn't need to stay all night at this one, thank God. I thought we could get a takeaway. Where are you? Shall I join you? Do you want me to pick you up?'

And when he says that every single bone in my body seems to scream: yes.

So maybe I'm having my first-ever real-life conversation with Dark Knight. So maybe he's telling me all about Schwartz. So maybe this is something I would have put top of my wish list a few weeks ago, or even a few hours ago. So what? My boy, my darling and my love is on the line and offering to drive here and whisk me away, away from this weird house full of weird people, and home, to bed and cuddles and boring, boring sex (oh, and a takeaway, don't forget the takeaway).

'Yes,' I say into the phone, 'yes, I would love you to pick me up,' and rattle off the address. Christian promises to be there in ten and I hang up, turning my attention back to Derek, who is now focussed on zombie mashing.

'Sorry, Derek, I've got to go. Something's come up.'

Derek doesn't even glance at me. ''K hon. See you around I'm sure.'

'Bye then.'

I close the door softly on my way out and pick my way back down the stairs, back over Xena and Alice (who are now topless) and, not wanting to risk the living room again, head for the kitchen.

The leather-bikinied bunch and their admirers have gone. The only person in the kitchen is Lorne, looking sad and drunk and green.

'Hey Lorne. I've got to run. Christian is coming to get me.'

'Oh shame.' Lorne looks really quite disappointed. 'We never got to have our chat.'

'No. Sorry.'

'Ah well, next time.' She takes a big swig from her glass. It looks like whisky. (Actually, it could be piss, for all I know. Actually in this place, it really could be piss. Actually, I think I won't start thinking about that.) 'I hear you nearly gave them a bit of a floorshow down the hall.'

'Oh,' I say, remembering the unpleasantness of the escapology room with a rush of shuddery horror. 'Well, not really, that just isn't my kind of thing.'

Lorne gives a long maudlin sigh. 'I know, honey. I'm well acquainted with the ins and outs of "not your kind of thing".'

I don't say anything back. I just stand there.

'Sorry,' says Lorne after a bit. 'Sorry I invited you here. I know this party's been, well, a bit shit.'

'Yeah, well, never mind.'

Lorne looks so sad it's quite hard to tear myself away, but I do and as I head out of the kitchen Lorne says softly: 'Nice shoes.'

I pull open the front door and hurl myself out into the vicious cold of the arctic cul-de-sac.

Making giant cartoonish stampy steps to keep my feet warm, I head down the slope to the main road and lean against the bus shelter.

It's not long before our Ford Focus rounds the corner and slides to a halt beside me. And, feeling just like Kate Winslet must have done when that lifeboat came back for her (except for the dead Leonardo bit), I open the passenger door and tumble into a comforting womb-like fug of blasting heat and blasting Joy Division.

As we drive away I look up at the house. Most of the windows are shrouded in heavy curtains, but one of the upstairs bedrooms isn't. Inside, I can see the countess and pussy. They're both in the window, her in her red rubber and him in his red skin. They're kissing, long and soft and sweet, and it's beautiful. They're beautiful. From a distance.

Isn't everything?

12

I spend the next morning with Christian. I'm sort of oscillating between loving him as only a damsel (who was previously in distress) can love her knight in shining armour, and eyeing him suspiciously. I'm still confused about what went on with Dark Knight aka Mr Fox aka Derek. I just can't quite believe Christian has given me the whole story. And his version just doesn't quite square with my conversation with Derek, somehow.

Derek didn't talk about their encounter like it was something that had to be suddenly cut short because of a camera being smashed and his partner doing a runner. In fact, Derek told me he asked for a second date right off the bat. Christian didn't tell me that, although I also know from Derek that Christian didn't agree to it either. But the basic fact is still that Christian was gone too long. I don't believe his story about networking and having no phone. It just isn't quite right.

So, I'm very relieved when Lorne calls and mutters through her hangover that she still has this thing she needs to tell me. The thing which she never got round to telling me last night. More information. Just what I need.

It's weirdly sunny – that kind of hard ultra-bright that only happens on clear winter days when the sun is low in the sky. It's come out of nowhere, but winter's here and it's made a stylish entrance.

Talking of stylish entrances, Lorne is waiting on the wooden footbridge that crosses the canal by The Moorings. She's hanging on the railings with a limp cigarette in her mouth, looking like a James Dean Athena poster, all scruffy denims and scruffier hair. God, she's looking really sexy today. Perhaps she's made a special effort – hoping to erase goat boy from my memory. If so, it's working.

When she sees me, clunking towards her on the mismatched planks of the bridge, she cracks a big smile and lopes over, lassoing me with arms that feel bigger and far more enveloping than they should.

Nestled in her grasp, I allow myself to be swished into the oak-beamed snugness of the pub. I don't go to The Moorings on a Sunday usually, and as soon as I cross the threshold I realise why, because it's absolutely rammed.

I'm thinking quite categorically that we shouldn't bother, and I'm about to say as much, when Lorne suddenly explodes with an ear-splitting whoop of greeting, directed somewhere in the middle of the crush of bodies.

Next thing I know I'm squashed up against Lorne as she steers me through the steamy throng to a wooden slab of a table, where a middle-aged couple are sitting and beaming at Lorne.

Clearly, from the exuberant greeting, these must be friends of Lorne's, but they are by far the weirdest friends of hers I have yet come across.

Mr and Mrs Blandford-Beige (NB real names have been changed here to protect the dull) are utterly indistinguishable from at least half of the cosy cardiganed couples in the pub, and also pretty indistinguishable from each other. They both sport comfortably beige hair and comfortably beige clothing.

These are the very last people I would have expected to be friends of Lorne's and the very, very last people I would have expected to be introduced as . . .

'Hey, Imogen, this is Tony and Sarah, the hosts of last night's party.'

And I'm really glad I'm not drinking anything as Lorne imparts this bombshell, because the top I'm wearing is Designers at Debenhams, and I'm certain Matthew Williamson doesn't create his wafty butterfly-gossamer clothes to look their best with a gobful of cranberry juice spat down the boob.

'Hi,' I say, as I'm boggling that these ordinary people could host a sex party (albeit a pretty low-rent one) and trying not to show any of my rampant prejudice in my face. 'Great party. I don't remember seeing either of you two there though.'

Mr Blandford-Beige laughs. 'Oh you did see me, darling. You might not recognise me though – I was wearing a gimp suit.'

I frown. 'A gim –, a what?'

Lorne nudges me. 'An all in one, in the kitchen, remember?'

'Oh, uh, yeah,' I say, cringing at being the dumb girl who doesn't even know what a gimp suit is.

Mrs Blandford-Beige leans over the table and squeezes my hand with her own. Her smartly painted beige nails still have flecks of a screaming fuchsia in the cuticles. She smiles, taking on the air of a Mother Superior to a wayward novice. However, instead of breaking into a verse and a chorus of 'How do we solve a problem like Maria?' she says, 'You met me too, and I wasn't wearing a mask.'

My mind races. Who the fuck was Mrs Blandford-Beige then? Definitely not Xena or Alice, snogging on the stairs. And really definitely not any of the leather-titted cocksucking women in the kitchen. So she's either the countess, or . . .

'The nurse,' I say gently, feeling like my heart is going to stop dead in my chest, which would be a blessing actually, because it would mean an end to what is fast becoming the most cringingly embarrassing conversation of my life.

'Yes,' she says and smiles in a way that squashes her lips together like two greasy beige slugs.

Oh God, the nurse! The nurse whose escapology floorshow I upset with my (completely justifiable) hissy fit. No wonder she's looking at me like I'm her wayward charge. 'Um, I'm sorry about that, I hope I didn't upset...'

'Imogen's claustrophobic,' Lorne interjects forcefully, stopping my bumbling attempt at apology/explanation/suicide in its tracks.

'Oh,' I say, flashing a quick smile at my gallant rescuer. 'Yes.'

Lorne grins. 'And you know what panic attacks are like, right, Tony?'

Mr Blandford-Beige gives me an understanding smile. 'Oh yes, honey, I do.' And then he gives his wife a bright look, which she returns with an equally unpleasant indulgent simper. 'You know once we were at this public play party,' he goes on, leaning over the table to me and acting as if, by telling me this, he is giving me some kind of naughty indulgent treat. 'And Sarah had me strapped down to this table and, well, I don't know what got into me. I just went ape shit, screaming and cursing. Ha. Do you remember, love?'

Mrs Blandford-Beige nods, racking up her indulgent look until it becomes full-on condescending, and not a million miles from the bizarre Mother Superior thing she had given me earlier – clearly the memory of Tony's little episode wasn't quite so amusing for her.

Which is lucky, because before we're mired into any more hilarious reminiscences of bondage antic past, though, Mrs Blandford-Beige calls a halt to our chat and shoves Mr Blandford-Beige off to the eight-deep bar to get a round in. Once he's gone, she leans back in her chair and smiles at us both, but, thankfully, we only have to make a bit of small talk before she excuses herself to the loo.

'Lorne,' I say, in a weirdly strangled voice, once we are alone. 'I don't think I really want to hang out with, uh, Sarah and Tony right now. I need to talk to you. About Dark Knight.'

'Derek, you mean.'

I frown at Lorne. 'How do you know he's called Derek?' My mind races, thinking maybe I told Lorne about my brief encounter at the party. But, I replay our parting conversation in my mind on fast forward, and no, I definitely didn't.

'Well, that's what I wanted to talk to you about too. That's the thing I was meaning to tell you last night,' Lorne says. 'I saw Derek at Schwartz, well, I was there with him, kind of, and then a bit later I saw him with Christian. You know I told you'd I'd seen Christian when we were looking for him. Well, anyway, it didn't click what seeing them together might mean until I got home that night. I mean, I knew Derek liked to pick up bunnies online, but I never dreamed that he'd be your very own bête noire.'

Lorne nods, sort of thoughtful, and continues, 'So anyway, that's what I meant to tell you at the party – that your Dark Knighty chap had turned out to be my mate Derek, but it didn't really work out like that because by the time you arrived I'd had one voddie and coke too many, and about five poppers too many and, well, it all went a bit shit-shaped.' Lorne shrugs.

Lorne seems different here, under the oppressive beams and surrounded by the oppressive crowds. My gorgeous androgynous James Dean has metamorphosed into a shrugging, ratty little apology, rambling on about

being too out of it last night to give me crucial information, and making me spend my Sunday lunchtime
with the hosts of the fucking fuckerware party.

I've had enough. I decide to take action. 'Look, Lorne,
let's get out of here, pick up a tram into town. I don't
think I can bear to look at Polaroids from last night.'
Polaroids were indeed promised by Mrs Blandford-Beige
before nature called. Actual Polaroids! Haven't these people heard of the digital camera?

Rattling our way into town on the tram, putting steady
miles between us and those Polaroids, I turn to Lorne.
'He's not just Derek you know, Dark Knight, he's Mr Fox
too.'

'Oh,' says Lorne, with a slow steady nod of her head,
which goes on just a beat or two too long before she
frowns and says, 'Mr who?'

I laugh. The tram clatters on towards the town centre
and I slip into the rhythm, oscillating in my seat. My
denim-clad thigh is pressed very closely against Lorne's
denim-clad thigh and I still feel quite odd. Too many
strange things have happened in too short a space of
time and I don't like it. Mr Fox and Dark Knight, Dark
Knight and Derek, Derek and Lorne, Derek and Christian.
Mostly Derek and Christian if the truth be told. And it is
told. To Lorne.

I sincerely hope that the other tram passengers have
as much on their minds as I do right now, because I
really don't want them to listen in, as I explain to Lorne
about Christian's slightly odd behaviour, starting with
the general weirdness – as I am now perceiving it –
around the date itself, the missing hour or so, and the
lack of corroboration of his side of things from Derek.

'Hmm,' says Lorne, thoughtfully. 'So what you really
need is to find out for sure what happened at Schwartz.'

'Well, yeah.'

'If dear little Christian really did cry urgent camera maintenance and make his exit, or whether a little fun-time playtime happened after the lights went out.'

'Well, yeah.'

'So what you need is someone who was there on the inside and can tell you just what went on.'

'Well, yeah.'

'Now Christian doesn't seem to be an option here, because you don't feel happy with his version . . .'

'Yeah. Is that bad? I don't mean to be mistrustful, but . . . oh, I don't know.' I sigh and twist my hands in my lap.

Lorne halts my whingeing with a warning finger. 'Well, you could be right and you could be wrong, but the fact is you're suspicious and the only way you'll relax is if we get a second opinion. Right?'

My mouth drops open and I shake my head. 'We are not asking Dark Knight.'

'Can you call him Derek? I can't quite get used to him being called Dark Knight,' Lorne says with a light chortle in her voice. 'And, anyway, no, we're not going to ask Derek. He's not best pleased with me anyway after I dragged him along to that do last night. Besides, we're not going to ask Derek because we don't need to.'

'So who're we going to ask? Christian and Derek were the only people in that room. I know. I saw.'

Lorne shakes her head at me. 'Oh, Imogen. It's not nineteen-ninety-one any more, you know. No one is ever alone in a room these days. You, of all people, should know that.'

Lorne has something incredible up her sharply tailored sleeve. It turns out that Lorne, my little drag king goat-boy admirer, doesn't spend her spare time cavorting with nymphs in a forest. She has an actual job – and she's in security. Well, she works part time for an agency that supplies the door staff for most of the clubs and pubs in the gay village.

And Lorne, through her office, has access to any number of keys and pass cards, and security codes to most of the bars and clubs in the little criss-cross of cobbled streets that calls itself the gay village, and beyond.

Which is something of a revelation, frankly.

So, before I know it, we're key in hand, and motoring down the street, almost-but-not-quite running down to Schwartz.

Schwartz looks completely dead and even emptier than it had before it opened. Now it's not just empty, it's used – all used and abandoned – with uncollected rubbish scattered on the front steps and scuff marks in the shiny new paintwork on the front door. The same front door that Lorne is unlocking right now so we can dive inside.

Instantly, the alarm starts to squeak its preliminary warning, and Lorne scoots over to jab at the panel of buttons, checking the numbers against the reef of paper she's brought from her office. Jab, jab, a few last squawks and the alarm is easily placated.

Schwartz is a silent kinky cathedral before us and our short, excited pilgrimage is all but over.

I'm trying not to breathe too loud. Lorne has made it clear that we are not supposed to be here, and under normal circumstances this would be more than her job's worth. So although I'd love to waltz off in the shadowy maze of Schwartz, I can't. Instead I follow meekly as Lorne leads me through a door behind the reception desk, clearly marked 'Staff Only'.

It's funny, but as soon as we step over the threshold of that door the whole atmosphere of the building seems to change. Whereas the entrance hall was imposing in its grandeur (OK kitsch grandeur, but grandeur all the same), through the door it's all industrial-strength carpet tiles and work-a-day paintwork.

We creep down a flight of steps covered in some particularly horrid blue lino, across a small, and very dirty, staff area, and through another door and there we are: security-camera land. A least twenty televisions are showing us the monochrome bleakness of empty rooms in Schwartz.

'Now,' says Lorne, crossing the room and taking up pole position in the big swivel chair in front of the screens, 'I warn you this might take sometime. I don't know this system and God knows how they catalogue their tapes – I'm just hoping they keep them for at least forty-eight hours. So you trot off and find us some coffee and I'll get rifling.'

My heart sinks at this – what happened to my furtive fun? Get coffee. Great. So I'm demoted to runner, already. I'm surprised Lorne doesn't pat my bum on the way out.

But I bite my tongue and do as I'm told; after all, Lorne is doing me a massive favour. So I don't say anything, despite the fact my quest for coffee is at the expense of sitting about in the security-camera room watching Lorne fast forward through videos of Schwartz antics.

I trot back to the sordid staff room we passed earlier and find a kettle and a jar of instant. That, I decide, will have to do. I might have resigned myself to getting coffees, but I am also going to take the path of least resistance – I'm not traipsing all the way to Starbucks, or anything like that, no matter how revolting this instant is.

And I soon find the Schwartz staff room isn't such a bad place to hang around waiting for a kettle to boil, mostly because I find a magazine called *It's a Dog's Life*, which is pretty damn sexy. The basic premise of *It's a Dog's Life*, which I gather pretty quickly, is attractive young men, pretending to be dogs. Page by page, they're posing in collars and leads, in kennels, lapping water from bowls and fetching sticks. It's all very erotic, but in a playful way – there's not even much nudity, and it makes me smile and even laugh as much as it makes me squirm and sigh.

Then the kettle clicks off before I've even finished the letters page, and I shove the crumpled mag in my handbag, before slopping boiling water into two polystyrene cups of granules. I don't trust the milk so I leave them black, hedge my bets with one sugared and one not, and head back to the camera room.

In the dark room Lorne is rewinding and freeze-framing some grainy footage of two men snogging. I pause in the door and peer at it.

'That's not Christian,' I say coolly, after a quick squint. I'd know his kissing style anywhere.

'Nope,' says Lorne, 'but it is Derek, which is a good thing.'

'It is?'

'Well, yes. If Derek's getting off with what's-his-face here, then it implies Christian did leave him hanging.' She looks over her shoulder and gives me a look that is pure Hercule Poirot.

But I'm not convinced. It isn't proof Christian left Mr Fox hanging – this here snog could have happened anytime. It's good and very fun to watch, but it isn't what I came here for. I give Lorne a pleading look, and we soldier valiantly on.

There's only the one chair in the room, and, as Lorne is the one who can work the technical stuff, I end up sat on the floor, leaning against a wall and craning up to see what's going on onscreen. Despite my excitement, it's all pretty boring. I never would have believed it, security-camera footage of Schwartz is boring, but it is. It's not like my video, it's not even like Christian's live feed; this raw film is mostly just blurry shots of crowded rooms, which might well have fun stuff going on in them, but the camera is just too far off to see anything clearly, even what people are wearing.

I scrunch up my coat into a ball and use it as a sort of fuzzy, lumpy pillow. My sleep patterns have gone to pot just lately – this duplicitous lifestyle is too much for me – and my eyelids feel awfully heavy.

Next thing I know something is tickling my face. Irritated, I shuffle and shift, still buried in my cosy blanket of sleep, but it keeps up – tickle, tickle, tickle. Maybe I'm dreaming about *It's a Dog's Life*. Then the tickling sensation changes to something wetter, and then to a soft melting sweetness and then to a vague taste of bad coffee.

Lorne is kissing me.

And now it's a replay of the women's section of Cruze, as I sputter and shake my head, confused and embarrassed, pulling my mouth free. 'Lorne, I . . .'

'Sorry, that was so stupid.' Lorne stands up quickly as she speaks, looking at me with wide panicky eyes.

I shake my head. I can feel my mouth moving, but I'm not saying anything. I can still taste her lips on mine, all sweetness and Nescafé and Styrofoam. 'No, Lorne,' I spit out eventually, 'forget it. It doesn't matter.'

And then Lorne bites her bottom lip, looking confused, and runs from the room.

I get up as quickly as I can, which is not that quickly, as I am near enough melded into my corner, and I'm about to dash after her, when I see what's on the middle of the five television screens.

Christian. Christian dressed in a scanty leather outfit, shadowy and backlit, so all I can really see is the glitter of his eyes and the buckles on his clothes – but I'd know him anywhere. He's standing in a familiar boxy room and there, looming over him, with more of a height differential than I realised, is Mr Fox.

There's no sound, but I can tell they're talking by the way their bodies are moving.

Undecided, I tear myself away from the screen for a moment and look over at the open door, half hoping Lorne will be standing there. But she isn't. She's nowhere to be seen. I know I should run after her, but I know I'm not going to. I slip and swivel into the revolving chair in front of the bank of twinkling screens, and fixate on the scene in front of me.

For a few moments it's story so far ('Previously, on secret cameras'), old news from a new angle, and then the magic moment: Mr Fox plucks the tiny camera from Christian's fringe and flicks it away, as if it were nothing more than an annoying bug – which is exactly what it kind of is.

Christian's mouth is stretched wide in shock and dismay. He speaks quickly, and then both of them are on their hands and knees on the floor, out of shot, clearly looking for the camera.

When they both stand up they both look worried and rather confused. Christian is talking again. I guess he is giving his line about using the camera for work. I'm already heaving huge sighs of relief: it's exactly what Christian said it would be. Camera plucked, worry all round, his line about monitoring. But it seems I sighed too soon, because the conversation goes on and on. Far too long. What the hell are they talking about?

I watch, dumbly, for about ten minutes. They both seem gripped. They're making very excited faces and moving their hands. Are they planning something? Are they planning a covert romance?

And then, as Christian finally turns to leave, Mr Fox reaches out and grabs him – suddenly and hard – by his left upper arm.

Mr Fox is strong – that grip is all he needs to flip Christian back into the room and slam him hard up against the opposite wall. Mr Fox is pinning Christian in place, each of his tight fists gripping one of Christian's biceps. A strong, controlling leg forces Christian's apart as Mr Fox leans in. It's the most possessive kiss I have ever seen. Mr Fox's mouth explicitly claims Christian's with a slick, hard, edgily violent kiss and Christian visibly gives in. Going soft and hard at once, he lets himself be taken.

I'm feeling all sorts of emotions at once.

When the kiss breaks, I hear a small noise behind me. I startle and spin round in the chair. Lorne is standing in the doorway holding the keys to Schwartz in her hand. Her expression is completely blank, but I guess it's time to go.

I walk home under a thunder cloud of guilt and confusion. Not just because I saw Christian kiss Mr Fox, although I am very confused about that.

A little voice inside me is telling me that was exactly what I wanted Christian to do, i.e. get off with Dark Knight. I dressed him up to cock tease the poor man to the max, so what did I expect?

But another voice – there appears to be an entire Greek bloody chorus of voices clamouring to be heard inside my head right now – is stridently pointing out that Christian kissed Mr Fox when he knew I wasn't watching, so he did it entirely for his own enjoyment. And what's more, points out voice two, he lied about it – a lie of omission at the very least.

And then there's the bloody infuriating question of what they were talking about for so long. Their conversation was about ten minutes. Was that Christian giving him some flannel? Was it the Dark-Knight-asks-for-a-date conversation? Was it some heavy flirting that led to that beautiful but oh-so-worrying kiss? I'm going insane with the not knowing.

On top of that there's the other kiss, the one with Lorne and comatose moi. I feel so bad about that kiss. I know it wasn't really my fault, the being asleep being a pretty good defence. However, deep down I know that blamewise I should stand up and be counted for all the adulterous kisses that have gone on over the last few days. I feel like I'm such a terrible person, like I've been exploiting everyone around me in the most selfish way possible. I actually ought to get my comeuppance. It's no more than I deserve.

The thunder cloud of misery is still there as I walk up the echoey steps to the flat, still there when I open the front door, still there when I go into the kitchen and pour myself a glass of water, and still there when I see Christian in Mr Fox's kitchen window.

And that's when the lightning strikes.

13

In the film of my life the glass I am holding right now will slip from my hand and splinter into rainbow shards all over the lino. It'll look very pretty, but it will be artistic licence, because this isn't what happens. In fact I don't think this sort of thing ever really happens. I don't think shock makes people drop things on the floor in real life – it only ever happens in films. Just a little something I've observed.

So, I keep the glass in my hand as I stare blankly at Christian through the window. After a moment, Mr Fox comes in and smiles indulgently at him, and he and Christian move and gesture as if talking about something. I don't have much to go on, but they seem quite earnest.

I pause to consider all possible actions in response to this strange situation. And after that I muse for a while, weighing up the pros and cons of each possibility. This oh-so-rational process takes me, what, about half a second? Or less. Then I run.

I crash-bang out of the flat and head for the identical block across the courtyard. I've never been into it before, but it's weirdly familiar because it's just like the one we live in. Before I know it I'm standing on his doorstep, feeling shaky and sicky on the communal lino.

Before I can knock, though, the door opens and Christian walks straight into me.

'Shit, sorry, mate,' he says, before he twigs who I am. The penny drops from a hundred storeys up. 'Oh! Genny!' And then, 'Oh God.'

'What are you doing?' I say, level and even, as Christian looks about as guilty as he ever has.

'Uh,' says Christian.

And then, from behind Christian, Mr Fox says, 'Imogen Taylor? Hey, nice to see you again.'

As I reach out and shake Mr Fox's hand he smiles at me, with the weirdest expression on his face.

And I don't know why I think it, but once I do I know it's true: he knows.

He knows everything.

Somehow Christian manages to use this confusion to take charge and persuades me to come back to our flat with him before I say, or even think, anything else. Eager for an exit, I agree and find myself sitting on our sofa drinking tea and listening to the tallest story I have ever heard.

'OK, babe, look, I was going to tell you this when I got back anyway, so I might as well tell you now.'

'Well, that is telling me when I get back,' I say, like Captain Logic, clinging to my tea like a warm-brewed lifeline, because at least that makes some sense. Milk no sugar, perfectly straightforward.

'I felt kind of guilty about Schwartz, you know, with the camera being broken and everything –'

I interrupt, my heart sinking at the mention of the ruined camera, 'Oh, don't remind me.' I'm not looking forward to Monday morning. I'm not sure yet if I'll have to confess. Maybe I'll find a way of covering it up by clever cunning – or something. Maybe I could blame Justin...

Or maybe I should keep my mind on the matter in hand.

Unaware of my brain tangent Christian continues, 'Well, I thought I should arrange another date with Mr Fox. I knew how upset you'd be about the camera going dark, so I . . .' Christian tails off, finding it hard to express himself just like he does in bed every once in a while.

'You what?'

He swallows. 'I told Mr Fox. I told him what was going on. He didn't really swallow the line about me wearing the camera for security anyway, so the game was kind of up as it was.'

I don't speak. I can't.

'So I explained what was happening. I told him everything. And we hatched a plan that night. That was where I really was all that time – not hanging with the Fandango crowd. I was planning your surprise. I'm sorry I lied to you, baby, but I think you'll forgive me.'

And the weird thing is my first thought as Christian spits all this out is a little surge of triumph that I was right all along.

So Mr Fox does indeed know all, because Christian has told all. Apparently Mr Fox took it all quite well, from the news that his online pup was me, to, well, everything else really.

'I'm not quite sure,' Christian explains, 'but I think he really liked the devious deviance of it all. He laughed a lot when I explained what had been going on. Especially the phone-call part, oh, and the fact you sent that first photo without telling me – he loved that.'

'But wasn't he angry that he had no pup, no slave boy? That he's not going to get his jollies?'

'Well, that's just the thing, Genny. He is going to get them.'

Christian fires up the laptop and launches Explorer. A few key taps and a little grainy window appears. It's a live feed from another web cam. I stare at the murky image, for a few seconds, trying to make it out. It's a room – a dark one – with a shadowy closed door and a single window swathed with heavy red velvet. The room is brimming with sinister atmosphere and bulging with kink – it's like someone took the stage from the Schwartz dance floor and stuffed it into a box room. And then it all becomes clear when the door opens with a creak (because, yes, this cam has sound too), throwing a long, lean shadow across the dark floor. The long, lean shadow of Mr Fox.

After Christian has kissed me at the door, and promised me The Greatest Show on Earth, I don't rush back to the computer. I don't even go into the living room. I go into the kitchen. I sit at the rickety picnic table in the window, with my comfortingly weighty binoculars sitting sturdy in both hands, because I reckon they'll both know I still like it old school, just every now and then.

And then suddenly there they are, bang on cue.

They stagger and tumble into the kitchen. Christian is in white underpants and Mr Fox is in black ones, topped with his tiger jacket. Their lips are practically glued together, as their hands grab at limbs and flesh and hair. They're desperate for each other like some kind of crazed lust spell has been cast over them. And it's all for me. Yum.

Mr Fox slams Christian up against the fridge in a replay of the Schwartz kiss that I saw on the security cameras. His hands are down the back of Christian's underpants, fondling and groping his neat arse, pulling them down just a little and giving me a peek at his delicious honey-nut skin. Meanwhile, Christian's hands are scrabbling hopelessly for purchase against the ice-smooth surface of the fridge door.

Hot stubbly skin grates and chafes across hot stubbly skin. The symmetry is delicious, with every elegant similarity between them balancing with a delicious contrast. Mr Fox is so tall – effete and regal – and, while he isn't pale, he looks quite porcelain next to Christian's small and dark pixie looks. Mr Fox's additional height means he can bear down on Christian, firm and controlling, while Christian acquiesces beneath him, in every way his obedient slave.

And then Mr Fox is tugging him roughly out of the room.

I dash into the living room to find the computer has shut itself down for some unknown, stupid reason. I curse at the stupid lump of plastic, urging it on with a number of swear words as it starts up and insists on scanning the drive for errors no matter how loudly I protest. I'm jerking up and down with frustration as the screen goes as blue as my face must be and I wait impatient and impotent.

Finally I get my familiar desktop in view and I launch the net browser, praying that Christian saved the site link. I'd so hate to have to go and interrupt the sexy couple across the courtyard with yet more technical hitches.

But no need, it's there, tucked away in the favourites. I get clicky with it sharpish. And, oh wow. They're well on their way, but I caught up with them at just the right moment.

They're both there, in the dungeon/box room. Christian is wearing a gag – a dark-red ball buried deep in his mouth and held in place by dark straps that criss-cross his face. He's nearest to the camera, kneeling on the floor with his head bowed a little, and Mr Fox is behind him, moving closer. Oh God. And suddenly my hands are wet with sweat, cold and clammy and so very furtive.

I can hardly bear to look at the screen. It's too bright, like looking right at the sun. I need one of those pieces of paper with a pinhole in it that were supposed to make it OK to look at the sun (but in actual fact still burned your retinas to ashes). And my retinas are blowing away in the breeze right now, as Mr Fox moves in close behind Christian and swiftly binds his hands behind his back.

I don't breathe. I don't even exist. I'm less than a fly on the wall. I'm without substance, floating in the air. I'm the place where Mr Fox ends and Christian begins.

More rope follows – rope on rope. Mr Fox ties Christian's ankles and, then, lying him down on the floor, attaches his bound ankles to his bound wrists, making a very neat and very helpless little package. Christian's eyes are distant – vague and glassy – and his mouth is still gagged. He looks like he's in another world.

He moves just a little, a sort of writhing grind, and it's enough that I can tell he's hard and wet between his legs, aching for a touch there but unable to even move. I see a tiny movement of his lips, stretched taut around the red rubber ball gag, and those movements are enough to tell me that the gag is uncomfortable and frustrating and that it tastes horrid. My right hand, which is resting on the mouse, begins to shake with anticipation. I bring it to my lips and bite my knuckle hard.

Poor bound Christian is alive with tiny movements. Once I see one I see them all – a writhe here, a struggle there. Mr Fox is already looming over him, holding a short black riding crop. He leans down and places the crop in front of Christian's face, right in his line of vision and then says, 'If you manage to get free, maybe I won't whip you, naughty pup.'

Mr Fox leaves the room. And leaves all the prettiness for me to watch.

Christian is writhing around on the floor, struggling against the ropes, but with his ankles pulled up and back, nearly touching his wrists, he can't move any single rope more than an inch or two without it tightening another. There's no way he's getting free. He can't even sit up or roll over.

My mouth is so dry and my cunt is so wet. And it's not just me that's wet. I can see a damp patch in the white cotton crotch of Christian's underpants spreading slowly over a very pronounced bulge. It seems my boy knows how to enjoy himself, and the prospect of a beating from Mr Fox doesn't seem to have dampened his ardour at all (just his underwear). I always knew Christian liked bondage, but never knew what a connoisseur he truly was.

I watch him writhe some more, all pretty twists like a prima ballerina. His face is flushed now with the effort, but he's made no impression on any of the ropes binding him in a tight little circle on the floor. He can't even move enough so that the cruelly placed crop is out of his direct line of vision. There's sweat on his brow, and he can't do anything to prevent it running into his eyes as he jerks around desperately and gets absolutely nowhere. Oh God.

And then it's too late. I gasp out loud as I spot a big booted foot in the corner of the screen. Mr Fox is back.

He sneers at his victim, which sends real chills racing along my spine. 'Oh dear, oh dear, you don't seem to have budged these ropes an inch – not that I expected you to, my poor little pretty.'

He smiles a thrilling and sickening smile, as he crouches down to inspect the flushed, damp and heaving mass on the floor that was once Christian. 'Now, I promised you a whipping, didn't I? So I think we need to have you over the horse.'

Leaving the squirming Christian, Mr Fox drags the wooden 'horse' from a corner of the room. It's a simple enough device: two wooden frames, each about waist height, and hinged together at the top. So simple, and yet so complicated when poor Christian is untied and made to bend over it, secured firmly at wrist and ankle. With a thin smile Mr Fox takes down a blindfold from a hook on the wall. It's much better than the one we use – a sturdy leather contraption that I have no doubt will block out all light. As Mr Fox brings it up to Christian's face, poor trussed Christian moans loudly into the gag, but not with trepidation – he wants it.

Mr Fox chuckles lightly as he buckles the blindfold fast around Christian's eyes. 'So you like to be blind-folded?' he says, almost conversationally. 'Well, pup, your wish is my command.'

With Christian blind, silenced and unable to even twitch, Mr Fox finally retrieves the crop from the floor and swishes it ominously through the air. Even through the still-present gag, I can tell Christian catches his breath.

The first blow is light, yet still enough to make Christian buck and twitch in his bondage. The second is far more pronounced, hard and sharp. He screams this time, a strange strangled noise through the muffling of the red rubber ball. A softer third stroke follows, then a very hard fourth.

And so it continues, a mixture of hard and soft, impossible to predict, up to ten. By which time both of them are sweating and panting and looking about as ready for a good hard fucking as any two people I have ever seen. And I've seen people.

And then Mr Fox stops what he's doing and looks right into the camera. I feel weird. It's sort of like he's staring right at me. Slowly, he curls his fists and raises them both to his eyes, like a mime of binoculars. Then he turns and walks out of the door.

I know straight away what he's getting at. He wants to tell me something. I get up a little stiffly, and walk into the kitchen, grabbing the binoculars from on top of the fridge, and peer into Derek's kitchen across the courtyard. Derek's there. He's standing by the window pulling on his coat. I watch, puzzled and then he holds up a key. I recognise the key. It's identical to our own front-door key.

Then I get it, and I run. I scoot into the bedroom and grab the secret box from under the bed, and then I sprint out of the room.

I hurtle out of the front door and down the echoey well of the communal stairs.

C-lang, c-lang, c-lang.

I heave open the heavy exterior door and sprint along the gravel path that cuts the courtyard diagonally.

Cr-unch, cr-unch, cr-unch.

And dash straight into Derek's block. Then it's up the stairs, a mirror of what I've just done. Three flights. C-lang, etc.

Half-way up the last one I meet Derek coming down and we exchange furtive wordless glances. Derek holds out the key, eyeing the box under my arm with satisfaction, and I take it.

I'm at the top of the stairs, about to put the key in the lock when I realise I've overlooked something. I turn and pelt back again, catching Derek on the middle flight. At first he's confused at the tiny object I press into his palm, I think he thinks I'm giving him his own front-door key back, but then he gets it.

And back at Derek's door I unlock with my new key and ease it open.

Derek's flat is weird, because it's just like a mirror image of ours. The layout of kitchen, bathroom, living room and bedroom is just the same. The only difference is that he has no door off his living room to a second bedroom. At least he has no useable door. The place where the door should be has been boarded up leaving just an alcove. A ghost of a dead door – the door that wasn't.

I know at once why Derek has no entrance into his spare bedroom from the living room. It's because his spare bedroom is the room he's converted into his secret playroom, and the entrance to it is from his master (ahem) bedroom. (Not a conversion any estate agent would ever recommend.)

So I head for the master bedroom, trying not to feel too much like I've gone through the looking glass. But it's a hard feeling to shake. Derek's mirror-image flat is a strange place. And kind of like Alice, I am struck by how everything I was able to see from my flat is just as it should be, but everything I couldn't see is totally different from how I imagined. For example, in Derek's bedroom all I had ever been able to see before was the bed and a bit of white wall above the headboard. I had imagined the rest of the room IKEA-stark and minimal – all chrome and black ash. I simply hadn't reckoned on a faux fur throw draped over a chaise longue, or a bright kilim rug on the floor.

But now is not the time for admiring Derek's unexpected flair for interior design. The door to his playroom is now right in front of me and I feel like it's glowing, all throbbing and red in the silent, and surprisingly airy, bedroom. Inside that door Christian is waiting for me, no doubt confused and in some discomfort. Yum.

I push it open. And there's Christian, in the puddle of golden light cast by the open door. He's still bent helplessly over the sawhorse. And he's still blindfolded, but the gag has been removed and it lies on the floor at the foot of the horse. Christian turns his head, sensing some-one has come into the room.

'Please,' he says, his voice soft, 'please, sir, don't make me wait any longer.'

Straight away I slide into the strap-on cock, achingly slowly because I don't want to make a single sound that will give the game away. While I'm easing the buckles home Christian moans again. 'Please, are you still there? Please, make me come, sir. Sir, would you fuck me? Please fuck me. Fuck me hard.'

And I'd feel so mean if I didn't oblige.

Once I'm strapped in I walk around behind him, and rip down his underpants, sudden and mean – just the way Dark Knight would – and Christian just melts in my hands.

And then I positively glide inside him, like flying. Mr Fox is a clever boy: somehow the angle Christian is held at is just perfect, so I don't have to scramble and struggle like I normally do when I'm trying to fuck him. It's just beautiful.

He moans. I've only sneaked the tip into him so far and he reacts like it's a lightning bolt, bucking and moaning and wanting, so desperate. He's every last bit as turned on as I am, and he's been kept waiting too.

I withdraw completely and tease the head of my cock around his arsehole and up and down between his cheeks. I nuzzle it forward and stroke his hidden balls and he twitches and flutters, panting.

And I just don't want this to end. I couldn't bear to plunge my cock right back into him and get us both off in minutes. I decide to get creative.

I walk around him and crouch down near his blind-folded face. He is so beautiful. It's like poetry. Close up, I can see the pretty twin red chafe marks the tight gag has left, one in each corner of his mouth. I touch one of them with a fingertip.

'Fuck me,' he moans, his voice cracking all over the place with need. 'Please, sir, fuck me, now.'

I keep on stroking his face slowly, running a finger along his cheek and jawline with feigned coolness.

'Please,' he almost shouts this time, his voice a whole new shade of desperate. And the really cute thing is, no matter how much he pleads, there really is nothing he can do about it until I decide it's time for him to get fucked.

I lean in and kiss him, pressing my lips against his, hard and claiming. I try and kiss him the way Mr Fox would, the way Dark Knight would. And he responds so vigorously that the sawhorse nearly topples over as he struggles to press closer and closer to my mouth. We kiss for a long time, wet and messy and delicious. When I pull away he gasps with frustration, but I don't let him have any more. I straighten up and reach out.

I stroke his cheek softly, and then slide my index finger into his mouth, just the tip at first, and then more and more, pumping it in and out like a tiny cock. And that gives me an idea.

I shuffle round a little so I'm standing square in front of my baby. His head is just below waist height, at groin height, cock height. And I butt the head of my silicone cock up against his lips, I have to do it a couple of times, and then he gets the message.

He opens his mouth just enough for me to slide inside and, oh wow, it looks amazing, seeing my beautiful boyfriend suck cock from this close quarters. Suck a cock that is attached to me and is just ghosting a little pressure against my cunt. He takes it deep, sucking it with greedy desperation, and so very well. I keep going, sliding in and out of his willing wet mouth for such a long time, until it becomes almost hypnotic (if there is such a thing as insanely arousingly hypnotic).

And then I really do want to fuck him. I can't wait any longer.

I pull free from his mouth, almost run around the saw-horse and plunge my well-lubed cock deep into his arse.

He cries out, and then softly mutters, 'Thank you sir,' as I begin to fuck him, rough and fast.

And I'm doing it! I'm Dark Knight!

I fumble underneath him to find his cock, hot and hard, pressed tight against the wooden horse. Grabbing it tightly I begin to stroke him in time with my deep thrusts, a flurry of movement, banging and fast. And, thanks to the sweetly perfect angle Christian is pinned at, my clit is purring happily and I'm rapidly working my way up to the point of no return.

My mind is alive with images, my perfect fantasies of Dark Knight and Christian together, merging and blurring with the reality that I watched of Christian and Mr Fox, in this very room. And me, I'm there too, fucking Christian in the mouth and teasing his slutty arse until he begs.

And then I can see it. It's the home straight, and it's in easy range now, just a matter of reaching out, reaching out and taking it.

I'm coming. I think Christian is too, I hear him cry out, feel him twisting underneath me, I bask in his heat. But I can't really be very sure of anything because wave after wave of pleasure is pulsing over me, peak after peak, until I think I might die from it.

But I don't die. I realise later that I'm not actually dead, but my feet don't touch the floor any more. I might look perfectly normal, but I'm not. I might look like I'm walking slowly down the steps outside Mr Fox's flat, but I'm not. I'm floating on air, so relaxed I'm shocked I'm actually upright.

Christian is huddled against me pretty much unscathed, apart from being a little creaky from being finally released from his bondage. He exploded out of the ropes like a tight wound spring, and when he saw his tormentor was me, he just grinned the world's biggest grin – breaking his own record.

We help each other home, neither of us have a front-door key, so we have to ring the doorbell. And the door is answered by Lorne.

Which is awkward.

'Lorne, oh, look, I'm sorry about...' I start, because even though this is neither the time nor the place, something deep inside me is desperate to apologise to Lorne. That last bit of negativity, my Lorne guilt, is still burrowing inside me.

But Lorne interrupts. 'Don't. It's OK, really.'

Christian, oblivious (but that's understandable), suddenly seems to notice where we are and who we are talking to. 'Lorne, hello, mate. What are you doing here?'

'Um,' says Lorne, 'um, actually I called by to apologise to Imogen, but somehow, well Derek was here and he, well...' Lorne twists her mouth and looks rather shamefaced. It doesn't take Sherlock Holmes to figure out how she's been passing the time until we got back, especially as the laptop, complete with freeze-framed Christian and Imogen ass-fuck perve-o-vision is still in full view.

Derek, who is seated in front of it, turns and looks over his shoulder at me. 'I saved it all for you,' he says.

I gaze around the room, at Lorne, at Christian, at Derek. I'm very happy, and very, very lucky.

* * *

In bed, just before I turn out the light, Christian says, 'I've got you a present.' And he twists round to rummage and rustle around in a carrier bag on the floor by the bed.

'Christian, you nutter, you don't need to buy me a present. You've just given me the biggest present ever, ever.'

'Well, yeah, but . . .' Christian tails off as he straightens up, clutching a tube of Jaffa Cakes.

I smile happily, because confused as I am, I really do like Jaffa Cakes. I take the tube, but before I crack it open I ask the obvious. 'Christian, what are these Jaffa Cakes for?'

'Eating.'

Rather than answer, I give him eyebrows-of-doom in response.

'They're because I feel guilty, all right,' he says, while I take a Jaffa Cake and take a big bite.

With my mouth all full, I splutter, 'Guilty? Guilty about what?'

At first he doesn't say anything. I can see by the way his mouth is wriggling all over his face he's trying to make himself spit something out, and then he does, all in a big tumble. 'Because I kissed Derek, Dark Knight, um, whatever it is we're calling him these days. Not today, but in Schwartz on Friday night, after the camera went out. So I can't say it was for you, because I knew you couldn't see it. And it was his idea, he initiated it, but I didn't really stop him. And I enjoyed it. And I feel guilty. Hence Jaffa Cakes.'

'Oh,' I say, taking another bite of the cake, 'is that all?'

Christian gives a sort of muffled snort of laughter that makes me think he doesn't know whether I am joking or not.

'Well,' I say, 'if this is true confessions then I better

tell you I kissed Lorne, twice. And it was all her idea both times, once when we met, in Cruze, and once today, when we were at Schwartz, watching security-camera footage of you and Derek snogging.'

And it's Christian's turn with the 'Oh'.

'So,' I continue, turning over the half-eaten biscuit in my hand, 'I'm not sure I really deserve Jaffa Cakes.'

'You're right,' says Christian, coolly, 'you bloody well don't. I should have just got you digestives.'

14

I don't often cook properly – out of sheer laziness. But today I've pulled out all the stops and followed Delia to the letter. I'm flushed and glowing, but it's all worth it, because they're worth it, my wonderful team.

While I'm in the kitchen putting the finishing touches to the gravy, I can hear Christian regaling Lorne and Derek with tall tales about the sexual perversions of a number of celebrities. To listen to him anyone would think he knew all these divas and stars of the silver screen personally, when, of course, the truth is that he is merrily recounting bits of half-remembered gossip columns and snippets from *Popbitch*, hastily embroidered with the very best his fevered imagination can come up with.

My boy. I really do love him.

The meal goes down well.

'Roasts,' I confess, when the praise gets overwhelming, 'are all in the timing, and when you've got a minute-by-minute Delia countdown to keep to, well, nothing to it.' But I get impressed nods and appreciative noise all the same.

By the time we've demolished a leg of lamb, a sticky toffee pudding (M&S's finest) and several bottle of wine, I'm merry enough to agree to anything, which means I allow Christian to pull out his PlayStation 2, and challenge Derek to a duel. It's like a fight for my honour, except if it actually was I'd probably be keener to watch it. But watching boys play PlayStation is boring – even these boys. So I wander off into the kitchen to start on the washing-up (this is meant to be my treat for them after all). Lorne follows.

Without speaking, she picks up a tea towel and starts to wipe the soapy offerings I am stacking on the draining board. We work in silence for a while and then Lorne leans over and gently kisses the top of my head. 'How are you feeling?'

I sigh and gaze down at the sink-full of kaleidoscope bubbles. 'In all honesty, Lorne, still overwhelmed. Seeing you and Christian and Derek together and realising how much you've all done for me, not just last weekend, but over this past however many weeks. I'm so lucky. And I really have no idea why you all did so much for me.'

'Well, you're kind of addictive,' says Lorne, and although I'm not looking at her I can tell she's got a semi-smirk on.

'Yeah, yeah.'

'No, well, actually I suppose we all had our reasons. Derek, well, you can see why Derek went along with it. Actually, he didn't even know he was going along with anything at first, and then when he did, well, he'd seen the merchandise up close.'

I give a splutter of a laugh. Lorne has a good point. 'Er, yeah.'

'And Christi, well, he's in love with you. I mean, I think you had a point, I think there was a time there, somewhere in the middle of the muddle, where he might have got a bit carried away with the part he was playing and the exotic wrongness of Dark Knight, and maybe started taking his part a bit too seriously, but it was still about you. He only slid into the role he was playing so deeply because that was what you wanted. The bottom line is, it was always about what you wanted, maybe it intersected with some stuff he wanted, but that's just luck.' And Lorne shrugs her shoulders a little, while polishing the glass she is holding to near oblivion.

I let out a long whizzy sigh. Lorne is being very perceptive this afternoon. I don't remember her advice being this good before.

'And what about you?' I say. 'Why did you do so much to help me?'

'Like I said before, you're very addictive.'

'Lorne . . .' I'm not sure what to say.

'Don't say anything, Imogen.'

'No, I have to, because you've got it all wrong, Lorne, it's not what you think.'

There's a pause and then Lorne says, 'Yes it is. I understand, and it's not the first time I've heard it – you're straight.'

'No, well, yes, yes I am, but that's not why I'm not interested in you, Lorne. You're as much of a man to me as either of those bloody game-boys in there.' I wave a hand towards the almost closed door to the living room. 'I am interested in you, Lorne, I am attracted to you. I found that really confusing at first. I'm over that now, but, the fact is, I'm with Christian and, whatever else I might get up to, I'm faithful to him, and that's that.'

'Oh,' says Lorne.

We wash the dishes for a little longer, lulled by the soft sound of soapy crockery clunking together. Then Lorne says, 'You could have asked me to, you know.'

'Asked you to what?' I say. Even though, really, I sort of know what.

'Asked me to be Christian. To do the call and go to Schwartz. I would have done it. I could have smuggled you into the security-camera room too, I expect. You could have watched it all from multiple angles.'

I don't look at Lorne. I carry on washing the dishes, looking out of the window above the sink. Then, eventually, I say, 'But, Lorne, Derek knows you.'

'Well, yeah,' Lorne says in a wheedling sort of tone, 'but I didn't know it was Derek back then did I?'

'Um, I suppose,' I say, confused by these high-level hypotheticals, and give a sort of laugh.

Later, after I have had to threaten to smash the Play-Station with a bloody hammer, we're all lolling around the living room, still stuffed full of food and wine.

Derek is sprawled on a sofa all to himself, while the three of us are scattered over the other one. I'm sitting on the carpet, leaning back against Christian's shins as he perches next to Lorne. And I'm tipping my head right, right back so it's resting in his lap. I can see right up his nose. I've been telling tales, the story of the countess and pussy boy, and they've all been finding my aversion to being caught on camera myself hugely amusing. Which I suppose it is, kind of.

'Oh God, babe,' Lorne sort of snorts, 'I didn't know you had such a surreal time.'

'From the goat opening the door to the friendly chat over dead zombies with the man who might or might not be fucking my boyfriend, I've never had surrealer,' I say. I'm still sort of drunk, and I stumble the last word – which may or may not be a real word – giving it about four l's.

I roll my head to one side, and look over at Derek. He's so stunning, I can't quite get over it, so much better than I could tell from my spying across the courtyard. So much better in the flesh, and even better in the flesh after a healthy share of three bottles of wine. His body seems to be about five miles long, and every one of those swimmer's muscles is clearly visible through his light-blue shirt. I almost have to do a double take to make sure it isn't painted on.

Derek looks over and catches me staring. I could blame the wine, but I definitely get a glow in my cheeks when our eyes meet.

'Genny,' he says softly, and it's sad to admit but I do kind of get goose pimples on my arms when he speaks to me, 'why don't you fetch that empty bottle off the table.'

'Why?' I ask with a frown, but even before I've started speaking I've stood up and taken a couple of steps on my errand. What can I say? Derek just has a way about him. So when he suggests a friendly little game of Spin the Bottle, we're all very up for it.

Derek, taking the lead, steps up first. He spins the wine bottle with a slow and knowing smile, and gets what I assume he wanted, in Christian, who returns his grin with an amused and put-upon expression that I really like.

I get up from my position at Christian's feet so Derek can get at him. And he wastes no time moving in, straddling Christian where he is sitting on the sofa, forcing him back into the cushions, as he pushes their lips together, slow and soft for the first moments and then suddenly hard and hot and greedy. In that short moment he owns Christian. There is no doubt.

I sigh audibly.

But the kiss ends suddenly and far too soon. Derek flips off Christian's lap and shuffles himself in the gap between him and Lorne, even though there isn't really a big enough gap there. But that doesn't seem to matter, because Lorne slips off the sofa and grabs the bottle, ready for round two.

Lorne spins and the bottle stops, pointing at Derek,

who eyebrow-flashes Lorne and stands up smartly. In two big strides he is over by the fireplace, where Lorne is squatting by the bottle. He bends down, and practically drags Lorne upright by the collar, pushing her up against the wall next to the fire surround, and near-enough tongue raping her: kissing her with a bruising intensity, while holding her pinned firm. It's a beautiful sight, with Lorne up on squirming tiptoe as Derek takes her.

I can't help myself, I sigh again. It's almost as good as the one with Christian.

When Derek drops Lorne in a quivering heap on the floor, it's Christian who steps up next. He spins the bottle with a pout and a flourish, and gets Lorne.

Lorne is still in a crumpled, well-kissed heap on the floor by the fireplace, but she reaches out her arms greedily to Christian, who crawls over to fill them. They kiss delicately, both lying full length on the carpet. It's amazing. With their faces pressed so closely together it is hard to tell that they are not, actually, the same person. They look like mirror images. It's like watching one very hot man snogging his reflection. It's delicious.

And then it's my turn to spin. And, as it turns out, my turn to kiss Lorne, whose lips are looking rather red and swollen, by this time. It's the third time we've kissed, and it's the first time that I initiate it.

Lorne sits up from where she is lying on the floor, and I hold her chin, pulling it close until our lips touch, feather soft. Just like the other times I've kissed her, it's when her lips are on mine that I can feel the ways in which her mouth isn't like a man's. It's not just softer and smaller, it moves in a whole different way – delicate like a butterfly. I've never noticed before that she tastes amazing. Yum. I can't help taking maybe a little more than I should.

I'm still in the land of Lorne kissing, when I hear

Derek say, in that commanding tone he manages to have, 'I want another turn. Come on you two.' So we break apart, just in time to see Derek's bottle spin come to a halt, pointing right at me.

I am going to kiss Dark Knight.

I'm still sitting on the floor next to Lorne, and suddenly Derek is on top of me, straddling my knocking knees. He has one hand behind my head and the other on my chest, as he lowers me to the floor, sliding a muscular thigh between my legs to rub teasingly against my crotch. Then he leans down and gently licks my bottom lip. I open my mouth to try and draw him into the kiss, but he pulls away, stopping me from chasing his mouth with firm hands on my shoulders.

He looks down at me – I'm so aroused, all panting and wanting him – and smiles. His tongue darts out and flicks his own bottom lip – blatantly teasing me. I find myself pushing my crotch down to grind against his hard thigh, but it's just far enough away to be frustrating rather than satisfying.

Derek leans down again and runs his tongue back and forth over my top lip, resisting all my frantic squirms and moans as I try and get him to kiss me properly. Then he pulls away again, looks down at me for a moment, and then whispers, in a voice I'm sure that only I can hear, 'You're a very bad girl, Imogen Taylor.'

And then he finally kisses me, just before I burst in flames. He jams his thigh hard against my cunt, rubbing back and forth. I see sparks behind my eyelids and feel an orgasm begin to build. I squirm and writhe in his arms and then, with no warning, it's over. He pulls away properly, and I'm back in the room.

I sit up, trying (rather pathetically) not to seem flustered. But I'm on fire, wondering if I could make some excuse and dash to the bathroom to finish off what Derek has started, without it seeming too obvious.

And then, when I become properly aware of the room around me, I see that Christian is spinning the bottle. I swallow and compose myself, getting ready for a replay of the pretty sights of Christian and Derek, or Christian and Lorne. And I'm so totally shocked when the bottle neck ends up pointing at me.

But Christian doesn't kiss me. Instead he walks over to where I'm sitting, takes my hand and leads me away into the bedroom, which seems like another world.

The bedroom lights are off, making it seem cool and calm, compared with the cheek-flushing bright intensity of the living room, as Christian tumbles me onto the bed.

I laugh in the semi-darkness. 'What are you doing?'

'I got you. I get to kiss you, don't I?'

'Well, you're not kissing me,' I say, not wanting to be obstructive, but nice as this cuddle is, semantics-wise, it isn't a kiss.

'Oh right, sorry.'

And Christian pulls up my long denim skirt and pushes his face right in between my legs. His tongue sneaks out and presses gently against the soft cotton of my underwear – so soft and teasing, through the damp fabric.

'Oh God,' I say as my well-teased cunt springs to vivid and insatiable life. Involuntarily I close my thighs on either side of Christian's head – as if I'm scared he might pull away and leave me hanging – which has the delicious side effect of forcing his face deeper, harder against me.

He laps the damp cotton with his tongue and I rock back against it, my mind alive with images from the delicious kissing game. In my ears, that voice rings over and over, 'You're a very bad girl, Imogen Taylor.' And, oh God, it's too, too good. I can't last long.

And I come, cotton knickers and all, screaming loud enough for Derek and Lorne to give a muffled cheer out in the living room.

I'm a bit embarrassed after my outburst, so I make Christian go and get me a glass of water, so I can hide in the bedroom. I'm not feeling quite able to face my public just yet. As he leaves the room, I curl up on the bed, feeling so sheepish I've near enough grown wool.

When the door opens again, I sit up for my drink, but it's not Christian, it's Derek.

'Oh, hi,' I say, trying not to look him in the eye, which is hard. He's that kind of guy.

'I thought we should talk,' Derek says, crossing the room and sitting down on the end of the bed.

'Oh, OK.'

'You see,' he says, in a soft voice, 'I really can't let you get away with all of this, Imogen, or should I say, pup.'

I gulp. 'Get away with what?'

'Imogen, you can't just lead people on online, pretending to be something you're not. It's not fair. What if I'd really fallen for Christian, the Imogen version, or the real version for that matter – someone could have got hurt, and not in a good way.'

And he's right. Of course he's right. 'I know,' I say, shrugging awkwardly, 'and I'm sorry. It's just, well, you know what online stuff is like. I never really thought of you as a real person.' I shuffle on the bed, burning with discomfort.

Derek smiles. He reaches out and takes my hand, patting the top of it affectionately. 'Yeah, well,' he says lightly, 'as I got such a lovely little playtime with a normally unavailable pup out of it, I'll let it go. Especially as you're sorry.'

'I am, really, very sorry,' I say earnestly. Then I swallow and add, 'And I'm sorry for spying on you on Tuesday afternoons too.'

'What?'

Oh, and indeed, fuck. 'You didn't know about that, did you?'

So I have to apologise even more to Derek, who I suspect secretly finds my binocular antics a little bit amusing – not least because of my dedication. He even looks a little shocked when I tell him about how I deliberately swung working from home on a Tuesday afternoon so I could watch him on his half day off from the pool. So I pacify him with a few tales of some of the sights I have seen happening in a room mere yards from his own living room.

'Well, it's a good job my playroom faces the other way,' he says finally.

'Yeah, or looking at it another way, it's a real shame your playroom faces the other way.' I bite my lip.

Derek slaps the back of my hand, playfully. 'Hey, you've got nothing to complain about; you have your camera now, don't you?' He winks a lurid wink.

My heart leaps about a million miles in the air. 'You're leaving it in!'

'Well, you don't deserve it, but let's just say I could be persuaded.'

Uh-oh. 'Hang on,' I say, quickly. 'Christian's not an option, not any more. He's done me enough favours lately. I already owe him my immortal soul as it is.'

Derek smiles. 'Actually no, I wasn't thinking of Christian, lovely though he undoubtedly is. I was thinking of this guy.' Derek takes a crumpled piece of paper from his pocket. It's a print-out of a web page. A web page called 'Downtime'. It's a picture of Christian and Dan, snuggled up in bed together, a million years ago.

Derek taps the paper, flicking Dan smartly on the nipple. 'How about you get me your boyfriend's little chum here, and in return I forget that that camera is even there.'

I open and shut my mouth a few times before intelligible words actually come out. 'How did you get this?'

'I Googled your boyfriend's name, of course, just in case there was anything I should know about you two before you played your sordid sex games in my flat.' Derek shrugs.

I shake my head. I know what I ought to say to this. It's something along the lines of, 'Dan? I don't know. I'm not sure if that's even possible.' But what I actually say is, 'Well, I could try.'

'That's my girl.'

What can I say? Derek just has that way about him.

Visit the Black Lace website at
www.blacklace-books.co.uk

LOOK OUT FOR THE ALL-NEW BLACK LACE BOOKS – AVAILABLE NOW!

All books priced £7.99 in the UK. Please note publication dates apply to the UK only. For other territories, please contact your retailer.

BURNING BRIGHT
Janine Ashbless
ISBN 978 0 352 34085 6

Two lovers, brought together by a forbidden passion, are on the run from their pasts. Veraine was once a commander in the Imperial army: Myrna was the divine priestess he seduced and stole from her desert temple. But travelling through a jungle kingdom, they fall prey to slavers and are separated. Veraine is left for dead. Myrna is taken as a slave to the city of the Tiger Lords: inhuman tyrants with a taste for human flesh. There she must learn the tricks of survival in a cruel and exotic court where erotic desire is not the only animal passion.

Myrna still has faith that Veraine will find her. But Veraine, badly injured, has forgotten everything: his past, his lover, and even his own identity. As he undertakes a journey through a fevered landscape of lush promise and supernatural danger, he knows only one thing – that he must somehow find the unknown woman who holds the key to his soul.

Coming in February 2007

THE BOSS
Monica Belle
ISBN 978 0 352 34088 7

Felicity is a girl with two different sides to her character, each leading two very separate lives. There's Fizz – wild child, drummer in a retro punk band, and car thief. And then there's Felicity – a quiet, police, and ultra efficient office worker. But as her attractive, controlling boss takes an interest in her, she finds it hard to keep the two parts of her life separate.

Will being with Stephen mean choosing between personas and sacrificing so much of her life? But then, it also appears that Stephen has some very peculiar and addictive ideas about sex.

GOTHIC BLUE
Portia Da Costa
ISBN 978 0 352 33075 8

At an archduke's reception, a handsome young nobleman falls under the spell of a malevolent but irresistible sorceress. Two hundred years later, Belinda Seward also falls prey to sensual forces she can neither understand nor control. Stranded by a thunderstorm at a remote Gothic priory, Belinda and her boyfriend are drawn into an enclosed world of luxurious decadence and sexual alchemy. Their host is the courteous but melancholic André von Kastel; a beautiful aristocrat who mourns his lost love. He has plans for Belinda – plans that will take her into the realms of obsessive love and the erotic paranormal.

Coming in March 2007

FLOOD
Anna Clare
ISBN 978 0 352 34094 8

London, 1877. Phoebe Flood, a watch mender's daughter from Blackfriars, is hired as lady's maid to the glamorous Louisa LeClerk, a high class tart with connections to the underworld of gentlemen pornographers. Fascinated by her new mistress and troubled by strange dreams, Phoebe receives an extraordinary education in all matters sensual. And her destiny and secret self gradually reveals itself when she meets Garou, a freak show attraction, The Boy Who Was Raised by Wolves.

LEARNING TO LOVE IT
Alison Tyler
ISBN 978 0 352 33535 7

Art historian Lissa an doctor Colin meet at the Frankfurt Book Fair, where they are both promoting their latest books. At the fair, and then through Europe, the two lovers embark on an exploration of their sexual fantasies, playing intense games of bondage, spanking and dressing up. Lissa loves humiliation, and Colin is just the man to provide her with the pleasure she craves. Unbeknown to Lissa, their meeting was not accidental, but planned ahead by a mysterious patron of the erotic arts.

Black Lace Booklist

Information is correct at time of printing. To avoid disappointment, check availability before ordering. Go to www.blacklace-books.co.uk. All books are priced £7.99 unless another price is given.

BLACK LACE BOOKS WITH A CONTEMPORARY SETTING

- [ ] ALWAYS THE BRIDEGROOM Tesni Morgan — ISBN 978 0 352 33855 6 £6.99
- [ ] THE ANGELS' SHARE Maya Hess — ISBN 978 0 352 34043 6
- [ ] ARIA APPASSIONATA Julie Hastings — ISBN 978 0 352 33056 7 £6.99
- [ ] ASKING FOR TROUBLE Kristina Lloyd — ISBN 978 0 352 33362 9
- [ ] BLACK LIPSTICK KISSES Monica Belle — ISBN 978 0 352 33885 3 £6.99
- [ ] BONDED Fleur Reynolds — ISBN 978 0 352 33192 2 £6.99
- [ ] BOUND IN BLUE Monica Belle — ISBN 978 0 352 34012 2
- [ ] CAMPAIGN HEAT Gabrielle Marcola — ISBN 978 0 352 33941 6
- [ ] CAT SCRATCH FEVER Sophie Mouette — ISBN 978 0 352 34021 4
- [ ] CIRCUS EXCITE Nikki Magennis — ISBN 978 0 352 34033 7
- [ ] CLUB CRÉME Primula Bond — ISBN 978 0 352 33907 2 £6.99
- [ ] COMING ROUND THE MOUNTAIN Tabitha Flyte — ISBN 978 0 352 33873 0 £6.99
- [ ] CONFESSIONAL Judith Roycroft — ISBN 978 0 352 33421 3
- [ ] CONTINUUM Portia Da Costa — ISBN 978 0 352 33120 5
- [ ] DANGEROUS CONSEQUENCES Pamela Rochford — ISBN 978 0 352 33185 4
- [ ] DARK DESIGNS Madelynne Ellis — ISBN 978 0 352 34075 7
- [ ] THE DEVIL INSIDE Portia Da Costa — ISBN 978 0 352 32993 6
- [ ] EDEN'S FLESH Robyn Russell — ISBN 978 0 352 33923 2 £6.99
- [ ] ENTERTAINING MR STONE Portia Da Costa — ISBN 978 0 352 34029 0
- [ ] EQUAL OPPORTUNITIES Mathilde Madden — ISBN 978 0 352 34070 2
- [ ] FEMININE WILES Karina Moore — ISBN 978 0 352 33874 7 £6.99
- [ ] FIRE AND ICE Laura Hamilton — ISBN 978 0 352 33486 2
- [ ] GOING DEEP Kimberly Dean — ISBN 978 0 352 33876 1 £6.99
- [ ] GOING TOO FAR Laura Hamilton — ISBN 978 0 352 33657 6 £6.99
- [ ] GONE WILD Maria Eppie — ISBN 978 0 352 33670 5
- [ ] IN PURSUIT OF ANNA Natasha Rostova — ISBN 978 0 352 34060 3

To find out the latest information about Black Lace titles, check out the
website: www.blacklace-books.co.uk or send for a booklist with
complete synopses by writing to:

>   Black Lace Booklist, Virgin Books Ltd
>   Thames Wharf Studios
>   Rainville Road
>   London W6 9HA

Please include an SAE of decent size. Please note only British stamps
are valid.

Our privacy policy
We will not disclose information you supply us to any other parties.
We will not disclose any information which identifies you personally to
any person without your express consent.

From time to time we may send out information about Black Lace
books and special offers. Please tick here if you do <u>not</u> wish to
receive Black Lace information.   ☐

Please send me the books I have ticked above.

Name ....

Address ....

....

....

....

Post Code ....

Send to: Virgin Books Cash Sales, Thames Wharf Studios, Rainville Road, London W6 9HA.

US customers: for prices and details of how to order books for delivery by mail, call 888-330-8477.

Please enclose a cheque or postal order, made payable to Virgin Books Ltd, to the value of the books you have ordered plus postage and packing costs as follows:

UK and BFPO – £1.00 for the first book, 50p for each subsequent book.

Overseas (including Republic of Ireland) – £2.00 for the first book, £1.00 for each subsequent book.

If you would prefer to pay by VISA, ACCESS/MASTERCARD, DINERS CLUB, AMEX or SWITCH, please write your card number and expiry date here:

....

Signature ....

Please allow up to 28 days for delivery.